Scourge of Dawn

Volatile Eclipse

ISBN: 979-8-9934121-0-8

Summery: Colton, while trying to obtain a good living for him and his best friend, meets a girl with psychic powers, and has to survive his mutated bully while his home city burns in civil war.

This novel was made completely without any use of generative AI. All words were hand-typed by the author, and all concepts thought up without the use of generative AI systems.

Published in the United States of America

Book Cover artist:
Tathena Tubbs

Editing by:
Allister Thompson
James Powell
Alison Smith
Aimee Hales

Beta Readers:
Samuel Smith
Meg Jensen
Aimee Hales
Amos Olsen
Rae Jones

Table of Contents

To those who were my partners in 'crime'
Hyrum, Connor, Jeramie, and Grace

Alfeon
Scourge of Dawn
Volatile Eclipse

Caleb DM Smith

Prologue:

Demons and angels weren't real, nor were their otherworldly abilities, powerful magical tech, or destructive global wars.

As far as anyone knew.

Yet here I am, being called a demon child.

Colton stood with a blank gaze, spacing out from the lecture he was being given.

As usual.

"—and as I'm responsible for you, I must pay for da damages," the man said, his accented voice struggling to be heard over the tumultuous rain.

Yet you're gonna make me pay you back, Colton thought.

The man continued on his spiel, right in front of everyone in the street. Colton groaned, feeling his insides twist a little as a haggard woman cast him a glare as she trundled by.

A man wearing rags for clothes, carrying bundles of food bumped into the dark-skinned man, ending his lecture and sending various edible items all over the ground. The two men grumbled and began hurriedly picking up the mess, which Colton observed for a moment.

He moved to turn away from the two men, his legs twitching and eager. He glanced up at the dull, gray clouds. Off in the distance and far above them was a massive mountain range, practically a wall. Framed against it on a plateau, was a city, with skyscrapers poking the clouds and gold lights shimmering from rain-soaked windows.

I bet the Auratus District is nice and warm.

Across the road, a soldier dressed in sleek gray armor was busily putting up a poster on the dilapidated wall of an abandoned wooden house. A sad attempt, as the rain peeled and soaked the paper, warping the image slightly.

Even their posters don't wanna be here.

Curious, Colton waited until the guardian had moved away, before he weaved through the crowd, brushing against the itchy clothes of a passerby until he came to stand a foot from the wall.

Colton felt his stomach drop to his feet, his own face staring back at him from the soaked paper. A large number hung beneath the sketch of his appearance, with the words 'Wanted dead or alive' leering at him.

Two—no—twenty-five hundred acunar? That can't be real. That's enough to feed someone for three years.

Colton kept staring at the paper, feeling his shoulders itch as he heard sounds behind him mix with the rain. He sporadically glanced around him, seeing only heads bowed against the weather, and all eyes to the ground.

I don't see any—

A small mass of shiny gray pushed through the crowd to his left, bearing guns and talking with distorted radio voices, marching in sync. One soldier with a bright green stripe on the front, pointed at Colton, radio voice emitting from a box under the throat, before they all rushed his way.

Grabbing the paper, Colton tore it off the wall before turning and dashing down the road, recklessly knocking people to the side as the sound of muddy footsteps mixed with the sound of the rain drowned out all other noises.

Please tell me those are just my own steps.

Colton turned down one alleyway, vanishing into the shadows and skidded to a stop, his lungs burning and limbs protesting at him as he bent over and gasped for air.

He straightened up and turned back around to peer out of the alleyway, backing up slowly, only to bump into someone behind him wearing a cloak.

"Watch where you're—It might just be *my* day" said the stranger, the voice was oddly digital and harsh. Two yellow lens-like eyes peered out from under the hood, and sickly warm breath emitted from the shadows.

"I—" Colton stuttered, frozen.

Scourge of Dawn

"Now pick your method of pain," the stranger hissed, holding out two blades that glinted with the rain. Plasma burst along their edges, shrieking with hunger. "Freshly warm or cold as the rain?"

Colton turned and ran, just as he felt the blades scratch into his back like claws, the rain intensifying the sting. He rocketed out into the alleyway, body jittery with his jaw clenched tight.

"Come back here, little prey!" roared the stranger, close behind.

An old woman wearing a raggy shawl protested, and a middle-aged man dressed in a dingy jacket cursed as Colton shoved past them, his pursuer slashing the two out of the way, sending red flecks everywhere.

Colton glanced back, seeing the distance close before he tripped and slid across the mud, landing at someone's feet. He looked up to see sleek gray armor and heard a distorted radio voice.

"Hey, there's the kid!" the guardian exclaimed.

Colton rose to his feet, just as his original pursuer lunged and swiped with intended lethality. Ducking again, Colton dove forward, avoiding the stranger, who became entangled with the guardian, dropping both to the ground.

Holy nosk!

"How dare you!" the guardian shouted. "I'll make you—"

Shkk!

Colton felt his insides go cold, eyes wide and glued to the guardian's crimson-stained armor as the stranger pulled out two swords. The guardian dropped to the ground, two holes in his chest. The stranger hunched over, shoulders starting to shake, muttering before breaking into muffled laughing. More guardians charged, and the stranger let out a cry and picked off two guardians.

"Just you wait, pathetic rat," the stranger said, leaping away, "I'll hunt you down, and claim that bounty on your head."

Slowly backing away into the alleyway, Colton clung to the shadows, his lungs refused to inflate, his head swam from millions of thoughts, and his muscles were painfully tight.

"Doth thou wish to cover thy head from rain?"

Colton jerked hard, nearly breaking out into a run again as he whirled with a yelp, catching sight of an old man hunching down against the wall, robes wrapped tight.

"I—The rain doesn't bother me," Colton muttered.

"Then why doth thou peereth over thy shoulder?" the man asked. "What hast thou done?"

"Nothing, just—looking for someone."

"Thy friend art in danger?"

"Who are you exactly?" Colton looked over his shoulder.

"Hide thy face for thy countenance betrayeth thy words."

So, he's old enough to have a broken brain.

"Right. I'll keep that in mind. Why d'you talk like that?"

"Careful of thy feelings, Colton. Lest thy friends fate mirrors thine but worse."

Just some crazy old guy. Probably a friend of Bristol.

Colton shook his head, turning and leaving until something cold caught hold of his wrist. A glance back and he saw a handmade of solid water sprouting from the muddy ground, gripping him tightly.

The old man twisted and twirled his fingers as he stared at Colton with whitish quartz eyes that felt like a needle injecting medicine.

That's not normal. That's not normal at all!

"Harken, for thou knowest little of this world," the old man said. "Nay, the darkness and doubt of Alfeon hath hidden the truth of thy blood. Thine own mind hath closed to thy genesis."

Colton froze, his heart pricked and thrashing as the cold of the rain seeped into him. He remembered the paper still clutched in his hands, and he looked down at it, his face now misshapen and horrifying.

A face that could have belonged to a demon.

"How do you know my name?" Colton asked, voice wavering.

"I hath witnessed thy tarrying here. And heard of thy exile from thy homestead."

"So, you've been watching me?"

The old man slowly rose to his feet, regally spreading his hands, causing the water hand to burst. Colton felt a small itch at the back of his neck, like a weight that bowed his head and dropped his eyes to the ground.

4

It feels right to bow to him.

"What doth thou desirest, Colton of Aquila Mons?" The old man asked.

This is freaking me out!

"What do you know about Aquila Mons?" Colton raised his eyes with a forced glare despite his heart thrashing in his ribcage.

"Thou fled thy first house, thou shalt flee thy second," the old man said. "Yea, the day cometh, to flee will cost thee thy life. Yea, on that day, thou shalt be questioned again, 'what doth thou desirest?'"

Colton stood frozen, his grip slackening until the paper fell from his hands, sinking into a puddle as the image warped more, and something inside him twitched. Something that was alive but apart from him.

An image flashed in his mind of a burning house. He recognized it, but it felt *different*. Something about the image was off. The fire was black with white outlines, the sky was red, and the sun had been turned to a void.

Colton shook his head and glanced down at the poster, the sensation in his gut starting to writhe and fester, like something he ate began to disagree with him so severely he felt the urge to vomit.

The rain pelted him, and his limbs began to shiver. The tumult was all he could hear, keeping away the outside world with its chaotic downpour.

What'm I supposed to do? I feel like I'm always messing up and all on my own.

5

2 years later

Chapter 1

A Humble Dawn

Upon initial viewing, one might think he was a pretty clumsy teenager. On a closer look, one would find him devilishly mischievous in his clever schemes.

"Oh, excuse me!" Colton exclaimed, forcing a smile, his gut twisting.

The haggard man Colton had bumped into glared down at him. Colton raised his hands defensively, pulling down his hood around his face before turning and shuffling down the street, leaving the man to give a huff and walk the other way.

Colton wound his way down a street, passing by houses made of whatever materials were available, stone, wood, mudbrick, tents. All crowding each other and invading on the dusty road occasionally littered with trash.

Colton flipped the wallet out from his sleeve, glancing about to ensure nobody saw before he opened it, dumping four coins into his hand.

One, two, three, yes! Jackpot!

One was a rectangular copper coin depicting a man, standing in the center, and a rifle on his shoulder. Two were triangular silver coins with a star in each corner and a tree pictured in the middle. The last was a circular gold coin with a square hole through its core.

One halkai, two chrimata, and one valyuta. He must've been saving for the Auratus District. Sorry, but I can't get there if I starve to death.

Colton replaced the coins and hid the wallet under his ripped, dusty shirt before scampering away on bare feet. He turned a corner, vanishing into the shadows of an alleyway, just as a squadron of guardians walked by.

Colton watched them, instinctively his hair stood on end at the sound of the guardians' clinking gray armor. They carried rifles in their arms, and the crowd parted before them as if afraid to touch them.

One man, dressed in clothes that had more holes and dull colors than they should, bumped into a guardian. The squadron immediately stopped as the man muttered a hasty apology, trying to slip by only for a guardian to grab him by the shoulder.

"Have you seen this boy?" asked one, holding up a poster. Their voice projected from a glitchy voice box, giving the tone a hard digital edge.

Even after two years.

The man shook his head. "N-no, I haven't."

"Shame," said another guardian, "would've saved you from your crime."

"I didn't do anything wrong!" the man suddenly screamed, falling to the ground, arms flailing as he rubbed his nose in the dirt. "I never broke any laws."

"You practically assaulted a guardian," said the first guardian, drawing a baton. "You won't get the death sentence, unless you're weak."

The man wailed, begging for mercy as he kissed the boot of the guardian, who kicked the man in the face, sending him rolling.

"Disgusting dog," the guardian said.

Colton looked away as he heard the fleshy *whump!* Followed by the man's wails intensifying. More fleshy *whumps,* and soon enough, the man fell silent, replaced by distorted digital laughter.

Looking back, the man lay spread-eagle on the road, face covered in red, nose almost entirely gone, and shirt shredded to bits. His chest was barely moving up-and-down, and anybody who passed by, simply stepped over him.

Oh, but I need this money. Colton thought, his stomach grumbling.

He continued watching, witnessing none to help the poor man before Colton groaned. He checked both sides of the road for guardians, before he hurried over and crouched next to the man.

"You okay?" Colton asked.

The man groaned, sitting up as he stemmed the bleeding from his nose. "Those cursed Richmen-scum think they own us."

"They almost do."

The man rubbed his eyes, clearing them of reddened dirt. "One day, we'll see their skyscrapers burning to the—"

The man paused, staring at Colton before his expression twisted into a scowl. Colton's gut dropped, and he stood up.

"You're the boy they're looking for!" the man shouted.

"They are. But I came over to give you some money to help you out. I—"

"Guardians! He's over here!"

"Wait no—"

"Guardians! I found the boy."

Colton cursed under his breath and darted back to his alleyway, sprinting to the other end. He raced across a couple roads before stopping, peeking out from the shadows between two encroaching mud-brick huts, and hurrying forward to blend in with a small crowd shuffling forward on a side road.

Colton wrinkled his nose, the stench of the crowd burning his nostrils. Every time someone brushed up against him, the sackcloth clothing felt like sandpaper. Faces were hardly visible as most kept their eyes toward the ground, and the shuffling of bare feet was like a discordful, lamenting melody.

He kept his eyes toward the ground like most everyone else, but his hair standing on end kept him glancing at a few of those around him. He saw a distraught mother clutching a frail baby that cried endlessly, a young man with eyes horribly sunken who gnawed on a piece of bare-bone, and a decrepit old man who wheezed and coughed each time he breathed, nearly stumbling with each step.

Most around Colton were human, though a rare few had skin like scales, and fingers like claws. Their eyes were serpentine and cruel, with matching ominous mouths and cloaks that hid most of their bodies, movements mimicking the crowd around them.

Even rats wouldn't enjoy ripping your face off, like they would. Colton shivered.

He was brought out of his rumination as another boy emerged from the crowd and sidled next to him, keeping his head down before painfully nudging Colton in the side.

"How're much did yah get?" the boy whispered, slightly hopping with a grin.

"Where did you come from?" Colton asked.

"I got secrets I ain't tellin' ya till I'm dead."

Colton cast a dirty look before huffing with a smirk, flashing out the valyuta. "Enough to keep me eating for a few days."

Fisk flapped his hands before picking at his ripped trousers, shaking the dust from his worn shoes. "Yuh know, Mr. Daas'd say—"

"I know what he'd say."

"He'da disapprove."

"This was your idea."

"Yuh but I can' have yoo be gettin' me en trouble."

"How's he gonna know?"

"Bristol mighta tell 'em."

Colton rammed his shoulder into Fisk. "Bristol wouldn't do that. I got the job done. We had a deal."

"Who'd ya steal from? A kid frum teh rich district?"

"You think I could pull off breaking in there again?"

"If ya did, yoo wouldn't be in this city still."

"Right, dead or finally escaped here."

"Yuh, yoo are the reason the guardians come done here."

"They're paid to. They wouldn't care about me breaking in if they weren't paid."

Fisk whistled, snatching the gold coin before holding it up to the noon sunlight and examining it with a broken-toothed smile, "Ets a real shiner, a valyuta."

"Yeah, and it's mine, Fisk," Colton held out his hand for the coin. "You get the rest. That was the deal."

Fisk glared at Colton for a few seconds before pocketing the coin and pointing a stern finger. "Consider it yer taxes."

"So now you're gonna act like one of the guardians?"

"I'da never be like wun o' them brats. A politician boot-kissin' city guard they are."

"That still sounds like you."

10

Fisk began a ramble as they walked, complaining about owing debts, snitching to their caretaker, and other things. Colton's gaze lingered on him before switching to a cloaked creature behind, making his hair stand on end and his shoulders begin to itch.

Why's that Kekamoto staring at us?

Colton watched the stranger, finding them shorter than most Kekamotos, and with a few strands of pale blonde, almost silver hair spilling out of the hood.

Hair? Wait no, no one down here has blonde hair that looks like that. At least, clean like that.

The hood shifted as if the head was tilting. Colton stopped in his tracks. The figure strode towards them.

"—an' owe quite a bit of people, Jace too fer all dat!" Fisk finished.

"Yeah, great talk," Colton mumbled, tapping Fisk's shoulder, "but we gotta go."

Fisk looked at Colton with a scrunched face before following Colton's gaze.

"Well, hawt darn! Yuh got one o' dem kekamootoos angwee?"

"Fisk, only the Richmen have blond hair."

The stranger broke into a sprint and Colton's senses went into overdrive. The two boys pivoted and dashed away, shoving their way through the crowd, some complaining and others issuing threats.

"Yah see, this the part weer we uhh, take covur," Fisk shouted right before he turned into a narrow alleyway.

That son of a kretch!

Colton took after Fisk, nearly tripping as he followed into the shadows. Fisk stopped, grabbing Colton by the shirt and tugged him back just as the cloaked figure ran into the alleyway from around the corner.

Wait how—?

Did they raise the bounty on my head? Hired a professional?

The two boys shot out and rounded a corner, ramming past the crowd. Colton nearly cramped his neck as he watched his pursuer leap off the buildings with fluid dexterity to land on the wall of a dilapidated stone house ahead of them, sliding down and gliding into a brisk walk in their direction.

Without a word, Fisk turned and dashed down the road to the side, shoving Colton into a trio of strangers. The strangers shouted in protest and shoved Colton back, sending him into the cloaked stranger.

A hand with a winter-cream complexion, small and gentle, covered in thin scars, caught Colton and tugged him forward.

Flee away with me. It's not only the guardians nor Lizard-folk who hunt you.

Colton stared at the stranger, swearing he'd gone crazy from hearing the feminine voice in his head. He shook his head vigorously and yanked his wrist from the grip of the cloaked figure. He turned and dashed the way Fisk had gone before the stranger could react.

Not stopping to look back, Colton weaved between people until the road finally spat him out into the Central Market. He quickly ducked into an unattended stall, crouching down in the shadows amongst crates of mushy fruits that were mobbed by flies. Swatting them away, Colton peered out, eyes darting to-and-fro between all the people and things.

A bustling town square of stalls selling various goods, formed circular patterns towards a broken fountain in the center that was currently flooding everything around it. Guardians from the Auratus District, dressed in sleek gray armor, marched around looking for their entertainment, bearing rifles in their arms. Other guardians stood watch over a platform near the fountain as if it was a trophy.

On the platform, with pale skin that had just lost its color, blank eyes that stared toward the ground, and necks viciously clawed, hung several limp bodies. They were victims who swung lifelessly from ropes like demented windchimes.

Three new hangings today. I wonder how many were actually criminals? Looks like they didn't even get their necks broken.

Colton lifted his eyes, squinting as the morning light reflected back at him from the arrays of metal and glass buildings of the Auratus District. Set high on a plateau amongst the massive mountains, it was above the rest of the city like a crown compared to the Scintilla Initium.

12

Imagine ruling the whole world and living in the top of those buildings.

Colton turned his attention back to the Central Market, eventually finding Fisk laying low near a stall not far from Colton himself. Keeping to the shadows, Colton hurried over, trying his best to avoid the puddles from the fountain as he drew close to Fisk.

"You must be *so* popular with your friends," Colton growled.

"I ain't dead yet," Fisk said.

"Maybe you will be."

"I ain't got no boun'ee on me head."

"Not like the guardians would care."

"I dur-not know 'bout yoo, but I ain't ter wun whoo stole turday!"

"What? I only stole because—"

"What have I told you about stealin'?" a third voice said.

Colton cursed himself under his breath as Fisk snickered, the two of them turning toward the man who towered over them.

Dressed in a fraying red sweater, shirt, tie, and brown slacks, the man gave a stern look from behind cracked glasses perched on a weathered, olive-skinned face. His posture was straight-backed and his hands had no calluses.

"What d'you think yur doing, Colton?" Mr. Daas demanded.

Colton resisted making fun of the man's accent like he sometimes did. Instead, he withered beneath the man's glare.

"Fisk was—"

Colton didn't finish as Mr. Daas grabbed him by the ear and dragged him from the Central Market to a small alleyway, Fisk hooting the whole way. People glanced at them as they passed, one man frowned, while a woman commented on the poor state of the next generation.

"You dur not know how to keep out of trouble d'you?" Mr. Daas admonished, letting go of Colton but smacking him on the backside of his head.

"Fisk made me do it!" Colton argued.

"Fisk is scrawny, and can't make anyone do any'ding," Mr. Daas stated. Fisk nodded hastily behind Daas's back.

"He doesn't need muscle like Jace does," Colton said.

Caleb DM Smith

"Colton, you keep stealing dings. You've committed like twenty crimes today."

"I only stole the wallet."

You're an idiot, Colton.

Mr. Daas rubbed his temples, "Oh, for love of ammi, Colton. You will rob all of Central Mesica and Malelentos dry."

"More like making you poor," Colton said. "What happened to actually *taking care* of us?"

"How much did you steal?"

"Fisk has it," Colton said.

"I don't dink so."

"Yes he—" Colton began, before shutting his mouth and throwing a glare at Fisk. Colton handed over the wallet of coins, which Mr. Daas dumped into his hand, counting it with a frown before pocketing it.

"Coulda stolen more, not much left for me to use. Fisk, keep Colton in line," Mr. Daas said before walking off into the Central Market, muttering something in another language.

Once the man was gone, Colton kicked the dirt into the air, shouting as he clutched handfuls of hair. "I can't—Stupid little—AAH!"

A rat scampered by and Colton chucked a rock at it, before punching the wall. He collapsed against the wall, sliding to the ground as Fisk snickered.

"Weel, looky at poor yoo," Fisk said, "lost yer dinner turnight."

"Shut up," Colton muttered.

"Wha'? Yoo don' like Daas stealin' from yah?"

"It's not like I could steal back from—" Colton paused, frowning.

Or, maybe I could. He would know if I did though. But maybe if I had Fisk do it… Not like he'd get blamed.

Colton leaped to his feet, a grin spreading across his lips. "Fisk, you know where Mr. Daas's stash is, right?"

Fisk's face contorted with a brow raised. "Yeh, maybe I doo? Why yoo wannuh know?"

"Let's consider it Daas's taxes."

14

Chapter 2

Partners in Crime

Daas'll beat the lights outta me if he finds out.

Before them stood a building, more sturdy stone than its neighbors, dust floating through the windows. A sign above the entrance depicted a hammer breaking open a large boulder, and Colton's instincts did their best to pull him away from the building.

"Hope you don't have asthma," Colton muttered.

"Well, whatur yoo waitin' fur?" Fisk whispered.

Watching the small crowd shuffle past, Colton threw his hood on and snuck across the street to cling against the wall and peer in the window. He coughed a little bit at first but squinted his eyes against the dust and waved a hand in front of his face as he peered in the building.

Empty of people, but full of plenty of desk-like stations designed to hold large stones. Crude tools were laid on weathered wood; pebbles littered the floor. Against one wall were large stone columns and boulders, and on the opposite, a series of doors leading to other rooms.

"Maybe this wasn't such a good idea," Colton said, slowly withdrawing from the wall until his stomach growled.

Fine, fine. If you say so.

Reluctantly, Colton entered into the room, turning towards the series of doors, finding there to be three, with the center one being the only one not made out of rotting and half-broken wood. A plaque on the front about eye-level read 'Mr. Daas.'

Well, he makes it hard to fail. Colton thought with a smirk, striding toward the door.

Finding it locked, he backed up, peering outside the window, seeing Fisk standing and keeping watch. The scrawny boy rapidly flapped his hands, gesturing wildly.

15

Studying the door, Colton took a deep breath, gritted his teeth, and sprinted right at the door. He leaped and slammed his foot into the wood with all of his weight. He crumpled to the ground, shocks running up his leg, and pain blossoming in his ankle.

The door hadn't even creaked.

Colton crawled away from the door, eyes watering as his leg stung from earlier impact.

"Ow, maybe not," Colton groaned.

He clutched his leg, slowly regaining his footing as he waited for the pain to subside.

Looking around, he took in the stations, finding a few objects. A bowl under a station, an array of chiseling tools beside a large stone block, and a sledgehammer beside the wall.

Well, what do we have here?

Colton grabbed the sledgehammer, nearly getting jerked into the wall at the surprising weight. Hefting it to his shoulder with a grunt, he shuffled to the door, his muscles weakening quickly.

Hefting the sledgehammer again, Colton raised it, groaning as he hurled it over his head, nearly losing his balance as he sent it spinning to smash right through the center of the door.

Colton winced at the loud crack, glancing at the window.

"What'r wassat?" Fisk called.

"Just getting my way in," he answered sheepishly.

"Wella hurry! Daas mighta be heer shoon."

Colton hustled up to the door, freeing the sledgehammer from the wood, allowing him to reach his hand in and unlock the door.

Inside he found an office-like space, though extremely meager in quality. Its contents were in such disrepair that the covers of any books appeared to have been completely replaced with mold.

A quick search through the drawers and shelves yielded little result. Only a few scrap items and sad excuses for office tools. The most extravagant things the office held were a cushioned chair with feathers sticking out all sides and a small statue of a deity-looking humanoid on the desk looking like it was made by a toddler.

Did Jace make that? Or did Daas?

Colton snatched up the statue before hurrying out of the office, grimacing at the massive hole in the door.

16

"Thatall yah got?" Fisk jeered from the window.

Colton held up the statue, causing the two praying arms to fall off. Fisk wilted, frowning with his broken teeth, giving a pitiful expression.

"He doesn't have it here," Colton said.

"I figured hey'da have sumthin'. Stealin' froma everyone, he is," Fisk said.

"Daas's probably smarter than to hide his stash in his office."

Colton hurried to the door, throwing it open to find a large boy standing there. pudgy, expression upside-down, large arms crossed, and his entire dark-skinned, rotund shaped form bristling like a balloon ready to explode.

This day just can't get any worse, can it?

"You stealing from my dad?" Jace demanded, leaning forward.

Colton cast a glance at Fisk, who had a sour look in his eyes, but a gleeful smile, like a soldier flanked by an ally tank.

Of course, Fisk set me up!

"I was asking you a question, short-head," Jace clocked Colton on the side of the head, sending him into the doorway for a double hit.

Colton cradled his skull, casting Jace a glare. "Nosk off, kretch!"

Jace swung again, but this time Colton was ready, side-stepping the blow.

"What'd you call me?" Jace bellowed.

"I don't have anything you'd want," Colton retorted, giving Fisk a fierce glare, who seemed to be enjoying watching the exchange between Colton and Jace.

"Yes, yoo do," Fisk said, "the money you stole. Give it heer!"

"You threw away my money?" Jace howled, swinging again.

Colton barely contained his frustration as he resisted the urge to swing at Jace. The bully grabbed Colton by the neck, who countered by smashing the statue on Jace. A valyuta and a few chrimata fell to the ground.

The two paused, glancing down, with Jace's grip going slack. Colton ducked down, snatching the coins, and dodging past Jace. The large bully shouted, with Fisk hooting angrily. Colton grinned, looking back at them, giving chase. He gritted his teeth as pain shot through his leg, his ankle protesting from its injury.

He collided into a man covered in heavy metal armor that clicked like steel cogs of a machine, facial features and armor hidden by a black cloak. Metal covered hands grabbed for his arm, but Colton twisted out of the way. The man led out a grunt that sounded digital.

Weird guardian.

Colton rounded a corner, with Jace lagging behind. Fisk, with fists balled and swinging, could almost grab Colton's collar. Colton veered off the road, dashed through an alleyway, popped out the other end, and merged with the crowd. Fisk grabbed at his clothes, and Colton tugged free, sprinting away.

At last, Colton reached his destination, adrenaline pushing him the last few yards as his legs nearly gave out. He kicked open the door, groaning before he slammed it shut behind himself. The wood groaned as Fisk collided into it.

A quick scan of the room revealed a host of kids Colton's age sitting on a frayed rug with a stout teacher, book in hand, glaring down the bridge of her nose at Colton.

"Colton Diaíresi Toa!" the teacher shouted in ire, "you should *not* be here."

Colton smiled sheepishly, pulling off his hood. His eyes shifted to see his friends, Liam and Bristol, sitting on the rug, both staring at him.

"It's an emergency," Colton said.

"What're you doing here?" Liam asked.

"Give it back, short-head!" shouted Jace's behind the door.

Liam and Bristol shook their heads at Colton, the girl more horrified and Liam more annoyed.

"You did *not* steal from Jace," Liam muttered.

Colton bit his tongue. "I may or may not have stolen from his dad."

"You're so dead," Bristol covered her face with her hands.

"It was Fisk's fault."

The teacher pried Colton away from the door, allowing Jace to crash into the room, stumbling and nearly crushing a small redheaded kid beneath him, with Fisk close behind.

"Give me my stuff back!" Jace demanded, his arms pushing him back onto plump feet.

Colton wrenched himself from the teacher's clutches, dodged past pudgy grasping hands, and dashed out the door, shoving Fisk to the ground in the process as he threw his hood back on.

Bristol looked at Liam expectantly, and he sighed, scratching his head and gritting his teeth.

"Let me go save him. *Yet again.*"

Liam climbed to his feet, apologizing to the teacher before rushing out the door.

* *

Colton collapsed onto the mudbrick roof, his heartbeat slowing down a pace as he took a few steadying breaths. He tore his cloak open, a cool breeze giving respite as the jitteriness slowly left his limbs.

Stupid life of a criminal.

Propping himself up, Colton watched from the edge of the building, catching sight of Fisk and Jace conversing at the edge of the market. Jace knocked Fisk in the head, sending him to the ground before striding away. Colton grimaced, rolling to his back and letting out a sigh of relief as Liam popped over the edge and stumbled over to him.

"Why'd you think it was safe to steal from Jace?" Liam asked, running a hand through his muddy-brown hair.

Colton sat up, the dizziness hitting him and his pain throbbing from the bruises he had acquired.

"Like I said, it was Fisk's fault," Colton said, examining his ankle.

"Why do you keep hanging with him? He doesn't do you any good."

"It's not my choice"

"But you keep talking to him."

"Like I said," Colton huffed, "it's not my choice."

Liam folded his arms. "You always have a choice."

"Not when you're gonna die."

Caleb DM Smith

"You're not gonna die."

"I will if I don't eat, so will you."

Liam threw up his calloused hands. "You ever gonna listen to me?"

"I know what I'm doing," Colton said, moving his gaze toward the massive nearby mountains.

When has listening to people gotten me anywhere?

Colton shook his head before treading over and began descending the side of the building via a series of cracks.

There's been only one time it helped me. And that was with Kai.

Colton paused, giving Liam a frown before rolling his eyes. "Fine, I'll try it for one day, tomorrow."

He dropped down, landing on the packed dirt in a crouch, his feet stinging slightly.

"Where're you going?" Liam popped over the edge of the roof.

"Home. You wanna stay here for the guardians' nighttime routine?" Colton asked, "I'd rather leave now before sunset."

"Two fifteen-year-olds have no chance of beating a guardian," Liam said, scaling down the building.

The two of them made their way down the streets, doing their best to keep Colton hidden. The buildings slowly became lower in quality as they walked. Turning into shacks and sheds made of scraps. Branches, rotting wood, and foliage piled together.

They left the packed dirt roads huddled amongst humble shelters, walking on barely formed paths amidst reeds and dry grass. Ahead of them, a small forest lay, and next to it, a quarry buried into the mountain side.

Into the small forest they went, their trail slowly steepening more and more, until they were forced to begin climbing sheer rock and navigating a treacherous route up the sides of the mountains.

Colton glanced back at the city as he climbed, seeing entirely the stark contrast between the two districts: one with parks, and lights, and music. And the other quiet, dark, and dirty.

Weird. Deja-vu. I wonder what the Auratus District is like.

Colton twitched, shaking his head as his neck complained at him, and he felt the writhing sensation, like a serious upset stomach. He cast a glare at the city again.

No. I wish I could burn—no. Not that. I just want to leave this place behind.

Chapter 3
Memory Lapse

The boy huddled amidst the two trees as he did his best not to be found.

His pursuer slowly crawled over the rock, not yet within line-of-sight, but drawing closer, breath heavy. The boy scrunched himself closer to the ground, apprehension rising in his gut, his pursuer let out a growl.

"You can't run forever."

The boy snickered. "Yes, I can."

The pursuer let out another growl and leaped down, swinging his arms wildly, face twisted furiously. Colton laughed, fending off the pretend blows before his attacker stopped, standing up and smirking down at Colton.

"Looks like I won!" he said.

Colton watched his younger self throw his hands in the air, feeling the same sensations as if in both places at once. "That's not fair! You're older than me."

"You shouldn't compete with someone who's double your age."

Shut up, you're not—I'm not eight. Of course you'd win. Why'm I having this dream again?

"I'll beat you one day!" Colton protested, leaping to his feet and not gaining much height.

"I'll find you every time. I'm the inevitable end. *Maybe* one day you'll beat me in a fight."

"I can beat you!"

"Yeah?" Kai challenged, grabbing a stick and tossing it to Colton.

Colton caught the stick and immediately charged, swinging it wildly while Kai nimbly dodged.

"You can't swing it aimlessly like that," Kai said, "you'll take someone's head off."

"That's what I'm trying to do!" Colton said, swinging again.

Kai blocked with a swing, snapping both sticks, and Colton groaned, chucking the remains away. Kai chuckled and grabbed a large stick, snapping it, and holding the two smaller parts in both hands.

"It's not about pure power; it's about playing to your opponent's weaknesses."

"But you don't have any weaknesses."

"Everyone has a weakness, Colton."

"Then what's yours?"

Kai laughed. "I can't just tell you; you have to figure it out. And remember, not all weaknesses are physical."

Kai kicked up a stick and tossed it to Colton, who grabbed it and gave Kai a smirk, the older boy holding out a hand and beckoning.

"Try again, sword master," Kai said with a grin.

"I'll use my superpowers and blow you up!" Colton said, swinging the stick stylishly.

Kai's usual smile fell and his bright blue eyes lost their glimmer, sinking down to dulled cyan. "No, Colton, you don't have powers. Forget whatever your parents told you."

'But they said—"

"NO!" Kai shouted.

He swung his sticks, snapping Colton's, and knocking him to the ground. Colton felt his palms scrape as his whole body jolted with the sudden stop.

"Colton, listen to me," Kai said, kneeling, "never bring that up to your parents."

"But what about all the scary needles?" Colton asked, lip quivering.

"Forget whatever they said! They're delusional. You *don't* have powers."

"But they said—."

"You're nothing to them; they say that to make you behave. It's not power. It's a disease you have."

"But they they always spend—"

23

"NO!" Kai screamed, shaking Colton roughly at the shoulders.

Colton stared at Kai with wide eyes, his brain going haywire and he tugged at Kai's grip. Tears started brimming in Colton's eyes as he began shaking with fear.

"Colton, I'm sorry," Kai said, "but you are a normal, nobody kid, alright? You have to believe that, for yourself. I'm trying to protect you. You're just a stupid kid."

Colton felt the urge he had to run intensify, he tugged harder. "Let me go."

"No, Colton—"

"Let me go!"

Colton tugged his wrist out of Kai's grip and turned and ran up the slope, almost sprinting toward the town set upon the massive conical hill, like a swirling wedding cake.

He ran as his tears streamed down, his gut writhing and thrashing as it always did. The sensation of it trying to burst out of him proving hard to fight down.

Why can't I control myself—that weird thing inside me?

Colton ran and ran until he was among the glorious mansions and people dressed in expensive clothing. Many stared at him, faces twisted in disgust and Colton subconsciously looked down at his dirty silk clothes, the tears surging from his eyes again as he continued his exhaustive sprint.

Comments and murmuring followed him, and the thrashing continued. He rounded a corner and ran into someone, knocking himself backwards on the ground.

Looking up, he nearly screamed, his wrists and arms itching under their bandages as he felt the intensity of his father's glare.

"Where've you been?" His father demanded, grabbing Colton by the collar and shaking him. "We've wasted our time looking for you!"

"I was—" Colton began.

His father slapped him across the face and pointed a rigid finger.

"You'll never run off again, understand?"

Before Colton could protest, he was dragged up the road, slowly winding up the hill. More gasps, more muttered comments, more stares, as if reacting to a piece of pollution.

His father turned, striding off the road and onto a walkway leading to an impressive manor. The windows leered at Colton, and the door gaped open to swallow him.

Into the darkness of the interior he was dragged, and Colton screamed, pulling against his father's grip. Down the stairs, through dark hallways, creaking doors, and to a room only occupied by two things. A bed with chains at the corners, and a bedside table beside it, holding a syringe with gold liquid and a second with magenta fluid.

"NO! Please, no! They hurt," Colton wailed.

Colton tugged as hard as he could, only resulting in his father throwing him on the bed. Before Colton could do much, he felt a sharp pain across his back, digging into him.

A glance revealed his father held a thin short whip, the end stained a dark red, almost as dark as the expression his father wore, nothing darker than the eyes.

Those tired, worn, furious eyes.

"Show me your back," he commanded in a gruff voice.

"Please, no," Colton whimpered.

"I said, show me!" screamed his father, raising the whip.

Reluctantly, Colton lifted his shirt, tears streaming down his cheeks as sputtering sobs escaped his lips. He squeezed his eyes shut, the whip cracking with heat, before he felt a coldness spread over his skin.

The whip cracked, a flash of agonizing hot, then more cold.

It cracked again, more heat, and deeper cold.

A third time.

A fourth.

Again.

Again.

And again.

Colton winced, bracing for another crack, blood dripping down his skin. He felt strong hands force him down to the bed, flipping him over, followed by cold metal clamping around his wrists and ankles. His father reached into a closet, pulling out a large dagger.

"Your own foolishness brought your agony," his father said, pricking him in the shoulder. "If you hadn't been so idiotic, this disease wouldn't have existed."

"I didn't do anything," Colton cried, thrashing against the chains, only for his father to spit on him.

"It's a shame we had to disgrace the family with you. With your cursed *heritage*."

"Father," said another voice. An older boy, eyes like his father's, tired and worn, coupled with a devilish smile. "Has he produced the Blood Eye yet?"

"We shall see," replied the father.

"You're going to take my eyes out! Bleed me to death? My eyes aren't bloody."

"Idiot boy, the Blood Eye comes from one sick like you. Maybe by your illness we can heal others."

"No, please!" Colton wailed.

"Submit, or do you let your darkness overtake you?"

"No, no no!"

Colton screamed as his father reached for his eye with the large dagger. The writhing sensation thrashed inside him so hard he felt it rise in his throat. His fingers burned and his veins felt ready to burst, like a gale of dark flames.

Bury it, bury it, bury it!

Looking at his father's murderous eyes, Colton writhed, his father's form warping and twisting like smoke. The surroundings seemed to disform, losing shape.

No! Let me see what happens!

Colton coughed, a sense of vertigo overwhelming him as he was torn momentarily from his younger body. He lost all sense of direction, his eyes being blinded by smoke until he found himself standing upright in a basement hallway.

Wha–? It just teleported me.

A glance behind himself revealed a door, scorched black, and set at the end of a hallway. Fire erupted from its crack as it gorged itself on the walls. Colton cried, stumbling forward as part of the house collapsed behind him, flames licking his back.

"Colton?" called a voice.

"Help!" Colton wailed.

A second later, Colton collided with Kai, finding him badly burned, but more alive than Colton was.

"Colton, what happened?" Kai asked, eyes wide.

"I–I–I didn't mean to, I—" Colton cried.

Kai shook his head, moving Colton down the hall. "Come on!"

The house creaked as flame and embers roared, cracked, and popped all around them. They made it to the stairs, and Kai shoved Colton forward up them. Kai slipped behind Colton, a loud *smack*, cracking, and he cried out, legs caught in flaming debris. Colton stopped, turning to help, but Kai slapped his hands away.

"Colton, run from here!" Kai shouted. "Before they come get you!"

Colton shook his head. "No! I have to help."

Colton grabbed Kai's hand and helped slowly drag him up the steps, eventually reaching the top. The house groaned, shifting as cracking filled their ears.

Kai grabbed Colton's wrists, pushing him and sending Colton tumbling down the hall. Wood and debris popped and cracked, crashing on top of Kai who let out a scream that devolved like a digital buzzing from a machine shutting down as flames roared in Colton's direction, engulfing him.

"Kai!" Colton screamed.

He sat upright, shoulders heaving, the searing sensation lingering on his shoulder and arm. He shook his head, mind swimming, and heart thrashing in his ribcage.

He glanced around, seeing no black fire, no collapsing house, and no Kai. Only the dark concrete room he slept in inside the mountains beside Malelentos was visible to him.

Colton groaned, hanging his head in his hands, his throat closing as he felt that writhing sensation slowly rise up before he pushed it down.

No! Bury it! Bury it!

Why does that keep coming back? I know I can't remember all of it, but I know what happened.

A wildfire burned down the town. Took everything.

No one's gonna help me.

27

Chapter 4

In Quarry

Colton hunched down on the rock, bundled cloak in hand, watching Liam slowly and expertly climb down the small rock face.

He better not fall.

Liam immediately vanished below the cliff edge, and Colton's senses pricked up as he rocked forward on his toes. A moment later, Liam called for Colton to follow. Colton rolled his eyes and slowly approached the edge, turning to scoot backwards, and place his feet on small footholds in the stone.

Why're we taking this route from our hideout?

Colton slowly lowered himself, his feet touching foothold after foothold. Meticulously preventing himself from falling onto rough rocks on a steep slope.

I can't believe I let Liam talk me into a job. I'd literally make more stealing.

Reaching the last foothold, Colton descended a little lower till he was hanging by just his hands before dropping the last eight feet, landing in a crouch.

"Maybe you could be an explorer. You've got the skills," Liam commented, his ruddy face winding into a smile.

"With my luck?" Colton asked, dusting off his cloak, adjusting it. "Plus, most people come *into* Malelentos. Not out."

"But there *are* some who leave, right?"

"Not any who're poor like we are. I'd have to break into the Auratus District or find a treasure horde to get any chance of leaving this city."

"Who knows? Maybe we'll find a way," Liam shrugged.

Colton scoffed. "So, you wanna break in now?"

"No, but I have faith things will turn out for the better."

"Right, because *faith* is gonna feed us."

Liam turned and began strolling into the small forest, Colton following, heading in the direction where the sound of pickaxes ringing out against rock was audible. Past small oaks and tall fir trees they walked. A series of farms were visible a ways off beside a small path that led to the Scintilla Initium.

Colton and Liam slowly emerged from the trees, stepping foot onto the gravel-covered dirt. The scent of dust hung in choking clouds and the ambiance of hundreds of workers filled their ears.

Liam led the way to a particular section of the quarry, where a massive man wielding a pickaxe stood, dark skin rippling beneath raggedy, sweat-soaked clothes as dust around him nearly hid him from view.

There's no way that pickaxe handle isn't just a tree trunk.

"Morning, Dromus," Liam greeted. "I brought extra help."

Dromus growled, setting down the pickaxe and nearly causing an earthquake as he took a long glower at Colton.

"More hindrance than help," he growled.

Colton raised a brow, and Dromus flared his nostrils, picking up his pickaxe and striding off to another section of the quarry, muttering as he stomped. "Get to work."

Liam walked over to where a bin held piles of rubble and rock, which he began sorting through. "We'll sort through these, picking out the prettier rocks."

"Looking to build your collection?" Colton teased.

"No, it's for the mason shop. Auratus District needs more ornamental pieces."

"Why do you even work for those Richmen?"

"Honest money."

"There's faster ways to make money."

"*Illegal* ways."

"No one's keeping track."

"The guardians are," Liam said.

Colton shrugged. "But they haven't caught me."

Liam stopped working, letting out an exasperated sigh before turning to Colton with a stern look. "You wanna know why I work for Daas even when you won't?" Liam asked. "So, he doesn't turn you in and get you killed."

Colton opened his mouth to retort, but no words came out.

"Oh," Colton said, "I didn't know…"

Liam shrugged and Colton hurried over. They hefted stones for a while, with Colton feeling his muscles complain each time he grabbed a boulder, and his legs groan each time he carried it to another bin.

As they worked, Colton stole glances at the other workers hacking away at the hillsides, a few Kekamotos among them, hissing at anyone that got too close.

"How many races do you think there are besides Kekamotos and us?" Colton asked.

"No idea. Bristol might know," Liam said.

Colton pretended to push glasses on his nose, making his voice nasally. "Kekamotos have been here since the First Great Calamity due to weapon usage. And they've only survived here through mutual crimes with humans."

"That's kinda mean."

"It's what she'd say, right?"

"She's smarter than us," Liam muttered.

"Yeah, I'm not too sure about Bristol's theories," Colton said. "I don't think you can create something like Kekamotos from a war."

"Like, what?"

"Well, Nessa agrees with Bristol that the Kekamotos came *from* it. Like the weapons used caused mutations."

"How does a couple bombs make a whole new race?" Colton asked.

"Beats me."

Colton groaned and hefted another boulder into the bin, making it smash into pieces, sending sparks everywhere as chunks of obsidian became visible.

"Careful!" Liam exclaimed.

Colton gave a grimacing, apologetic look.

Definitely not my dream job.

Someone smacked Colton on the back of the head, nearly strong enough to send him stumbling to the ground.

"Get back to work!" Dromus rumbled.

Colton muttered a mocking impression under his breath, rubbing the backside of his skull, feeling it swell up.

"Go back to where you came from," Colton spat.

Dromus smacked Colton on the back, sending him tumbling into the rocks, scraping his hands and knees.

"The Crossroads where I came from," Dromus growled, hefting his pickaxe threateningly. "Be glad you ain't livin' there."

"Sounds nicer than here," Colton said, shaking his hands and blowing on them gently.

Dromus crouched low and Colton felt as if a mountain was threatening to hit him with a landslide.

"I said, get back to work."

"What if I just left this stupid place?"

"You wouldn' last a day out'a Malelentos. Not a broke stupid kid like you."

"I'm not dumb," Colton spat, climbing to his feet.

Dromus narrowed his eyes. "Last person I heard say that, left his baby daughter and went into an Arachnotaur forest, called the Plummeth of Groff. Didn't come back ever."

"Arachnotaur?"

"Half-human-half-spider creatures. Kretchs'll eat your face off."

"Sounds like a Kekamoto."

"Colton," Liam said, shaking his head ever so slightly.

Colton raised a brow at his friend before sighing and grabbing another rock from the bin.

"Whatever."

Dromus sneered, hefting his pickaxe, turning and leaving once again. Colton threw a glare at the man's back.

No way there's Arachnotaurs or anything like that, right?

* *

By the time Liam had selected his rocks and they wheeled them to the stonemason shop, Colton had nearly passed out from exhaustion.

His stomach rumbled and his throat was parched as he hid in an alley-way.

Finally! Colton thought as Liam emerged from the building, dusting off his palms.

Liam raised his brows, frowning. "So, why's there a massive hole in Daas's door?"

"Can we go eat now?" Colton complained.

"Didn't Daas take all your money? Or did you steal more wallets?"

"I don't steal," Colton said, "that much."

"Instead of stealing to eat, we can visit Nessa. She loves to feed us."

"Ugh, not that crazy lady."

"She's just old and lonely. You'd be a little crazy, too."

"Yeah, maybe," Colton conceded, pulling his cloak hood over his head.

Liam took off down the road, heading to the opposite end of the Scintilla Initium District from the quarry with Colton in tow. Every so often, Colton had to duck into an alleyway or hide in some form from guardians that marched by.

This is stupid. One of these days, I'm gonna learn to fight them off.

Once the guardians were out of sight, Colton hurried down the street, head on a swivel and shoulders itching.

At length, they drew close to a large plaza with very few people in it. Colton studied it for a moment, before his eyes widened and he threw himself into the shadows of two buildings. Liam gave him a confused look, brows raised.

"What're you doing?" Liam asked.

Colton gestured to the other end of the plaza, where the slums slowly turned into concrete and steel.

It was a heavily fortified zone with iron gates, twenty or so stationed guardians that were armed to the teeth, cameras, alarms at the ready, and plenty of other defenses fit for war.

"You remember the last time I was there?" Colton hissed.

Liam nodded. "Looks like you got them to upgrade a bit."

"You think? They only had three guardians stationed there two years ago."

The two watched for a moment, with Colton keeping tabs on each guardian. As far as he could tell from the tilting of their helmets and relaxed bodies, most looked bored, and others half asleep.

Except one was looking right at Liam.

"Liam, get down!" Colton hissed.

Liam looked between Colton, and the guardian. "I haven't done anything wrong. Why would he—?"

"What're you looking at, gjinx?" the guardian called. The voice was distorted and partially glitchy, like a digital machine struggling to reproduce an organic voice.

"What's with the slur?" Liam began.

"You're from the Scintilla Initium District? You're a filthy gjinx."

"Sorry, if I disturbed you. I was just passing by to somewhere else."

The guardian kept strolling closer, and Colton could feel his muscles prepping, with his brain running through a dozen or so scenarios.

"Then why'd you stop here, huh?" The guardian asked.

Liam shrugged, his fingers twitching as he took a step back.

No, stop! You look nervous and guilty doing that, Colton thought.

"I was just—" Liam began.

The guardian raised their rifle, jamming the barrel into Liam's chest hard enough to nearly make him stumble back. The muzzle glistened in the sunlight, and the faint smell of gunpowder was detectable.

"You thinkin' of try'na get in?" The guardian asked, tilting their head.

Liam hastily shook his head, rubbing his hands on his trousers. Colton bit his tongue, eager to leap out and cause a distraction, but his itching shoulders warned him to stay hidden.

Don't try and help. You'll just cause more problems like always.

"You know what would happen if you tried that?" the guardian asked. "You wanna know what happened last time a kid tried it?

33

The dark-facial visor hid any human features, reflecting no light as it leaned closer toward Liam. Colton watched as the guardian moved a finger, slowly flipping off the safety, then placing it on the trigger.

Nosking kretch! He's gonna blow a hole in Liam's chest.

Colton balled his hands into fists, slowly standing up to rush out. He stopped as the security gate let out a blaring beep, drawing everyone's attention.

The guardian turned their head, watching the gate slide open as a dozen more guardians entered the Scintilla Initium District. Turning back to Liam, the guardian lowered the rifle.

"You lucky I'm off the clock," the guardian said. "Next time you get your filth too close. It's a bullet through your head."

Colton crouched back down, watching the old guardians swap with the new, the retired ones beginning a hike up a long road, switching back to the tops of the skyscraper adorned plateau.

Liam stumbled back, nearly crashing into Colton as he took a few steadying breaths. Colton winced, patting his friend on the back.

Liam let out a shaky breath. "I've *never* had one approach me like that."

Colton chuckled nervously, slowly rising to his feet. "Not everyone who gets hung on the gallows is guilty. It's a game to them."

They turned and briskly walked down another road, taking a long route to avoid more guardians. They drew close to a lake that wrapped around the cliffs of the Auratus District. On the shore they stopped at a house of green painted wood and stone, standing out against the other houses of rotting lumber. Proper shingles, windows, walls, and a door made of solid fresh oak.

It's a surprise it's not burned down or raided by guardians every day.

Colton walked up the steps to the door, rapping his knuckles lightly on the wood, only for silence to answer back. He did it a second time with the same result.

A third time Colton heard a cough and the sound of someone shuffling inside the house. A few moments later the door creaked open, revealing a woman with cracked glasses, blazing red hair, and looking so old that Colton compared her to a toad. Squat and not a pretty sight.

"Oh, well hello there, Colton!" she exclaimed as if in a hurry.

"Hi, Nessa," Colton said, looking at Liam.

"Could we have lunch with you?" Liam asked.

"Weel, yes, of course ye can." she said, stepping back, accent bleeding through.

Colton hung back, the stench hit him instantly. It was as if a dozen animals had been stuck inside for a month, only removed an hour before.

Does she ever clean this place? Colton thought as he wandered into the house, pulling off his hood.

"Sit, sit," Nessa invited, pointing to a rotting couch. Liam sat down, with Colton preferring to lean against the wall.

"Are you doing better?" Liam asked. "I heard your leg got worse for a week."

Nessa waved a dismissive hand. "Oh, that ol' thing has been right bags for a good wael now. But it's on the mend."

"We're glad," Liam answered.

Colton raised a brow, averting his gaze.

Nessa nodded at Colton. "Not very happy. Not much a chance to steal today?"

Liam smirked. "No. He might throw a tantrum."

"Shut up, Liam," Colton said. "Why'd you tell her that?"

"He told me nothin'," Nessa said, "I jus' know how to use me eyes n' ears."

"Why do you talk like that?"

Nessa bobbed her head. "The local dialect of me town. Protected all the wae from the First Great Calamity when me country took shelter underground, as is the case wit' many a town and their people. The isles of Megral are where I'm from, before I traveled here to Central Mesica."

"So, you've traveled a lot, huh?" Liam asked.

"Wael, yes. I first stayed in Aquila Mons before here."

Colton nearly choked on his own throat. "You lived in—but you can't—I lived there."

"I know. I traveled wit ye here. Wit the other survivors that be."

"What's Aquila Mons?" Liam asked, looking at Colton, who averted his eyes.

"A wealthy town that met a terrible end," Nessa said. "I was one of a small group of fifty survivors."

In response, she pulled down the collar of her woolen sweater, revealing a large burn scar on her neck and shoulder, though oddly shaped.

It looks like someone painted it badly. Is it fake?

"Huh, okay, I guess," Colton said, frowning.

"Ah, wael, I'll get you two a fed now," Nessa said, slowly shambling into the next room. Liam gave Colton an excited look, who rolled his eyes and shook his head.

Her food never tastes good.

Colton turned his attention to the house. It was small, but cozy. Plenty of furniture crowded the rooms, as well as an assortment of almost every other item in existence. The most numerous of which were hundreds of papers hanging from strings tied to the ceiling, many being diagrams of machines, places, or even articles about different people.

Was she a guardian at some point?

Colton reached up and grabbed one piece of paper, pulling it down. Liam threw him a glare, but Colton shrugged. He looked over the drawn picture, seeing a woman with red hair, freckles, and an ever-grinning smile. Written text gave information that Colton didn't understand, with a label reading 'Constance Jensen - Shapeshifter.'

Looks like her cousin, or a sister. Is this all Nessa's random folklore?

Another paper, this time seeing a young girl with golden eyes, void-black hair, and the purest expression. A title in the top-right corner read 'Theos Mortem - Heritage.'

Yup, sounds like some god of death.

Putting the paper back, Colton took down another, seeing a picture of a mean-looking boy that packed a good amount of muscle, and with cruel cold eyes. The name read 'Paisie Silenus - Frostbite.'

36

Frowning, Colton replaced the article for a fourth, finding a boy, much older than the rest, with bright blue eyes, blond wavy hair, and a brave smiling expression.

Why does she have a picture of Kai?

Colton gripped the paper, the writhing sensation starting to crawl up his stomach as he felt a spike hit his limbs, making them numb and jittery. He barely noticed his teeth grinding so hard his jaw hurt.

The name printed: 'Kai Winder - Experimental Chimera One.'

Chimera One? The kretch is that? Why does she have this? He died years ago in Aquila Mons.

"Oh! do excuse meh," Nessa exclaimed, shuffling back into the room, steaming pie pan in hand. "It still needed a wee bit more time."

Colton jerked his gaze up, dropping the paper and settling his eyes on Nessa who was setting a pie onto a coffee table. She looked at him, then the paper at the ground by his feet, then back to him.

This time with a knowing look.

Colton scowled. "Why do you—?"

"Thank you so much!" Liam exclaimed, butting in and ending the staring contest Colton and Nessa were holding.

"Eat, eat," Nessa encouraged, serving and shoving plates full of chicken curry pie into the two boys' hands.

Colton grimaced down at his food; the aroma was deceptively pleasant. Hesitantly grabbing a fork and stabbing the slice, he nibbled a small bite off before quickly swallowing.

Ugh! That tastes so—slimy! Colton thought, setting the plate down on the arm of the rotting couch.

"You think that tastes a wee bit awful?" Nessa asked with a grin. "Wael, wait till yeh try Demon meat."

Colton and Liam shared glances, both looking unsurprised.

Her folklore is fine, as long as she doesn't describe eating or killing something.

"Sounds—good," Liam said with a forced smile.

Nessa bobbed her head. "I hear you had trouble. I made a wee thing to help you."

She reached into a pocket of her dress, fumbling for a bit before she held out her hand, displaying a small bag in her palm. Hesitantly, Colton grabbed at it, keeping his eyes mostly trained on the frail woman.

This better not be one of her tarts.

Colton picked up the bag, having more weight than expected as it let out a small metallic jingle. Furrowing his brows, Colton opened the bag, finding a couple valyuta inside.

No way! She's just giving this to me?

"You don't want this money?" Colton asked wide-eyed. "Not that we couldn't use it" he hastily added.

Nessa shook her head, smiling with her all-gums-no-teeth mouth. "Keep it. It's nothing to a frail old hag like me."

Colton nodded hastily, pocketing the money, looking at Liam with an overly happy expression, who also seemed pleasantly surprised.

"This is enough to buy proper beds, or maybe even get us real close to getting outta here," Colton said humbly. "Where'd you get it?"

"Thank you, Nessa," Liam said hurriedly.

"Yes, never mind where it came from," Nessa said. "I have work to do. Go spend your lot."

Colton practically skipped to the door, his mind running through all of the things he could buy as he obsessively patted his pocket to make sure it was there. Liam uttered another thanks before closing the door.

Colton jangled the bag again before slipping it back into his pocket. "I'm rich! I could buy almost anything."

Liam folded his arms. "You could. But, we should spend it wisely."

"Like how? We're so much closer to leaving!"

"I know someone that's pretty smart."

Colton scowled, glaring down at his bag, admiring the golden glint of the coins as he lightly shook them. He gave Liam a look.

Of course he wants to talk to her. She's a know-it-all.

"Fine," Colton groaned, donning his hood, "we'll go talk to Bristol."

38

Chapter 5

Informal Information

Colton felt tempted to bang his head against the wall as he glared at the circular building with a small dome on top. He tried to burn the red paint-peeling door with his eyes, almost convincing himself as light wafts of smoke drifted out from behind the door.

Great, the end-scents are being used. Or whatever they're called.

Colton creaked open the door, peeking inside to a poorly furnished room with collapsing bookshelves, torn rugs, pillows, and a makeshift desk made out of a door and four stone blocks.

Just as shoddy as ever.

Colton slowly walked into the room, pulling off his hood, Liam in tow as they approached the desk. Behind it, a woman crooked as a bent nail, sat with miniscule eyes peering at the two boys through cracked glasses with a chain of rusty beads hanging down.

She looked between Liam and Colton, her already frowning expression deepening into scowling canyons. She set down the book she had been reading and slowly took off her glasses.

"Colton Diaíresi Toa, I hope you're not here to cause trouble?" she growled, tapping a finger on the desk.

"He's here to learn," Liam interjected before Colton could answer.

Just not from you, though.

"Yeah, that," Colton conceded reluctantly.

The teacher considered him for a long while, eyes narrowing shrewdly at him. Colton resisted the urge to cough from the incense burners pumping out smoke on the desk.

"Not one disturbance out of you, understood?" the teacher demanded at long last.

She turned to Liam. "You'll be watching him, Liam Lewis, yes?"

Caleb DM Smith

Colton bit his tongue, holding back the urge to snap at her. He glanced at Liam, who nodded, and Colton bit his tongue harder.

"Yeah, yeah. I won't do anything," Colton said.

The teacher huffed, going back to reading her book, replacing her glasses on her overly large nose. Colton walked over and collapsed onto a heavily stained pillow that served as a seat, Liam taking his place beside him on a separate pillow.

"You should actually try and learn something. It's fun," Liam suggested.

Colton scoffed. "This place never teaches us anything useful."

"Maybe if you actually went to the classes."

"Why would I want to learn history when I can't even afford my own clothes? Not like I'll ever be a part of it."

"Careful what you wish for."

Anytime I wish for something good, the opposite happens.

They watched as other kids trickled in, a few older or younger, most their age. Among them was a young girl with a ruddy, dirt-smudged face. Her feet wore muddy and worn boots, paired with brown cargo shorts, and a shirt pulled tight by a knot near the bottom.

She looked at Colton and Liam, gave a cocky-grin, and strode over to them, throwing herself onto a pillow with a loud *thwump!*

"Colton's here!" She exclaimed with a mischievous smile. "Didn't you have a wanted—"

Colton lunged forward, slapping a hand to her mouth and hissing. "Shut it, Bristol!"

The girl bit Colton's hand before snarling like a wolf. "I don't ever 'shut it.' Do I, Liam?"

Bristol looked at Liam with batting eyelashes, who was busily picking at a loose thread on his clothes, a half-grimace on his face. Colton tut-tutted at Bristol, who threw him a nasty glare.

"Lee-um?" Bristol said in a sing-song voice.

No response.

"Maybe next time," Colton said with a smug grin.

Bristol muttered. "Shut it, wolf-eyes."

"My eyes are *not* that silver."

"They're like shiny metal coins. They work with your black-ish-gray hair."

40

"Shut it. You know why my hair's this color," he said, trying to hide his hair with his hands.

"I don't think a disease turned it that color."

Someone cleared their throat loudly, bringing Colton's attention to the teacher who was glaring at them. Colton gave a grimace as an apology, and Bristol made a mocking cough-cough.

"As I was beginning to say," the teacher began, "who remembers what we discussed about the Mesica Civil War?"

The teacher looked around the room, the silence dragged on, each kid looking at their neighbor or their feet. Colton felt both relief and dread when Bristol raised her hand.

Oh boy, here we go again.

"Yes, Bristol?" the teacher asked in a snide voice, clutching a book in her hands so tightly her knuckles turned white.

"It was that the war, also known as the Second Great Calamity, caused the Great Migration and a whole bunch of other societal changes and—" Bristol ranted.

"You're as smart as you are annoying," the teacher replied tersely.

"I love studying how the Great Migration caused evolution and cultural differences between races. *Especially* those two considered the 'damned and divine' and—"

"Well now, not another of your *preposterous* stories!"

"It's not *my* story. Someone told me that there's a race called Demons and—"

"Demons? How idiotic!"

Liam and Colton both shared a glance, shaking their heads and sharing the same thought.

Bristol's digging another hole.

Bristol clicked her tongue before continuing her rant. "They're a race like the Kekamotos but their difference is their point of origin and societal roles they—"

"Damned and divine? Demons? Whoever would consider that? It is pure idiocy!" the teacher cried.

Bristol shrugged. "Some girl who was really smart told me about it. Said they came from the First Great Calamity when people were messin' with stuff they didn't understand."

41

Caleb DM Smith

The teacher went berserk, throwing her book against the wall as she tore her glasses from her face. Colton winced, glancing at Bristol who seemed more annoyed than scared like the rest of the kids.

"There is no such thing!" the teacher screeched. "No such thing as devils, or gods, or magic. Nothing!"

"Yeah, well," Bristol began, continuing her argument.

Colton groaned and held his head in his hands. He glanced at Liam who was listening to the argument very intently.

He's always such a teacher's pet.

Staying tuned out of the conversation, Colton looked over the class, picking out different kids he thought he recognized. A wiry boy who had a middle part through his brown hair and an awkward smiling face, a young girl who looked younger than she really was with her incredibly short height, and one redheaded kid with glasses who was currently being picked on by two bigger kids.

Poor kid. Glad he's not me at least.

Colton continued to watch until he realized it was Jace and Fisk. He looked away, but a second too late to avoid making eye-contact with Jace, who shoved the kid to the ground and waddled over to Colton.

"What you lookin' at?" Jace asked.

"Nothing," Colton retorted, pretending to turn his attention back to the argument Bristol was having.

"I saw you lookin' at me!" Jace demanded, smacking Colton on the back of the head.

Colton scowled. "Go after someone else."

Fisk came over, cackling at Colton. "Looky who dursided ter show thar face!"

"What do you want?"

"We wan' ow-oor munny."

"That you stole from meh!" Jace added.

I swear—don't say anything, don't say anything.

Colton glared at them, before turning back to the argument. Jace growled and smacked Colton on the back of the head hard enough to nearly send Colton flat to the ground.

Do not say a word, Colton.

42

"Yoo afwaid o' Jace's dad gettin' ya?" Fisk mocked with a sneering laugh.

Don't, you, dare.

"He too scared to answer," Jace said. "Maybe he gonna get Liam hung."

Colton scowled, turning back to Jace and snarling. "At least they'd be able to get the rope around his neck. They'd need to save the whole gallows just to have enough space for you."

Way to go, Colton. You just signed your own death sentence.

Jace glared at Colton before glancing at Fisk, then back to Colton. "I what?"

You're kidding, right?

"Oh oh!" Fisk howled. "Jace, he call yah sumthin' mean an' nasty!"

"I'mma pummel you fer dat!" Jace bellowed.

Colton leaped back, avoiding a punch by Jace. Fisk lunged at him. Colton easily side-stepped. Colton stepped back, dodging another swing before shoving Jace, knocking him into Fisk.

"Colton Diaíresi Toa," the teacher screeched, grabbing Colton by the wrist. "We do not attack other students!"

"They're the ones who—" Colton began protesting.

"I have had it with you," the teacher hissed. She grabbed Colton by his hair and began dragging him toward the door.

"I didn't do anything!" he protested.

The teacher whipped open the door and shoved Colton through it. "Never show your face here again!"

The teacher slammed the door and Colton frowned, rubbing his head as he climbed to his feet, the pain ebbing away from where he had been grabbed.

Sometimes I wonder if good luck even exists.

He looked both ways down the road. No one paid attention to him, too focused on their miserable lives etched into the dirt. He yanked his cloak and hood around himself and crouched down in an alleyway, taking favor of the shadows as he watched the classroom door.

One day, I'll be outta this stupid city.

Caleb DM Smith

Colton sat there, waiting for Liam to come out. He occasionally glanced down the road at people passing by. One time, he caught Nessa shuffling by, her gaze settling on him for a few moments. Following her was someone cloaked in a brown robe, identity hidden entirely.

Was she watching me?

Colton shook his head, his shoulders itching again as he checked down the road, behind him, and repeating again before he felt a sense of security. He sighed, pulling his knees up to his chest and hugging them with his arms. He twisted his arm, glancing down at it. He traced a finger on the veins, the light blue barely visible under his damaged skin.

I wonder if those scars will ever go away?

He rubbed the scars on his wrist, the spotty memories floating to the surface. He shook his head and arms, his wrists itching horribly as if metal blasted hot under the skin.

No. I shouldn't think about that anymore. No point. I was born with a disease, and it won't go away.

They were trying to cure me, and I made it hard for them. It's my fault. They got tired of it. Just dealing with Fisk sucks. Eight years? Yeah, a long time to try and cure a doomed problem.

Colton sighed, rubbing his face.

Bristol sure knows a lot though. I could've sworn she came from the Auratus District with how much she knows.

Imagine living somewhere that rich. The day I live there is the same week this place gets destroyed. At least with my luck. Maybe even the world will get destroyed like the First Great Calamity.

Maybe.

Everyone fighting to control the world accidentally spawns new creatures? Hah, yeah right.

Colton rested his head on the top of his knees.

Who'd wanna rule the entire world anyway? Sounds like too much work. I'd rather just have a good life. No one believes me when I say that. I don't cause trouble because I like it.

I just want to—

Colton blanked and then snapped upright when he heard the classroom door open. His eyes were bleary and he felt drool on the corner of his mouth.

Oh—! I fell asleep.

He shrunk deeper into the shadows, surveying his surroundings as his shoulders itched intensively. Wiping his eyes and mouth, Colton watched the flood of youth stream out the door. A very dismayed Liam walked out, followed by a fuming Bristol.

"—no sense!" Bristol said. "Why's she a teacher?"

Liam shrugged. "She's an adult. And knows a lot."

Bristol groaned, banging her fists against the wall. Colton waved to Liam, who walked over.

"You guys took your sweet time," Colton said, standing up.

Liam shrugged again. "You caused trouble."

"You *know* I didn't start that," Colton retorted.

Both Liam and Bristol gave Colton a dubious look, and he glared at them. Behind them, Jace and Fisk walked out, both looking equally annoyed.

"What did you guys do in there?" Colton asked warily to his two friends.

Liam snorted. "Bristol ratted almost everyone out for everything they've done."

Bristol made a cutesy expression. "I aim to please."

"Yeah, well you overshot," Colton said with a withering sensation as Jace and Fisk headed their way.

They're so pissed. I'm screwed.

"Yur lucky we didn' end yah right thaer!" Fisk snarled at Bristol.

"Please, two of you couldn't fight a Monti-Otter and win," Bristol said.

"An' yoo! You owe us a lot," Fisk spat at Colton.

"I *never* stole anything from you guys," Colton muttered.

"Yah did when yoo got me n' Jace a lickin' from ter teacher!"

"You were the ones who started it. Why don't you just avoid me?"

"Why don' yoo go carmplain to Daas erbout it!"

45

Fisk and Jace both began laughing, with Liam and Bristol giving Colton warning looks. He threw a glare at Jace and Fisk, but bit back his retort, feeling his face burn a little.

I really really hate them.

Once the duo had calmed down from their fit of laughter, Fisk gave Colton a death-stare before muttering. "Tell yoo what. You get us a couple valyuta by tomorrow, an' we gon' forget yur little crime."

"That's not enough to—" Colton said.

"Wun day, o' we set teh guardians on yeh and yoo be hangin'!" Fisk spat. "Jace really needa be eatin'. Yoo don' wanna rope aroun' tur neck, righ'?"

Colton glared at them, before he grabbed Liam and tugged him, sprinting off down the road while Bristol stood confused.

"What are you doing?" Liam cried.

Colton shook his head. "We're going home."

Chapter 6

Home is Where the Hurt is

Colton popped over the edge, grabbing the rusty metal bars to hoist himself through the broken window. He crept past the window entrance, still fearful of stepping on a shard of broken glass, before he sat down on the inclined concrete floor.

Liam appeared in the entrance to their hideout, breathing hard, eyes half-closed, and body shaking visibly. Colton turned, grabbed Liam by the arm, and yanked him up. Liam crashed to the concrete, arms extended out in exhaustion, revealing a tattoo on his wrist of a fist holding a stick as if to attack.

Ruling-Hand, huh? Why'd you never tell me you were a slave in the Auratus?

Colton shook his head, standing on his feet and kicking a slab of concrete, stalking off.

"I still don't get how they can be such nosking—" Colton ranted.

Liam interjected. "They'll probably start being more kind after you give them the money you owe them."

"I don't *owe* them anything. They just want to steal it from me."

Colton paced further into the hideout, tearing off his cloak before throwing himself onto a depressing couch. He choked on the dust that rose up and waved a hand in front of his face.

The couch was the highest quality item they had in their hideout, which was located in a sideways skyscraper from a bygone era. Cracked glass windows gave an expansive view, and the whole steel structure creaked and groaned as the weight of collecting dust settled on it. Junk littered every corner, with some of it arranged to replicate furniture.

"Just wait. One day I'll be on the softest, nicest couch in a castle on my own island," Colton declared.

Caleb DM Smith

Liam gave Colton a 'you sound like an idiot' look before taking Colton's money and striding past him. He pulled a small bag out of his pocket, dumped a few coins into his palm, added Colton's remaining change, and stopped at a series of rusty fridges on their sides, serving as make-shift cabinets for an incomplete kitchen. Liam opened one of the doors before placing the money on a small pile there.

"In case you haven't noticed, we nearly got killed today," Liam said.

Colton rolled his eyes. "What's new?"

He felt a solid *whack* on the back of his head, and a piece of scrap clattered to the ground. He grabbed at where the pain blossomed.

"This'sn't a joke, Colton!" Liam appeared over the edge of the couch, more scrap in hand.

Colton grabbed the piece of scrap, a plate of metal with a couple random letters in the rusty surface, and the name 'Utah, Orem' above it. He chucked the scrap away and heaved himself to his feet.

"I'm not dead yet."

"You will be if you don't start taking things seriously."

"D'you like to think about dying?"

"No. But I don't do things that nearly get me killed."

"Why do you think I have to steal? We don't have food in those fridges."

Colton stormed off to the edge of the room, leaving Liam standing there, listless, as the light slowly dwindled from the setting sun. Colton shoved his hands in his pockets, nearly poking out the other end. He looked out at their resident city below them, the dirty window ruining the view.

Only half of Malelentos was lit up in the evening darkness. That being the only half that could afford to illuminate itself: the Auratus District.

I wonder how they keep all those lights going so long.

The buildings rose up like impressive columns, only to be pressed further into the sky by the plateau they resided on. It looked as if someone carved a slice out of the ground and removed it, only to change their mind halfway and leave it elevated above the surrounding terrain.

Everyone else was trapped in the dirty, lightless Scintilla Initium District. Crumbling streets were hugged by structures practically built from the earth, as if that was the only place that tolerated the vagabonds.

All around the city were wasteland plains, with the occasional ruins in the distance. Jutting out like sharp rocks from the ocean, one could only guess what the stark remains once were.

Colton's and Liam's hideout was of similar structures. Once-sleek-and-shiny buildings, more resembling those in the Auratus District as if they had been picked up and discarded to be half-buried on the cliffside with the sound of waterfalls echoing through the crumbling interiors.

I wonder if one day the Auratus District will end up like this?

"Colton, look," Liam began.

Reluctantly, Colton turned to look at his friend with a raised brow and crossed arms.

"I'm just trying to help," Liam muttered, coming to stand next to his friend.

"That's not gonna end well."

"And are you gonna tell me why that is?"

Colton picked at a scab that was standing out against his lightly tanned skin, "You think you could ever actually die?"

"I don't know. But you, on the other hand, can't be so reckless next time. We can wait a little longer to get outta here."

Colton nodded, keeping his expression neutral as he set his gaze on the city below.

I get so close and every time I just get kicked down. He's gonna end up like Kai.

Liam shook his head, turning on his heel and dusting himself off. "It's late. We should probably go to bed."

Colton barely glanced at his friend as Liam strode off toward the small janitor closet that served as their bedroom. Instead, Colton stayed staring at the city, his mind running with thoughts of the day, disliking the sensation he had in his gut that slowly turned and tumbled, starting to wake.

It's happening a lot more. Is my disease getting worse?

Caleb DM Smith

Colton shook his head, grimacing to himself as he hugged his knees. His thoughts turned to the strange pursuer he had, the words still echoing in his mind.

Flee away with me.

Colton scowled, clicking his tongue as he chucked a small pebble at the window, gaze fixated on the new crack.

Don't be dumb. You just imagined the voice in your head. Just an excuse to think you're special.

He ground his heel against the concrete, small pieces of gravel poking into his skin.

Same reason you have those dumb, weird, magical dreams.

Some dreams were of lizard-like creatures and celestial-looking beings, all vying for control of odd objects. Others were of a mechanical creature constantly chasing him, or of a peculiar group of fourteen creatures.

Half were menacing, varying in their twisted features, from cyst-covered to an arachnidian smile, or gluttonous jaws to jealous green eyes, spiky skin, screeching metal hands, or a deceitful gaze.

The other half were mirrored images, more pleasant and inviting, though murky as if hidden behind smoke and shadow. Masks that entrapped their true nature.

I wonder if Liam has similar dreams. Knowing him and what happened to his family. . .

Exhausted, Colton climbed to his feet, taking in the view of the city before he risked never seeing it again.

He didn't like his chances with Fisk and Jace prowling around. Or with the guardians hungrily looking for him. Among everyone else he had apparently caused trouble to earn their hate.

All I ever seem to do, huh? Cause problems.

Turning and vanishing into the shadow of the ruins, Colton gently pushed open the custodial closet door, having to hold the rusty, creaking metal as the slight incline of the building made it want to swing with more speed than intended.

Liam was already asleep and Colton's bed was nearby. Situated on a trio of rusty metal cabinets, with only a worn, itchy blanket and a rotten sack full of dirty clothes to give comfort.

The latest in royalty for a homeless gjinx.

Colton crawled into his bed, rubbing his head.

It'd be nice to have an actual soft bed for once.

He had grown used to it, but it never got any easier. Each time he turned his head, a grinding could be heard against his skull and whenever his knees bumped the metal, there was a hollow echo.

He slowly lost track of time, resulting in him banging his head lightly on the metal a few times.

Go to sleep, go to sleep, go to sleep.

He looked enviously at Liam before curling himself up, stubbornly forcing his eyes closed.

Each time he drifted off, he jerked awake, disturbed by that obnoxious falling sensation as his exhaustion slowly worsened. Ebbing away his patience.

Soon enough, he experienced the falling sensation yet again, only to crash down through the cabinets and rock and fall a long way until he collided with the dirt streets of the Scintilla Initium District.

Groaning as he pushed himself to his hands and knees, he looked around. A crowd stared at him, eyes unblinking as they surrounded him. All the while, ahead of him, a cloaked figure stood, the shadowed features reaching for him with wires that emitted from the sleeves. Behind the cloaked figure, from the cliffs of the Auratus District, a black sludge poured out of holes that raced toward him, devouring all in its path.

Woah, what? But I was just—a dream?

Colton rocketed to his feet, turning to run the other way, only for a disfigured man dressed in combat gear to lunge forward, rotten spit flying from his mouth, worms crawling between the teeth and holes in the sallow skin.

Colton tripped, scraping his hands and knees as smoke burned his lungs and eyes. He rubbed the tears from them and looked up, once again inside his old home as it burned to the ground with black fire devouring every surface.

Down the hall in front of him, he could see a boy, only a bit older than him, trapped under planks of burning wood, crying out for Colton to come help.

Colton climbed to his feet and rushed forward, the feeling of running through molasses bogging him down as flames licked at his back.

Come on, run faster, idiot!

"Kai!" Colton called. "I'm almost there!"

Before he got far, the fire blasted him, roaring forth and throwing him backwards. He crashed through wood and fell into an abyss. The earth never rushed up to meet him, nor did any solid structure pass by. Colton fell onward, endlessly, the wind howling in his ears like the screams of victims in a fire. Tumbling to perform flip after flip after flip, making him dizzy and queasy in the stomach.

Colton screamed, his voice torn from his mouth before his ears could hear. His eyes only saw the dark void, so deep it held its own reverse glow. Inexplicably dark and corrupting.

At long last, Colton slammed into an invisible floor, textured like glass at first, then, almost like quicksand, slowly pulling him into a venal darkness.

He pulled back, straining until his hands popped free, sending him sprawling backward and tumbling down unseen steps. He crashed to a charred wooden floor, warm to the touch and with an acrid scent stinging his senses.

He groaned, rising to his feet. Finding his new environment eerie.

The sky looked like cracked glass, stemming from the blotted-out sun. It was as if some form of dark power was trying to quench the light, resulting in crimson bleeding out in the sky down to the scorched ground.

The air was stifling, nearly suffocating him with its dread. Wails and screams came from the inferno upon a hill, a horrible image of orange and black.

A good distance afar off, the survivors trekked away, more burned than a sunset. All to leave one survivor crawling slowly, each movement making him groan.

Colton watched the survivor's progress, his perspective warping until he saw from the survivor's point of view. He felt the pain the survivor felt. The odd sensation of Colton *becoming* the survivor overcame him. Seeing what the survivor saw. Hearing what the survivor heard. Thinking what the survivor thought. All too aware of the weakness and the struggle to move muscles that were now his. Barely able to keep his unfamiliar head from dragging in the ashen ground.

Yet, in his hand—the hand blackened like a tree with leaves of fire and the fingers rigid as a body of rigor mortis—in this hand, he so tightly clutched *it*.

This object pulsed, a crimson glow slowly increasing in cursed luminance, only to dim to a barely perceivable glimmer. He could feel its presence, its power.

He could feel its *heartbeat*.

The fleshy surface of it was pressed against his ravaged body, intensifying the pain as the object healed his burns most monstrously, twisting and tearing. It gave him the strength he lacked. His once supple body struggled to inflate scorched lungs, yet now, efficiently filled with toxic breaths.

Shaped like a serpentine eye set amongst a fungal heart and emitting an unsettling aura, the object wriggled in his grasp.

It was merely an object, a vile token, but his senses screamed otherwise. Alive. Hateful.

He crawled just a bit further, dragging himself closer to a puddle that resided nearby. His hands dipped into the muddy surface and he cried out, forcing more of himself in despite the searing pain against ash skin.

He paused, glancing at his reflection, a charred figure that unsettled him. His eyes squeezed what little they had left to bleed tears that came with resistance.

He rolled to his back, clutching the bloodied eye to his chest, feeling its influence slowly spread over him, invisible tendrils from the organic artifact wrapping him like the strings of a parasite.

Each breath brought new, wet crimson leaking from his lips and fluid oozing from his eyes. His weak teeth ground to a white powder, leaving his gums bare.

Something moved, towering over him. He felt a pair of cruel eyes glare down at him. He heard a growl before a cumbersome Warhammer dropped beside his head.

"An arrival too late," the newcomer said in an almost slithery voice, "we needed the eye *with* the boy. Yet you've lost him and turned our two 'volunteers' watching him into Scourgers. Now, little remains of Kai Winder."

"No—please—don't—" the survivor rasped, "I tried—he—the Eclipse was ready. His Calibers were—*are* active."

The creature snorted, then a shadow crossed the survivor's face, and he heard a laugh, worm-eaten by evil and malice. Pain and cold rocked his body. His head began to feel like it would explode. The fabric of his delicate reality was torn and he snapped upright, slamming his head on the rusty pipe above his resting place.

Colton groaned, clutching his head as it throbbed. He leaned over, waiting for the pain to ebb away as his eyes watered and his body burned.

No. They couldn't have been talking about me. I have both of my eyes. Who were they?

Chapter 7
Soap in the Eyes

Colton hefted the chunk of obsidian, eyes glaring down at it with enough intensity he thought the rock would melt in his hand.

I'm so tired. Why didn't my brain let me sleep?

Colton chucked the obsidian, watching it slowly spin as it plummeted, vanishing into the trees far below. He frowned, kicking another piece of obsidian and watched it tumble down the cliff, shattering on its last impact.

A squeak off to his right caught his attention. He raised a brow at the Monti-Otter that had appeared from its burrow in the rock.

A fluffy brown weasel-like creature with silver lines racing down its back and sides, and auburn spots under its eyes. Slender and long, as if it had been stretched out.

"What do you want?"

Another squeak, and the Monti-Otter inched forward. Colton shooed with his hands, and the Monti-Otter nipped at him, drawing blood.

"Ow! You stupid animal."

The Monti-Otter squeaked again, and Colton grabbed a rock and hucked it, missing the little creature, which only snapped at Colton again, stopping short this time. Colton raised his fist, growling and the animal squeaked again, diving back into its hole. Colton sighed, lowering his hand.

Why don't you go infest the Auratus's hydro pumps? At least you'd be useful.

Colton looked down to where the animal had bitten his finger, finding the wound missing, but replaced with a strange purple crystal that covered Colton's knuckles.

Great, you brought it back. I hate this disease.

Colton tapped the crystal, before rapping his knuckles roughly on the stone ground, feeling somewhat flexible in his somewhat tanned

55

skin. Reaching over, Colton grabbed a handful of mossy Malelentos Sudsrea, squeezing it and covering his hand in a soapy substance, before he used the coarse cyan vegetation to scrub the crystal.

Why won't this come off?

Colton threw the moss away, punching the stone ground hard, sending painful shocks through his wrists as he chipped off a part of the stone, the crystal undamaged.

Colton stared, the writhing sensation bubbling subtly in his gut as he stared with wide eyes at the crystal. Twisting his fingers, he found the crystal moved with his skin, flexing and stretching. He punched the rock again, dealing a crack in it.

What the—? I didn't know it could do that.

"Colton?" Liam's voice called.

Colton began waving his hand wildly, trying to rid his hand of the strange purple-crystal.

"Come on!" Colton hissed under his breath as he shook his hand even more vigorously. Liam rounded a corner, and the crystal flew off, turning to dust that quickly dissipated.

"Your hand okay?" Liam asked.

Colton shook his head hastily. "No uh—Monti-Otter bit me."

"It triggered your uhh, thing?"

"Yeah, it did," Colton said sheepishly.

"I don't really mind your crystal condition."

"It's called a disease."

Liam frowned, shaking his head as he held out a hand, helping Colton to his feet.

"You're still human," Liam said, treading further down the cliffside path.

They carefully walked along the small trail, enjoying the sights, scents, and sounds. Water cascaded off higher cliffs, with the sunlight poking through a cloudy sky, turning the water to colored diamonds as they plummeted past dozens of ruined buildings of rusting steel and dirty glass. The falls were lower in volume than in the summer as the snow from higher cliffs had only just begun to melt from the meager warmth of spring. Hundreds of feet below, the falls merged into rivers that wound through a forest until depositing into Luna Lake, adjacent to the city.

The air reverberated with the roar, making hearing much else difficult. Only a few damp rooftops of the half-buried buildings were large enough to allow an individual to rest behind the waterfalls, with mossy carpets that took away all traction and Monti-Otters busy moistening their sleek coats.

The duo hurried along, wandering along the edge of a partially buried building, climbing through a broken window, treading carefully along a catwalk, and entering a large stairwell. From there, the two ascended to the roof, only to hop across a three-foot gap to a rusty ladder that adhered to the side of another building.

Colton clung to the ladder after the jump, glancing down at the crevice that fell a hundred feet or so, slowly narrowing the further down it went. He could feel his limbs struggling to stay still.

Can't we put a net here or something?

He shook his head and ascended up the ladder, arriving at the top where the falls fell at their gentlest, as was evident by the group of otters bathing there.

Colton shooed most away, with an oversized otter squeaking at him stubbornly. He gently grabbed it by the scruff of its neck and carried it to the small hole where the others had already vanished. A shattered window of an office space beneath the rock.

"Ow! You kretch!"

Colton flung the otter at the cavity as he shook his hand, a tiny bit of blood dripping from his finger. The otter squeaked, as if laughing at Colton before slipping away.

He kicked a rock at it, cursing under his breath.

Crawl back to your dungeon, you little kretch.

Colton glared at the bite wound, much bigger than last time, and free of any purple crystal.

That's weird. Didn't trigger it this time. Normally it's when I get super emotional.

"You must be really tasty to them, huh?" Liam asked, stepping toward one platform with a small trickle of a waterfall.

"Absolutely amazing," Colton spat.

"I wonder where they wander off to?"

"Probably have a whole kingdom hidden in the cliffs."

Colton walked to a separate area, around a corner and with more privacy. He took a deep breath, letting his shoulders slump as the tension slowly ebbed away from his muscles.

Time for some moss.

Scraping up some Sudsrea, he squeezed it above his head, sending a gush of mint-smelling suds all over his hair. Promptly, he hopped under a waterfall, drenching himself in the icy-cold water, his teeth chattering.

Ah! That's too cold!

Colton shivered, forcing himself to stay until his body stopped screaming at him and he began scrubbing himself and his clothes with the moss. Usually, the sounds of the waterfall, otters squeaking, and the odd hum of the mountains were peaceful, almost serving as a calming white noise. But now whenever Colton closed his eyes, he felt like the shadows were trying to suffocate him, forcing his eyes open despite the soap often getting into his eyes.

Colton glanced behind himself, scouring the cliffs with a shrewd gaze, subconsciously rubbing his right shoulder, the uneven scar beneath his clothes still itching despite being fully healed from any burns.

I swear I'm being watched. No one's there though. Maybe not.

Nothing obvious could be seen. Only a slight reflection of himself in the wet dark rock, depicting his semi-wiry frame, odd dark-gray hair, and bright silver eyes.

Wolf eyes, huh?

Colton rolled his shoulder, reluctantly turning his gaze as he continued his morning routine a little more quickly.

Finishing up, he threw the used foliage off the cliff before carefully walking back, his feet very aware of the surplus of water and soap on the rocks that slipped off the edge inches away. He rounded the corner and found the area abandoned.

"Liam?" Colton called.

He received no answer, only the roaring of the falls in his ears. He peered around the area, heart racing before he carefully tiptoed to peer over the edge.

Okay, doesn't look like he fell. I hope. So where could he have—

Something solid grabbed Colton's arm. He jerked away, spinning and letting out a yelp.

"Liam, what the—" Colton began.

He paused, seeing no one. Not Liam, Monti-Otters, or anyone. He stared at a spot that shimmered as if from heat, blinking rapidly and the effect vanished.

Weird. This's really starting to freak me out.

Colton rolled his shoulders, rubbing the spot he had felt something grab him. "Liam? This really isn't funny."

He paused, waiting, nerves on fire, silence echoing. He tilted his head, straining his ears for any sound but heard nothing. He opened his mouth to shout again, just as a high-pitched scream cut through the air. Almost animalistic.

"Liam!" Colton shouted.

He turned around and dashed back to where they had come. He hastily descended the ladder, cursing himself when he nearly slipped off and performed an ill-timed jump to the other building, scraping his hands and knees.

Quickly recovering, he raced down the steps and across the catwalk, leaping out the window without any regard for the sharp glass.

Rounding the bend, he carelessly sprinted even as he could feel the friction between his feet and the concrete wane to nonexistent, causing him to slip, falling on the rock. His momentum continued, carrying him further until he slipped off the edge and began plummeting.

He threw his hand out, body jerking to a stop, pain erupting in his arm as he held onto a twisted railing, saving himself from following debris that tumbled, snapping branches and chips of rock on the way down.

His body jerked down, making his guts leap in his throat as he heard metal creaking, slowly bending the railing under his weight. He tried to reposition his hand to hoist himself up, but his hand felt glued to the metal. While groaning and straining his muscles, he yanked himself up a little, grabbing the railing with his other hand.

Caleb DM Smith

The metal creaked more, with something snapping. Feeling his senses go into overdrive, Colton pulled at his stuck hand, finding it glued down by the magenta crystal. He tugged, causing the metal to groan horribly before his hand came free and he lost his grip.

KRETCH!

Colton's skin screamed in pain as he held on as much as he could with his other hand, having grabbed a sharp-rock handhold. Watching with a frozen heart as the metal stopped creaking for a moment, he slowly climbed up, body groaning, being careful to not tear the rest of the railing off with jerky movements.

Once he was back up on the building, he quickly dashed to the cliff wall, hugging it as he stared at the ledge, legs barely holding him and vision almost blurred by his heart and lungs racing the fastest they ever had.

Holy—holy son of a—no way I— Colton thought, shaking his head as he felt woozy. He looked down at his palm, the skin covered by the same flexible material, though it was dissipating on its own now.

Helped me for once.

Treading more carefully, Colton came to the quiet and empty hideout. Fearing the worst, he tore through the rooms, carelessly slamming doors, tearing off blankets, and opening the fridge cabinets.

"Come on, Liam." Colton cursed under his breath. "Stop messing around."

"Messing around with what?"

Colton cried out, falling back as Liam stood behind him, an oversized otter in his arms. Liam was smiling widely, while the otter resembled Liam the best it could.

"Don't scare me like that!" Colton shouted. "I thought you fell off the cliff."

Liam held up the otter, showcasing a leaf bandage on one of its legs. "I was helping this poor guy with his injury. He screamed when I accidentally bound it too tight."

"Well, tell me next time you go off somewhere."

Liam walked over and gently placed the otter on the couch, where it promptly curled up, using its tail as a pillow.

"I think I'll name it Wesly," Liam said.

60

Colton groaned. "We're *not* keeping that thing."

"He'll have a home here just for a little bit."

Colton threw his arms in the air, and Liam grinned.

"Today can't get any worse, can it?" Colton said. "Let's just go. The Central Market's gonna be busy today."

He grabbed his cloak from the ground and strode towards the exit, stepping past the dangerous debris and onto the winding path down the mountainside.

The ordinarily crisp cold air felt warm and stifling, making Colton's veins throb with pain as if something was trying to get out.

Ugh, I better not be getting sick.

The two boys trod across a narrow series of switchbacks, alternating from feasible trails to leaping down several feet of steep rock, taking a turn that led away from the quarry. They hopped onto a rooftop and descended crumbling stairs that threatened to drop them to their demise before monkeying their way past rusted metal supports that tried to stab them.

Exiting the building through its broken front doors, they ambled through a smaller part of the forest, the trees more shriveled and twisted, the ground heavily choked with fog. Sometimes small little creatures would scamper by or escape up trunks, mere shadows in the dim morning light.

What's up with today? Colton thought, shaking his head, removing the creepy atmosphere. *It's like it's cursed or something.*

The occasional ring of metal against stone could be heard echoing from the nearby quarry. Beyond the diminutive forest lay a series of small-scale farms, some growing crops, and others raising livestock.

The crumbling wooden fences ended and gave way to slowly collapsing shacks that served as homes, signifying the start of the Scintilla Initium District.

Soon enough, Colton and Liam merged into the crowd of people dressed in rags that hid their malnutrition and filthy skin. Colton threw on his hood and began looking around. His eyes settled on a small girl with pale blonde almost silver hair, then a man with a bald head and a bandage over an eye, and lastly an old woman with a gold and shiny bracelet.

"Don't even think about it," Liam said.

Colton splayed his hands. "I'm not doing anything wrong."

"Enough with the stealing."

"Who says I was gonna steal?"

"You really think I'm an idiot?"

"I didn't call you that," Colton muttered.

"If you keep stealing, you'll only be stuck where you were before."

"Not if I steal enough."

"No," Liam fumed, grabbing Colton by the shoulders, "you have to think of a more permanent solution than just stealing bracelets or wallets."

Colton looked away, a coy smile twisting to his face.

"No breaking any laws!" Liam said.

Colton knocked away Liam's hands. "I'm doing it so you don't starve."

"I have an honest job."

"That barely pays for a single bread loaf a day."

"And doesn't put a bounty on my head."

"Yeah, well I already have one," Colton said, throwing off his hood, drawing the eyes of the nearby crowd. "So, I got nothing more to lose. You think I steal because I find it fun? Because I like being a criminal?"

"I think you put yourself before others," Liam said quietly, as most people had put their heads down and ignored the duo.

"Only reason you're not skin and bones is 'cuz of me."

"The only reason you're not hanging from the gallows," Liam countered, "is because of me. Because I endure the job I have so Daas doesn't turn you in. You think I *want* to be cheated out of money every day?"

Colton opened his mouth to retort, then shut it. Liam shook his head, letting an exasperated sigh. He let his hands fall to his side before turning away.

"Don't get into trouble, and meet at our spot at twelve," He muttered before disappearing into the crowd.

Colton stared, watching his friend leave, putting his hood back on as his shoulders itched.

And that's why I keep trying to steal, Liam. I wanna get enough as quickly as possible to get us outta here.

Colton quickly hid himself in an alleyway, hurrying along in the shadows, and poking his head out the other end. He pulled back just as a large, dark skinned and burly man walked past, rifle in arms and dressed in heavy combat gear.

"Some kind of guardian?" Colton muttered under his breath. "Don't tell me they're still looking for me?"

"Yes, they still are," someone said from behind him.

Colton whirled, slamming his fist into a face that yelped and fell back. Colton's knuckles erupted in pain and he cried out, shaking his hand vigorously.

"What the nosk was that for?" Bristol cried, holding her nose, crimson leaking between her fingers.

"What do you think?" Colton said, wincing sheepishly. "Plus, what are you doing here? Aren't you supposed to be at the class or something?"

Bristol shrugged. "I got thrown out. Apparently, I've caused 'a disturbance of the peace.'"

"Almost like it's true."

"Aren't you usually off stealing something at this time of day?"

"I don't steal from people," Colton said.

Bristol huffed. "Last time I counted, you stole seventeen times last week."

"I'm temporarily borrowing."

"You caused about twelve hundred acunar in damages that week. That's enough to feed a family for two weeks."

"Wasn't my fault. Guardians decided to carelessly fire their rifles."

"Your bounty that you got for breaking into the Auratus District got raised to Seventy-five thousand acunar."

"The number isn't—"

"You're literally the most wanted kid in the Scintillia Initium District."

Colton clenched his fists, glaring at Bristol. "Not if I buy supplies to get away from here."

"You don't got enough money."

Caleb DM Smith

"Who says I need money?"

Bristol rolled her eyes. "You know it's at least a week-long journey on foot to the nearest town. A month or two to hike through the Montiwell Mountains. You gonna risk that?"

"Maybe," Colton shrugged.

"So, you have a death wish."

"No, I'm tryna get me and Liam out of this stupid place."

"And how do you plan to do that?" Bristol asked.

"Break into the Auratus District."

"And steal what?"

"People in the Auratus District have freedom," Colton replied. "Maybe I'll steal some of that."

"That's not how that works."

"Are you gonna help me or not?"

"I'm not breaking in with you," Bristol said.

"Just tell me how to get in."

"There's Vagabond's Venture."

"I'm not climbing that," Colton said. "Dozens of people have died."

Bristol shrugged. "More chances of living than your literal field trip. Welcome to real life."

"You almost make death seem normal."

"It actually is."

"Don't you know any other way in?"

Bristol rubbed her temples, groaning, before running her hand through her hair and giving Colton a shrewd glare.

"Why do you wanna get in?" she asked.

"I just told you," Colton replied. "To get away."

"Remember the last time you broke in?"

"That was two years ago. And that was mostly for the thrill back then."

"You think it'll be any easier now?"

Colton groaned. "Bristol, I didn't ask for a professional review of their security. Just give me ideas on how to get past it."

Bristol gave Colton a long look, pursing her lips as she huffed, scowling slightly.

She said. "You could cause a serious distraction for the guardians at the gate and get a large crowd to charge their way up the road."

"What kind of distraction?"

"A big one."

"Oh, yeah, you think?"

"You probably won't be able to break in anyways."

"You're not being helpful."

"Anything you try is gonna backfire and burn you badly."

"I'm not that bad at—" Colton began, he paused.

Maybe—fire seems to be pretty destructive from my experiences. Maybe I can get them to share in the bad luck.

Colton grabbed Bristol by the shoulders and shook her vigorously. "Fire!"

"Huuuhhh? What do you mean?" She asked with raised brows and wide eyes.

Colton grinned and adjusted his cloak. "I'm gonna give the guardians some fireworks."

"What do you mean by fireworks?"

"What happens with fire?"

"It uhh, burns things?"

"Exactly. I'm gonna burn down the gallows."

Chapter 8
Sound The Trump

Tck tck tck!

Liam repositioned the chisel.

Tck tck tck!

He gently bit his tongue.

Tck tck tck!

He pulled away, gaze gliding over the stonework. He hummed, his body relaxed as he took in the finished stonework. Each groove, curve, and corner. His stomach grumbled and he winced.

"It'll have to do."

Liam set down his tools on the little station, grabbing a raggy damp cloth and cleaned his hands of dust, as best he could. The poor cloth was so worn, it almost fell apart from the gentle scrubbing.

"Dromus!" Liam called, "it's done!"

Liam heard grumbling that shook the whole mason shop, followed by Dromus stomping into the room, face scrunched up in a scowl. He stopped in front of Liam's station and scoured the stonework with skilled eyes, before nodding.

"It is enough." Dromus said, "I'll carry it out tomorrow morning."

Dromus reached into a pocket of his dirty apron and dropped two Halkai coins into Liam's hand.

"Go, have lunch break," Dromus muttered, shambling off into a room, cracking the doorframe as he squeezed his body into the small opening.

"Thanks," Liam said.

He examined the two coins, counting in his head.

"I ate something two days ago, so tonight and tomorrow I'll save the Halkai, then the day after that, I can eat again," he grimaced. "And then another year and we'll be able to get away from here."

Liam nodded and put the coins away into his pocket, feeling a hole near the bottom.

"Already?" Liam shook his head, switching which pocket he placed the coins in. "Ugh, it's fine. Bristol can probably fix it."

He dusted himself off and quickly hurried outside. The warm, stifling air hit him and his skin instantly itched, like the few raindrops that splattered from the sparse clouds were bugs that bit at his skin. Pressing on, he trotted down the road, eyes roving, on the lookout for danger.

His thin shoes did little to protect his feet from the rough ground. Sharp rocks jutted into his soles, threatening to cut him with every step, becoming moistened from the damp earth.

Pausing and glancing down, Liam bent to pick up a soaked poster he had stepped on. He raised it up from the puddle, dripping dirtied water, the image horribly warped.

"You're kidding," Liam groaned.

He glared at Colton's deformed image, with a bounty of seventy-five thousand acunar, along with a date set a week ago.

"Not like anyone from the Auratus District would actually pay up if he got turned in," Liam muttered to himself.

"Not from the Auratus District, no," whispered someone behind him.

Liam whirled, leaping away from the newcomer in a brown cloak, letting out a yelp. The newcomer grabbed Liam and shoved him into the darkest part of an alleyway before passing strangers could cast prying eyes their way. The hood shifted, causing pale blonde, almost silver strands of hair to fall out.

"I am of no danger to you," the newcomer said, her voice was young and feminine, a refined accent as if from nobility.

"Are you someone who's hunting Colton?" Liam asked.

"On the contrary, I'm assisting," the stranger said. "But I'm limited in my ability."

"What you tryna do with him?"

"To place the both of you out of reach of those who'll cause harm."

"That's a little vague."

"I cannot reveal too much. I've risked enough talking to you."

Liam narrowed his eyes, trying to discern any facial features in the darkness of the hood.

"How can I trust you?" He asked.

The newcomer's hood shifted again, as if tilting the head side-to-side. "Find Colton and stay in your hideaway for the day. If he doesn't get himself killed today, someone else will come along and do it for him."

Liam blinked a few times at the stranger. "What? Who's going to get him killed?"

The hood twisted side to side before the newcomer leaned close, making known a fragrance like broken petals.

"All I know is they've sent a member of Red Dusk. One of their best, a professional murderer."

"Don't you mean assassin?"

"Almost. Assassins, in a way, have standards."

"His bounty is high enough for that?" Liam exclaimed.

The stranger slapped a cold hand to his mouth. "Quiet!"

"Sorry," Liam mumbled as the hand was removed. "Is he that wanted? And what's Red Dusk?"

"Not now. His bounty is of no consequence. It's his peculiar nature. His blood is of a different kind than yours or mine."

"What does that mean?"

"In due time. Go find your friend with haste," the newcomer said, beginning to retreat.

"Why can't you just tell me what's going to happen?" Liam asked.

"They're watching us. I can't speak more."

"Who? The guardians?"

"The Heralds of the Damned."

Chapter 9
Sparking Vindication

There's a lot of them today.

Colton huddled down on the rooftop, palms and neck sweaty, eyes squinted against the harsh noon-light. Puddles and damp surfaces doubled the sun's brilliance, with light rain falling from wandering clouds onto the guardians that stalked to-and-fro.

He took in the Central Market, the angle much different. His usual lookout was across the way, a frantic Liam looking for him atop it.

Colton shook his head, training his eyes on the dozens of guardians in the Central Market, like ants roaming around their hill, guarding religiously the Central Market, including the stalls which sold his needed supplies. A bottle, a cloth, and oil.

Shouldn't be too hard, if Bristol's telling the truth.

His eyes moved to the gallows, a large wooden platform standing in the center with a dozen guardians standing nearby. The ropes were all full, five people with cold and cruel, glaring eyes, swinging gently like fleshy banners.

Colton grimaced, his gut twisting. *Shouldn't be too hard to die.*

He bit his tongue, watching the guardians as his muscles refused to move from the edge of the building. He groaned, punching the mudbrick and forcing himself to slowly descend down the building, traversing piles of crates and windowsills as his means.

Pulling his hood tight around his face, he strode out into the road, swiftly entering the Central Market. Looks were thrown his way, most disdain or hate, some were confusion, and others were looks of superiority.

I think I'm too short for a Kekamoto. Some buy it though.

Eyes roving, Colton headed right for a specific market-stall. He stopped, slipping behind a pile of barrels as a squadron of guardians marched near. Their footsteps pounded by, matching Colton's heart-beat, each jolt he felt through the earth as he picked up the dizzying scent of chemicals.

Their footsteps faded away and Colton sprung from hiding. The adrenaline kicking in like a large dose of caffeine. Dashing into another market stall, under a series of beads, passing quickly behind the salesperson at the front. Colton wrinkled his nose at the heavy scent of the incense, grabbing a soot-ridden cloth and dashed out.

Three.

Stuffing the cloth into his pocket, he weaved past more stalls. Two trios of guardians approached from both sides, feet crushing the ground. Thoughts bouncing, Colton ducked into a stall.

"Hey! You're not allowed in here!" the salesperson exclaimed, wearing a dull red robe and sad hat.

Colton turned and the salesperson took in Colton's cloak and hood, their eyes growing wide and fearfully backed up, hands grasping around before raising a bottle and aimed to swing.

Colton held up his hands defensively, pulling off his hood. "I'm not here to steal anything!"

The salesperson tilted their head, expression twisting with a deep scowl. "You ain't no Kekamoto. You're that wanted kid!"

The salesperson swung, Colton ducked, and the bottle smashed into a couple others, bursting. One bottle fell to the ground, rolling into Colton's feet.

"News flash, I lied," Colton said, throwing his hood back on.

He ducked another swing, grabbed the bottle, and shoved past. Shouts followed him, with a new voice, deranged and digital, hissing. Colton sprinted away, a *whoosh*, and a *crack* above his head.

Two.

Guardians shouted, Colton cursed, and he raced forward, in and out of stalls, ducking and leaping. An older woman protested at Colton, who ignored her. He grabbed a pitcher and began filling his bottle with oil.

"That is not for—" the woman began.

"Keep the guardians off me!" Colton hissed

The woman folded her arms. "Why should I?"

"I'm getting back at them."

70

The pounding feet drew closer. Colton raised a brow and the woman threw up her hands. She began rummaging through boxes as the distorted voices came right to them.

The bottle overflowed and Colton pulled out the cloth, stuffing it in the top, placing the pitcher back. He looked around, eyes scrambling for anything to create a spark.

"Here," the woman said, holding out her hand, showing a series of small fully rectangular, semi-transparent berries, red with silver tops.

"Sparkberries!" Colton exclaimed.

He snatched the berries, stuffing some into his pocket and he grabbed another handful. The scent of their spiciness hit him, making his nose burn just as a group of guardians stormed into the tent, brandishing weapons. Colton leaped away, knocking over pitchers of oil, the woman screamed.

Shouts rang out, riddled with gunfire and bullets whizzing by. A pain erupted on the top of Colton's left shoulder, splattering cold over his cheek. He winced, gritting his teeth as the adrenaline drowned out the pain.

One.

Colton ran, guardians ran after him, closing in from all around, closing off escape to the sides. He slipped a turn, batons crashing through wooden beams beside his head. More guardians blocked his way; he ducked through a stall. Guardians charged ten feet to the left. Colton sprinted, weaving, dashing, ducking. He drew within line of sight of the gallows. He ran faster, pushing his legs to the tripping point, his balance becoming precarious.

He held the sparkberries close to the cloth, about to wrap them up. A fist shot out, slamming into the side of his head and sending him reeling. He tumbled across the ground, bottle flying from his hand and Sparkberries landing in the dirt ahead of him.

Nosk it! They're gonna get me.

Colton reached out for the Sparkberries, head woozy. He heard a laugh, a shadow crossed his field of vision, and a menacing Fisk stepped in front of him, crushing the Sparkberries beneath his feet, sending tiny flames along the earth.

Caleb DM Smith

"Yoo thought you curd run away from meh?" Fisk asked, sneering. "Yoo still owe mer ter money."

"Fisk, get outta the way."

"An' why werd I do tha'? Any plan ye got, aint gone do no good fer meh."

"You don't understand, I'm trying to get to the Auratus District."

"An' fer what? I can't yoos yoo there, now can I?"

"Look, I'll get you some—"

"I had ernuff of yah!" Fisk screeched.

He kicked into Colton's side. Another kick, and Colton's lungs seized up, curling him up, head becoming light from lack of oxygen. A third kick, he heard a crack, and felt something popping in his side.

I have to get away from him.

Fisk kicked, and Colton blocked. Pain rocked through his limbs, and he tried to stand up, only for Fisk to grab him and shove him back down.

"Stay down, ya filthy rat!" Fisk hissed.

The rabid boy grabbed a nearby wooden beam, raising it high as his eyes bulged with a violent spark. "I told ya tur get my munny!"

"Put it down!" someone cried.

Fisk looked to his side, only to be tackled by Bristol. The two began wrestling, grappling for control of the makeshift weapon.

"Colton, get outta—" Bristol shouted, getting smacked in the face.

Colton groaned, struggling to his feet, grabbing the bottle and limped past the scuffling pair. He rounded a corner and pulled the extra sparkberries from his pocket. He hurried toward the gallows, slowly gaining speed as he overcame his shakiness.

His guts thrashed, a cloaked stranger moved in his way. A flash of silver from the cloak, a blade that cut a stinging line across his cheek.

Come on! Why's everyone trying to stop me from—

Colton fell to the side, nearly screaming and dashing away. The sound of ripping cloth filled his ears and cold dripped down his spine. Glancing back, he saw the stranger chasing him, feet exploding the ground into chunks, catching up in an instant.

Colton barely ducked another swing of the sharp blade. A wooden canopy beam shattered. Colton ducked under a desk, and it became splinters. The stall fell on the stranger, and Colton ran for the gallows.

He wrapped the Sparkberries in the end of the cloth and crushed them, the juice igniting immediately, singing his hand. Colton readied to throw, fire racing toward the bottle's oil, and a boot knocked him to the ground.

He crashed into a stall, spilling boxes of cheap alcohol, the repugnant scent choking his throat. He kept his balance but lost the bottle a few feet away.

Colton reached for it, only for a heavy boot to smash his ribs, hurling him across the ground. Clutching his side, Colton propped himself on hands and knees, and the cloaked stranger approached rigidly.

"What do you want from me?" Colton shouted.

The stranger flashed a second twisted blade, dual wielding them with hands seemingly made of silver, black ring marks at every joint.

"I'll become you, and you'll become me." the stranger said, voice with a digital buzzing edge. "I will reclaim you, Eclipse."

What—? Is he some kind of nightmare guardian?

The stranger flew forward, and Colton ducked the swinging blades. He threw a weak punch, landing it firmly on the stranger's chest, crying out from his hand crumpling against solid metal hidden behind the cloak.

Colton dodged a strike, then attempted to tackle the stranger, who barely moved. The stranger knocked Colton to the ground with a kick, taking his breath.

"Fight, little pest, fight till you're dead," the stranger sang in a demented singsong voice. "Fight, and fight, till you've lost your head."

Colton held his side, body aching as he crawled slowly toward where the bottle lay, half of the cloth aflame. He reached out for it, only for his wrist to get crushed by metal.

"Run, run, run," the cloaked stranger hummed, the stench of oil stinging Colton's eyes. "Little more than bones is what you'll be when I'm done."

Colton cried out as the boot shoved deeper into the ground, causing cracking from Colton's wrist. The stranger raised the twisted swords, silver hands connecting until both arms ended in two weapons. The blades ignited with thrashing plasma, shrieking with hunger.

"Colton!" someone called.

Colton saw Daas walking toward him, expression angry, appearance disheveled as he splashed forward through the alcohol puddles, soaking his shoes and slacks.

"What did you do?" Daas shouted, picking up the bottle.

The cloaked stranger released Colton, striding toward Daas who raised both hands defensively. The cloaked stranger flew forward, blades ablur.

"No, don't!" Colton screamed, rocketing to his feet, stumbling sideways.

Time slowed down for a moment, the sound like glass shattering as a purple crystal covered the ground. The bottle shattered against the crystal, recreating the sound, spreading flames and causing the material to increase in luminance. Red heat covered everything, Daas being lost in it all, only for the fire to turn black, outlined by white heat.

A deafening roar erupted, shattering Colton's eardrums as light flashed brighter than noonday, blinding him. The heat matched in intensity, instantly burning his skin.

His whole body shook, throwing him back dozens of feet, like someone had landed a solid blow on every inch of his body. The ground became liquid for a split-second, knocking every person to the ground, turning every market stall to rubble. Flames leaped everywhere like frenzied orange lightning, fueled by exploding bottles of alcohol.

Colton laid still for a second, his body feeling broken. His skin felt entirely numb and shriveled. His ears rang, and his skull throbbed. The abhorrent stench of charred flesh overwhelmed him, making breathing difficult. Lifting his head proved near impossible as his neck resisted any movement, taking effort to view the carnage as his vision slowly returned.

The gallows were entirely gone. So was the fountain and everything else in a ten-foot radius. All of it was replaced by thrashing flames, ravaging with the sound of half-digital screams of guardians as they rolled around with what few limbs they had left.

"No," Colton muttered.

He stumbled forward, his eyes locked on a small piece of red fabric that floated just above him. His throat burned, a scream thrashing in his vocal chords like acid from vomit. His gut thrashed, trying to break free as if some kind of parasite was alive inside him.

But he couldn't let it escape. It stayed trapped. Maybe the fire wouldn't be real if the parasite stayed trapped.

He really just—Daas just—

Colton grabbed the fabric, the thread falling apart at his touch, dissolving into strands that were sucked into the inferno. Colton watched it, settling his gaze on the stranger standing in the midst of the fire.

Steaming metal skin, plates of metal for armor, and a face partially hidden behind a black respirator, tubes and wires connected to the wire-like hair, and all over the body. Ring marks were visible at every joint that separated and connected sporadically with a hiss of steam. The cloak was partially burned away, flames thrashing. A hell raged in the yellow, lens-like eyes.

Colton stared, unable to look away, his brain full of a buzzing cold that broke his thoughts.

"Beware Eclipse," the stranger hissed, voice breaking into a digitized death cry, "your blood'll stain the dusk red."

Colton's eyes stung from gritty char; his lungs barely took in any breath before they squeezed excruciatingly dry. His heart half-beating every time it pumped, exploding his chest with pain.

Then his body shut down.

Chapter 10
Sackcloth and Ashes

Fear. A buzzing cold that breaks your thoughts.

That was all Liam knew as he watched the fire ravage the entire Central Market. Smoke erupted in dark clouds, blotting out the sun. Most people stood motionless, jaws hanging, throats screaming, and terror glossing their eyes.

The guardians were in a frenzy of attacks. An old woman being rained upon by blows. A child huddling as armored hands grasped at him. A large mountain of a man, Dromus, held a limp guardian, his fist bloody, fending off more.

Liam stood staring, rooted to the road. He watched guardians swarming someone in the center of the Central Market, hauling them off, the body limp, and wolf-like eyes empty. An odd person stood amidst the flame, unharmed, watching, waiting.

Other people were busy with the chaos, some running from the inferno that devoured whatever it could, and other rioters rushing to turn guardians into corpse trophies, smashing their armor, stealing rifles, snatching batons, and spilling blood as other guardians fought back.

Liam made no effort to stop the guardians from grabbing and starting to choke him, pinning him to the ground and binding him. He thrashed, failing miserably.

He looked around for help, seeing Jace nearby, struggling against a dozen guardians. Fisk was scampering away down the street, howling. Bristol held a smoking rifle and looked pale as a ghost as she slunk into an alleyway.

Liam felt his brain slowly shut down, making everything hazy. He couldn't focus on anything. He couldn't see anything, hear anything.

The Central Market was gone.

And so was patience with the guardians.

76

Chapter 11
Then I Met Her

Everything hurt.

His body ached, his skin burned, his eyes stung, and his head throbbed. All of it felt like he had woken up, entirely sick, everything stiff and sore. But he could think clearly, the pain diluted to tolerable levels.

Am I dead? Dying?

The small rocks poked into his side, the hard concrete grinding against his skull. Yet he still felt sleepy, his eyes heavy despite the burning chill that seeped into him from the ground.

Where am I? Colton thought.

Any thoughts he had came packaged with pain, making it easy to lay mindlessly on the ground, hoping to be taken by slumber. He could almost snore as he began drifting off to blissful sleep again.

"Wake up, gjinx!"

Someone banged loudly on the metal, and Colton shot upright, all drowsiness gone as his eyes were blinded by a bright light emitting from beyond cell bars. A guardian held a tray of food in one hand, and a large electric lamp in the other.

"Enjoy it while it lasts," sneered the guardian, voice pitching high. "You'll be executed when I come back."

The tray slipped through the cell bars, crashing to the ground, and breaking some of the dishes. Sludge-like soup splattered all over Colton, smelling rank, and a dirtied fork nearly stabbed him in the eyes. He stared down at it, his gut twisting.

Execution?

The guardian withdrew down the hallway, leaving Colton to wipe the moldy food from his face and shake it from his hands. He glared down glumly at the fork as the light diminished to pure blackness.

Colton frowned, considering the food, brain hurting as he shook his head, temporarily worsening the pain. He picked up the fork, stabbing blindly to search for any of the food that had spilled. His knuckles were shot with pain, and he switched to his left hand, hurting less, only to hear the *'tink'* from hitting the cement each time.

"Do you happen to possess a night-vision Caliber? Or are you hoping to get lucky?"

Colton jerked his head, glancing around, fork held ready to stab. A loud *scrape,* then a warm orange glow quickly grew from a flickering flame within a lantern outside his cell.

A cloaked stranger stood outside, brown hood hiding any features except for pale blonde, almost silver hair strands that spilled out to the shoulders.

What's with the cloak?

"You're that metal freak that tried to kill me," Colton said.

"Not at all," the stranger said, sounding light and feminine. "I would be shocked if I found myself to be inorganic."

Lithe, winter-cream hands emerged from the sleeves, gently removing the hood, revealing a young girl in the dim light, scarcely looking a year older than him. She gave a coy smile before sitting on the ground, cross-legged, next to the lantern.

"I believed you would've found the luminance of a flame more soothing than the harsh brilliance of a flashlight."

Colton widened his eyes at the small, faint scars across her face, seeming to cause the color of her eyes. Sapphire raindrops.

"I uhh–" Colton stammered.

The girl smiled softly, holding out a hand through the cell bars. "I'm Lily Scientia Reine. Pleasure to meet you. Your name is?"

Colton sat, blinking rapidly. "Coal day toad."

The girl giggled and Colton grimaced, face burning as he smacked himself on the head.

"Don't worry," Lily said, "your name isn't hard to find, with all the wanted posters you have. I asked for the sake of pleasantries."

"Yeah, uhm," Colton muttered, he perked up, "how could you see me in the dark?"

Lily bowed her head slightly. "I couldn't see you, per-se. But there are tricks to navigating utter darkness."

"So, how'd you even get here? How'd I even get here?"

"Well, the guardians aren't too hard to bypass if you wave sufficient funds in front of their eyes."

"So, bribery?"

"I prefer 'purchasing entry.'"

Colton rolled his eyes. "Ugh, you sound like Bristol. Don't tell me you're a know-it-all kretch too?"

The girl sighed, re-tying the lace on her white combat boots into a neat little bow. "Perhaps now you're wishing you hadn't chosen the path of a thief?"

Colton scowled, tossing the fork at her, hitting the metal bars instead, creating a soft *tink*, and earning a reproachful look from her.

"I shouldn't even be here," Colton groused.

The girl scoffed before grimacing with closed eyes and muttering admonishment to herself.

"You didn't think very thoroughly through your plan," she whispered. "The damage speaks for itself."

Colton used a foot, dragging the fork until he could grab it with his hand. He began jabbing at the ground, more out of fidgeting than looking for the food.

Thoughts, pain, blurry images. It sucked to think, but he forced himself, replaying the earliest memories he could.

I think, I passed out when Fisk—

"I didn't get to do any damage. A kid stopped me," Colton said, forcing his fork into the ground so hard it broke two of the tines.

The girl frowned. "You attempted to set fire to the gallows, but the events had gone awry, and all of the Central Market was incinerated, with a tenth of the district itself burning."

Colton frowned, a weight dropping into his gut, disturbing the *thing* that slept away in his stomach, disrupting it from slumber.

"There's no way that's actually true," Colton muttered. "There's no way that's actually—th-tht's actually—that's ac—no"

He clutched handfuls of his hair, purple crystal emitting along his hands as pain rocked through from the injuries. "I caused that. I'm the one who—I caused—"

He felt his throat knot up and vision go blurry. His brain seared, ricocheting thoughts with the image of the blasting fire, the charred fabric, and those serpentine eyes.

How could I be so stupid? I actually—

He felt a gentle grip on his wrist, and something itched at his brain, like a slight fragrance of flowers. His bouncing thoughts slowed, the images vanishing from his mind as the crystal receded, and he could take a steady and slow breath again. He blinked, looking around as he remembered where he was.

"Colton," Lily said with a firm, but sympathetic look, her hand gently holding his wrist, "forget about it. What's done is done."

"But I'm the one."

"No. While your actions were careless and caused damage, there were other forces. And panicking about it now will do no good."

"How long have I been here?" Colton asked, voice croaking, rubbing his shoulder, a new bullet scar slowly growing.

The girl looked down the hall, pursing her lips, leaning slightly back before her cold blue eyes settled on Colton again, whose hands gripped the metal bars.

"Only a little more than three days. You suffered quite the injuries from your stunt, afterwards being hauled into the Auratus District and imprisoned here while unconscious."

"Three days? How am I not dead?" Colton asked, leaning against the bars, panic rising like a buzzing in his ears, "I gotta go find—

"Liam is alive," Lily said, "though, soon to be in the Auratus Prison as much as you are. He was caught amidst the chaos and is being interrogated."

"Did he get hurt?"

"When I last saw him, there were only a few bruises."

"I screwed up," Colton groaned, lightly banging his fist against the metal bars.

Lily tilted her head side-to-side. "Not entirely."

"What's that supposed to mean?"

"Before long, the Scintilla Initium District might've revolted and performed something similar. The Auratus District was far too oppressive, and as such, the morality or lack thereof is questionable,"

80

Lily explained. "Not to mention, I don't believe your intention was to blow up the whole of the market, simply burn down the Guardian's gloating device. You had no control."

"Yeah, sure worked, right? I should be dead."

"But you're not. A normal arsonist would've been."

"I'm just a normal nobody kid."

Lily tilted her head, frowning. "Those words are not your own. Why do you repeat them?"

"What?"

Lily shook her head, releasing her grip on the metal bars, pulling back and settling her eyes on the lantern.

"So how do you know about him?" Colton asked, the buzzing slowly diminishing.

Lily glanced up, before her eyes met Colton's again. "I've known about Liam for a while."

"Another one of his dumb admirers?"

"What leads you to such a thought?"

"You sound like Bristol, and Bristol is head over heels for him."

"Goodness, no. I have no romantic interest in anyone."

Colton folded his arms, giving Lily a long considering look, gently grinding his heel on the pavement.

She's weird, for sure. Is she even from the Auratus District?

"So, why're you visiting a stupid gjinx like me?" Colton asked.

"My current goal is to aid you and your friend," Lily said. "Ignoring the city now tearing itself apart, you have very desirable qualities that have caused one of the best of Red Dusk to be sent after you."

"What're you—? That I have a bounty?" Colton asked.

Lily leaned forward. "You're not what you think you are. You merely *look* human."

Silence in the corridor, intermittently interrupted by the barely audible ruffling of other inmates in their cells.

Colton stared, Lily raised a brow.

Colton continued to stare.

"So, you bribed your way in here just to mess with me and laugh at me being a screw up, right?"

Lily looked like she was trying to gouge her eyes out.

81

Caleb DM Smith

"I'd never do something so immature!" she shouted, scars flaring an angry red.

"Calm down, I was joking. Partially."

Lily hung her head against the metal bars. She took a deep breath, gently tapping her fingers. When she looked up again, she was more composed, and her scars were faint once again.

"Greatest apologies," she muttered. "I possess a bit of a temper, and do not have much patience for any imperfections."

Colton nodded slowly, studying her. He felt a weird instinct, like he was looking at someone who's trying to shatter their mask. It had a strange pull on him.

Those scars looked like they were tearing themselves apart.

"So, what did you come here for?" Colton asked.

"To meet you and potentially free you from your confines," Lily said.

"Why potentially?"

"That depends on your choice," Lily stated. "Do you intend to cause more chaos and harm?"

"What? No!"

"Or to run away and cause trouble?"

"Depends on that first part," Colton said. "Why do you wanna help?"

"We wish to keep you out of the hands of our enemies, at the very least. Hopefully to enlist you with the Celestial Lumanine."

"The nosk is that?"

"A righteous rebellion if you will."

Colton looked at the girl for a few moments.

"What if I don't agree?"

"You have an execution tomorrow, yes?" Lily checked.

"So, you're gonna leave me to die?"

"No, but you do not hold much choice to what fate we leave you in."

Colton huffed. "So, if I don't agree, you'll break me out anyways?"

"You'd still very much be incarcerated. Just by us until we can confirm you'd be of no threat," Lily said sternly.

"I'm a threat? How?"

82

"The Heralds of the Damned will take any opportunity to harm you. They value you as a threat and we must do the same."

"Heralds of the what now?"

"A group of evil beings with the purpose of subjecting all living things to their will."

"You just make up all these things?"

"They're legitimate organizations. One of which has sent an assassin after you."

Colton rubbed his head, frowning, and groaning. "I just try to help him, and I get caught in some war crap."

"Help who?" Lily tilted her head.

"Liam. I wanted to steal enough to get him and me out of here."

"I don't believe the way of a criminal is the best method."

"How else am I supposed to help him?" Colton asked.

"Not by decimating a city. However, I could provide an opportunity."

"You just threatened to leave me to die."

"Rather pointed out your lack of leverage."

"Great, I feel real safe now."

"I cannot promise your own safety, but I can promise you many other things."

Colton narrowed his eyes at Lily. He tapped his finger against his arm.

Why do they want me to join them? How in the world am I supposed to help a rebellion? Still—

"Can you promise that Liam will have a better life, and be taken away from any danger?" Colton asked.

Lily pursed her lips. "Better than he had or will now have if intervention does not occur from us. And I will personally see to his protection."

"You didn't promise what I asked."

"I cannot promise absolute safety for him. Only my best efforts will be put toward it."

"Fine, I'll agree," Colton said, keeping his voice level, "for now."

"Greatly appreciated," Lily said, smiling. "Now, as per my promise, we wait for Liam to arrive."

"He's not here?"

"Again, he's being put through interrogation. Especially since the guardians fear Red Dusk assassins may be involved."

"What's Red Dusk?"

"An assassin guild of the most lethal sellswords and mercenaries. To survive an attempt by one is nothing short of divine intervention."

"So that's who that was?" Colton muttered, more to himself.

"You saw one?" Lily asked, tilting her head. "How would you recognize—?"

"Said he brings the reddening of dusk, or something."

"Perhaps that was the occult guardian amongst the pandemonium."

"Uhm–what? Sorry, I only understand Plain-Speak."

"You saw an assassin, who others thought to be a guardian, because of the fire and chaos," Lily said, over enunciating the words. "You really ought to improve your language comprehension, you know."

"You know, you're as annoying as my siblings were," Colton muttered.

Lily huffed. "I bet they were quite exhausted with the way you acted."

"Kai would *definitely* be annoyed by you, too."

"Another boy you got roped into your troubles? Did Kai take the consequences of your actions?" Lily mocked.

Colton flung the tray at Lily, aggravating his hand injuries. It struck the metal bar instead, earning a loud *bang* as it crumpled to the ground.

"Was that meant for me? If so, you missed," Lily tut-tutted.

"Wow, you're such a genius," Colton said through clenched teeth. He shook his head, gaze falling. "I—sorry."

The girl squeezed her eyes shut, muttering a couple words before shaking her head and giving Colton an apologetic look.

"Forgive me if I was harsh," Lily said.

She produced a bandage-roll and a container of ointment from the fold of her cloak, holding it through the bars. Colton scooted closer and grabbed the bandage and ointment, giving her a dubious look as he leaned against the bars.

"You expected me to get hurt or sumthin'?" he asked.

Lily shrugged. "I witnessed your injuries in the Central Market."

"Assassin nearly broke my wrist. And I punched his metal armor."

"Conflicts with bare hands nowadays are more common, due to firearms being too costly."

Colton shrugged, meticulously treating his hand. The girl lightly dropped her head onto the metal bars, her nearly silver hair hiding her face. He heard a buzzing in his head, and the cold metal gained meager warmth.

He suddenly felt nauseous and his thoughts became muddled. Images flashed through his mind that he didn't recognize, half-blurry and warped as if peered at from a distance through a dirty telescope.

Did my brain get too fried?

One image was as if he was sitting on the floor, a maniacal man in a lab coat coming toward him with strange medical tools. The second, a terrifying, gigantic humanoid machine looming over him with glowing eyes while pleas for freedom echoed from somewhere. And lastly, a view looking toward the ground where a boy leaned haphazardly against the metal bars with a broken hand.

Wait—WHAT?

Colton jerked away, crashing into the opposite wall, protecting his hand as the buzzing cut out, dissipating the muddled thoughts and nausea.

"Are you feeling ill?" Lily asked, face blank.

Colton took a deep breath, shoulders aching and fingers twitching.

What is actually going on? This isn't funny!

"Y-yeah yeah, I'm fine," Colton muttered.

Lily nodded, her face twisting to replicate a smile, her irises reflecting the darkness. "Did you have strange images floating through your head?"

Colton snapped his head toward her so fast he tweaked his neck, making Lily give a slightly bemused laugh while Colton groaned and rubbed the pain out.

"Perhaps of a man dressed in a lab coat, unpleasant machines, or even the strange sight of yourself as if from someone else's eyes?" she inquired.

"How—?" Colton began, only to lose his words.

"Would you like me to demonstrate?"

"Demonstrate what exactly?"

"I shall show you. It will be pertinent that you touch the metal."

Colton studied her, the odd sensation in his gut twisting. Yet she seemed innocent enough, what with her soft blue eyes, her scars accentuating her gentle caring smile, and—

Shut up, Colton!

Colton gently slapped himself. "Why should I trust you?"

"Do you have anything to lose by doing so?"

"Not really, but—"

Colton considered her before he took hold of the cold metal with his left hand, cradling his right. Lily made sure to touch the same bar as Colton, placing her hand a mere two inches from his. A buzzing started in Colton's head, like insects were hovering next to his ears. He grimaced, shaking his head, but it persisted.

"Now, think of something you would—you wish you could possess if you could have anything. What would it be?" Lily said.

Colton gave her a slightly judgmental expression. "That's a weird question, but okay."

A few moments of silence, except with buzzing in Colton's head and nausea slowly returning. He thought about the question, but felt his mind drift, his eyes switching between the cell, to the metal bars, to the girl.

This is weird. Way weird. Where did she get those cracking-scars? She's kinda like Bristol. But more—attractive. Way better looking than Bristol.

Lily laughed and shook her head, playfully smiling.

"Though I'm flattered, think about the question rather than about me."

Colton froze, eyes wide frozen as his face turned bright red.

86

She can read my mind? Please, kill me now.

Lily laughed again before bowing her head slightly as Colton banged his head against the metal bars.

Okay, question. Question. Think about the question. I don't know! A lot of things. I just wanna be away from this stupid town. I wanna be happy, not worry about eating everyday. I should probably think of something else to tell her though. Can't say I wanna help Liam have a good life, that would just be awkward. I don't know. What if—

The buzzing ended as Lily removed her hand and clutched her cloak, wrapping it around herself as she hummed lightly. Colton looked at her, frowning.

"That is quite a noble want," Lily said.

"So, you *were* reading my mind?" Colton exclaimed. "How's that even possible?"

"Have you not seen such a thing?"

"No. There's a person—woman—uhh teacher we have and she says stuff like that isn't real."

"Perhaps I show you how it's possible?"

"Uhm, okay."

The girl gestured to the bar, then took hold of it herself. "Focus on letting your mind be free."

Colton nodded, squinting his eyes and following her command. He heard the buzzing again, followed by some nausea before the buzzing slowly cut out, taking the nausea with it.

Well, that was quite quick this time around.

Colton stared, hearing Lily's voice, exactly as he had heard it before, yet she didn't move a single muscle except for her eyes slightly narrowing.

How–? What?

"How–? What?" Colton stuttered.

Laughter in his head, followed by Lily shaking her head.

No need to say what I have already heard.

Colton looked to Lily's hand, then back to her, his expression slowly melting into a more confused one.

This is some stupid party trick. How's this possible?

Caleb DM Smith

Think of it like one computer trying to access another one. You do know what a computer is, right?

No.

It's a machine that performs complex mental tasks. But regardless, you can only connect to one through a wire, or if powerful enough, through electrical waves. Usually, you have to give access to see inside the secondary machine. That is, unless one possesses the correct toolset to force their way into that machine.

So, what was all that buzzing and headaches for?

Side-effects of unwarranted entry into your mind. It stopped when you gave me access.

Colton frowned. *So how much can you see of my brain?*

Lily smiled. *Only what you consciously think. Most basic form of telepathy. If I wanted to force my way deeper, I could.*

Tell–three? Colton thought.

Tel-lep-a-thee, Lily articulated mentally, *a Caliber, or supernatural ability, I possess. It's the ability to communicate with others mentally, with some deeper levels of mind-manipulation.*

So, mind powers? You really expect me to believe that?

Well, it is new to you. But I'd be happy to explain it, Lily gave a small smile.

Okay fine. What're these Caliber things?

Calibers function off a type of energy in our bodies called Bio-Energy. Your life force in a way. Generally, the more you have naturally, the stronger you are, and when you have none, you're dead. Only an uncommon few individuals possess Calibers as a way to vent off extra Bio-Energy, as the supernatural abilities are somewhat genetic. If you have too much Bio-Energy, it can cause harm, depending on the person. Much like caffeine can slightly affect you or kill another person.

You're making it sound like you're not human. You know that, right? Colton thought.

I am quite human. Yet, I'm known as a 'Caliber-user,' or a calitch. Someone seemingly like you, who appears to be without Calibers, is simply called a 'skiff.'

Pulling his hand away, Colton gave the girl a dull look.

"Nobody *actually* believes in magic," he scoffed.

"Your disbelief is not unexpected. Malelentos is well-known for its naivety," Lily answered, dropping her hand. "However, it is not magic. Merely a scientific system."

"You sound like you should either be in an asylum or one of those stood general—eye-thing Liam talks about going to."

"A Studia Generalia? Those're basic level classes of learning *you* should be in."

"No, not the one Liam goes to. The one after that."

"A Studia-Advancia?"

"Yeah, that."

"We possess a form of Studia Generalia, but no formal form for Studia Advancia. They're quite rare."

"How about an asylum?"

"Asylums are something you get comfortable with when dealing with the servants of the damned," Lily replied.

As if on cue, they heard the sound of footsteps marching down the hallway, along with a faint light. The girl looked down the hallway then back at Colton, who leaned against the bars.

"You have to get me outta here," Colton said.

Lily rose to her feet. "I'll return when the guardians have settled down."

"Can't you bribe them again?"

"They'd simply take the money and do what they wish afterwards, as I'm at a disadvantage *in here*."

"You've got to have some other way outta here, right?"

The girl doused her lantern, the sound of her light feet echoing softly down the hallway.

"They're gonna execute me," Colton cried, banging on the bars.

He stared at the spot she vanished, silence echoing back to him with a mechanical hum from somewhere underground. He groaned and banged his head on the iron bars as the darkness slowly gave way to a harsh beam of light.

The guardian strode to Colton's cell, stopping by the door, cuffs in hand, and a baton in the other, lantern dangling from the hip.

"Wait," Colton exclaimed, leaping to his feet.

Caleb DM Smith

The guardian paused, banging the baton against the iron bars. "Shut it, gjinx!"

"Come on, there's gotta be some way I can get outta this."

"If there is," the guardian said, "it's not while I'm alive."

"But I—"

"Shut it! Filthy terrorist scum."

"I'm really gonna be killed," Colton muttered, insides going numb.

"You killed a half-dozen guardians. I knew a good lot of 'em personally. The shamn lot of work you gave us."

The guardian brought out a keychain on his belt and inserted it into the rusty door lock, fiddling around with it.

How thick are those helmets?

Colton waited until the guardian shifted a little closer to the door before he lunged forward. He grabbed the guardian, slamming him into the metal. The helmet cracked, the guardian cursed, and dropped the handcuffs. Colton grabbed at the keys. The guardian punched at him, knocking Colton back. He fell, the guardian whipped out a pistol.

"I'mma blast your head off, rat!" the guardian yelled.

The guardian cocked the pistol, aiming it through the bars. Lily shot out from the darkness, landing a solid kick, knocking the guardian's hand away, sending the pistol across the floor.

"You! Your money won't save you from execution," the guardian shouted, brandishing the baton.

Lily dealt another kick to the stomach, doing very little. The guardian swung at Lily, she twirled out of the way and threw a punch. The guardian grabbed her wrist and pulled her forward, slamming her with the baton, knocking her to the ground.

Lily groaned as she fell to hands and knees. The guardian advanced on her, baton raised. She took a moment before rapidly scooting back, eyes wide.

She's so screwed!

Colton looked around his cell, not seeing much available to him except a plastic fork.

I know a distraction failed last time, but—

90

He grabbed the fork, rushed to the bars, and hucked it at the guardian, only for it to lightly *tink* against the helmet. The guardian froze, slowly turning to Colton.

"Did you just—" the guardian began.

"Kretch-face," Colton spat.

"You what—?"

"You got kicked twice, when you were ready," Colton mocked. "I could take you easily."

The guardian gave a sarcastic laugh, driving a kick into Lily's stomach before striding to Colton's cell. Colton stuck out his tongue, only for the guardian to grab him by the throat and slam him into the metal bars, the gray chlorine-smelling gloves holding him there.

I can't breathe!

"You were saying, gjinx?" the guardian seethed, voice jerking heavily, grip tightening, a creak emitting from Colton's neck joints.

He opened his mouth, but no words came out. His head swam with pain, and his vision started going dark, barely able to see Lily twisting her hand rapidly.

One of the metal bars creaked and snapped in half, wrapping around the guardian's own throat, who released Colton. The bar pulled tight. The guardian thrashed, kicked, and sputtered.

Lily tightened her grip, and the guardian's neck snapped, body going limp.

Colton stared, stumbling back into the cell, clutching his throat as he shifted his eyes from the dead guardian to Lily.

Woah woah woah, what was that? What the nosk was that?

"Well, that problem is removed from us," Lily said, rubbing a bruise on her head.

She walked over, grabbed the keys, and unlocked the door. Colton flinched hard, staring at the cell bar with a prick of fear in his chest, constricting his lungs as he tried to figure out what happened.

"How did you do that?" Colton croaked, wincing in pain.

"Telekinesis. Same thing as my first Caliber, but physical objects," Lily clarified with a smirk.

She waved her hand, and the electric lantern hovered into the air, floating as if hanging on an invisible chain and slowly spinning as Lily spun her hand.

Caleb DM Smith

"Let me guess, the hand movements help you focus?" Colton asked.

Lily smiled. "Hey, you do have some intelligence after all. And yes, especially as Calibers require exertion much like any physical action."

"Wait till we're outside before you give me another lecture," Colton said.

Lily nodded. "Then let's go liberate your friend."

Chapter 12

Smoke and murders

Colton hefted the baton in his left hand, his palm sweaty against the metal. He gave an uneasy glance at the pistol Lily let hang in her grip as they strode down the hallway.

Is she helping me or gonna backstab me?

She stopped at a corner, glancing down either way, before continuing. Colton followed, his skin tingly as he repeatedly glanced over his shoulder.

I feel like I'm being watched. Is this what it's like to be in that Arachnotaur forest Dromus talked about?

They walked for a good long while, stopping at another corner. Lily peered around it, before grabbing Colton and pushing him into an empty cell. She forced the two of them into a small corner, dousing her lamp as she held a finger to her lips.

Footsteps echoed as a harsh light slowly increased, followed by a guardian walking past, grumbling as they swung their light both ways down the hall.

Once the light fully vanished, Lily illuminated her lamp and snuck out of the cell. She peered around the corners again before stealing down the hallway. Colton stumbled out after her, trying to jog as quietly as he could.

"Where's Liam?" Colton asked.

Lily turned down another hall, stopping as they came in view of a guardian sitting on a stool at the other end of the hallway, head hanging down.

"Right there," Lily whispered.

Colton frowned and crept down the hall, tiptoeing as he avoided any pebbles that would skitter if he kicked them. He cast glances at nearby cells, seeing forlorn individuals who gave him murderous looks.

Caleb DM Smith

Stopping so the guardian was at the edge of the light, Colton held his breath, the shoulders of the guardian slowly lifting up and down, making the flashlight in hand gently bounce.

Good, he's asleep.

He looked over to the cell, seeing Liam asleep on a crappy cot, looking a little less roughed up than Colton felt.

And he's alive.

Colton looked back to Lily and waved. She quickly snuck over to him while he quietly felt along the cell door for any flaws to utilize.

"Psst," someone hissed.

Colton looked over, seeing a haggard Fisk, bruises, a black eye, and hair half-singed off. He stood in a cell across the hallway, clinging to the bars and face pressed up against the metal.

"It ain't just gonna swing open fer yah," Fisk whispered.

"You know how to get it open?" Colton asked.

Fisk pointed to the guardian, then pointed to his own hip, before making a shushing gesture with his finger pressed to his mouth.

Colton grimaced and crouched by the guardian. The keys were attached to a belt loop by a clip, fixed between the guardian's torso and hanging arm.

And Liam said my thief skills wouldn't help.

Colton gently reached forward, his hair standing on end as he gently touched the clip, eyes straying up to the guardian's face, the head still hanging lazily. Gently, Colton pressed down on the clip, hearing it click. He pushed it up, sliding it off the belt loop, barely brushing the arm before he adjusted his grip.

The keys slipped from his fingers, clattering to the ground. Colton froze, adrenaline flooding through his legs, the clinking echoing loudly down the halls like brash bells.

Colton slowly looked up at the guardian, body still limp and shoulders still bobbing. Colton gently reached down and picked up the keys, clinking slightly as he stood up.

He moved toward the door, just as someone behind him started grunting. Lily stepped over to the stirring guardian, gently peeling back the sleek grey sleeve as she touched a finger to the skin.

"What're you doing?" Colton hissed.

94

Lily closed her eyes, scrunching up her face as she grabbed the guardian's entire wrist. The guardian jerked, eyes flashing open, only to crash down to the ground limp again.

Lily stood up, sighing as she grabbed the keys from Colton and quickly began inserting keys into the lock, cycling through them.

"What'd you just do?" Colton asked.

"The mind is more vulnerable when asleep or afflicted," Lily said, "but sentients are hard to control. As he was leaving his deep slumber, I—made sure he stays asleep for a while."

"So, you killed him?"

"No. I shut his mind down. Think of when someone is knocked unconscious."

Lily yanked out the keys, clanging the metal loudly. Liam jerked, sitting up and staring bleary-eyed at them.

"Colton?" he asked, he looked at Lily. "Who's that?"

"We're getting out of here," Colton said.

Liam frowned. "How'd you get in here?"

"Long story."

"It's always a long story."

"As is fitting," Lily said, scowling and throwing the keys away.

"Who's she?" Liam asked.

"I'm Lily Reine," she said.

She pantomimed grabbing a small object before twisting. The lock began turning as a whole, the metal creaking as it disfigured the door. A loud snap, and the whole lock fell to the ground. She swung the door open, and stood back, looking somewhat more tired.

"How'd you do that?" Liam asked, leaping to his feet.

She proceeded into a shortened explanation of what she told Colton of Calibers and them being stronger the more effort is put in.

"And lucky people are born with mind Calibers?" Liam asked.

"My specific Calibers are telepathy and telekinesis. However, another individual could have similar Calibers or vastly different ones. They could even possess the ability to generate explosions, control vegetation, or produce frost," Lily said. "Only a few hundred out of a million will be born with Calibers."

"But if we're not born with them, we can never get them?" Colton asked.

Caleb DM Smith

Lily's eyes darkened to murky pools of oily ponds as her jaw tightened. Colton shivered, feeling like the temperature had dropped a few degrees, almost evidenced by the lantern light being dimmed by aura.

"There are other ways to receive Calibers. Yet, they are treacherous. Not just to your physical or mental well-being, but to your humanity. You may yet become a—"

Someone in the prison began sobbing softly. Metal thumping could be heard. Something caused Colton's skin to itch, like bubbling underneath.

What is this? Hell?

"Speaking of such things brings unpleasant spirits to our company," Lily stated in a grating voice.

Colton frowned, watching the girl cast her gaze around, her limbs fidgety and face more pale. She turned to walk down the hallway.

That was weird. Is there like—people experimented on or something?

Colton moved to follow her, only for Fisk to clear his throat.

"Aren't yoo goin'ter free meh?" Fisk asked, baring crooked teeth.

Colton looked to Liam and Lily, who both shook their heads. Colton looked back, frowning and Fisk snarled.

"Yoo bettah open up this heer cage, boy," Fisk growled.

Colton shook his head, turning and jogging down the hall with the others. Fisk thrashed against the bars, screaming at Colton.

"I'm gonna escape from heer, an' slit yer throat. I'm telling yah, I will make ya *watch* yer buddy's head fall to ter ground."

Colton squeezed his eyes shut for a moment as he ran, shaking the words out of his mind. The trio passed a number of jail cells, holding adults with filthy skin and matted hair. Other cells held young children, huddled in the corners, arms hugging their knees, eyes sunken into their skulls.

Colton stared at them. He recognized a couple of kids he met months ago. They had been in better shape than himself then. Others were more recent acquaintances he had known for barely a day or two.

At least, before I exploded the Central Market.

96

All were now brooding husks that rocked back and forth on bleeding heels, sobbing faintly, or faces replicating smiles as they laughed maniacally.

Colton peered into the bottom of one cell, and he saw a large boy huddled in the corner. The boy looked up at him, a bandage wrapped around his eye, a large red spot slowly spreading out. Bruises and slash marks covered much of the visible skin.

Colton stared. *It's Jace!*

The boy frowned, only to whimper, pressing further into the corner. He broke down crying, shaking uncontrollably as he let out gasping sobs.

"Get away from me. I won't cause any more trouble, I promise," Jace blubbered.

Is that really Jace? Is he really—?

Jace wailed, lunging forward and smashing against the bars, angrily reaching out like a rabid raccoon.

"Get out! Leave!" Jace screamed. "I told you to stay away from me. Else I'mma use you like they did me, stranger."

Colton took a step back, nauseated by Jace's bleeding lips and teeth jutting out jaggedly in his crazed, snarling scowl.

Use? What happened to him?

"Jace," Colton began, "I didn't mean for you to end up here."

"You didn't mean to? You got the wrong guy. I don't know you," the boy hissed.

Liam came up beside Colton, wrinkling his nose, looking somberly at the victim, with Jace snarling, flinging spit, and gnawing on the iron bars, crunching his own teeth till they were completely gone.

That black mark on his neck. It's like someone injected tar in his veins.

"Not all are lucky enough to be hung from the gallows," Lily whispered.

Colton lingered, his brain flashing images of the Central Market and the gallows with its hanging victims slowly strangled to death by the abrasive cords.

"Let's get outta here," Liam urged.

Colton nodded slowly, the veins in his arms like ice, infecting his whole body with arctic chill as he withdrew from Jace.

Caleb DM Smith

The eerie ambiance reigned supreme in Colton's ears as he hurried down the hall as quickly and as quietly as he could. The light slowly increased, revealing walls of poorly formed concrete and sporadic electrical light bulbs covered in black scorch marks, flickering weakly with a dim glow. The cell doors became full steel barriers, only a tiny window allowing a peek inside.

More voices came muffled from the containments; some were from down the hall toward the brightest of the lights. Lily ducked to hide at an off-shooting hallway, prompting the two boys to follow suit across the way.

They peered at a hexagonal center room just ahead of them. Guardians sat helmetless in cushy seats, playing cards in hands, a metal table laden with dozens more cards, and a set of three dice.

"That'll be a collect from me," said one guardian before grabbing a pile of cards in the center.

"Should've rolled the dice better," commented a second with curly blond hair, "Where's Henry? Shouldn't take that long to put a gjinx away."

"Off to go find a wizard or something," snickered a third with a sallowed face.

"Or hunting those demon things," mocked a fourth guardian, portly body shaking.

"Shut up and play your card!" demanded the fifth, nose crooked and bent.

Colton turned to Lily, her head tilted and a hand outstretched. His apprehension rose the more she emerged from behind the corner.

She whispered, "I wonder if I perhaps can—"

The table between the guardians shifted, ramming into the legs of one. Furious, the guardian shoved it back, hitting another, prompting all the others to join the argument, resulting in cards being thrown.

"What was that for?" accused one.

"Shut up! You're just mad I've got a good hand," shouted a second.

"I'm gonna–" started the third before getting a table slammed into the chest.

"Stop screaming and wailing like those bratty kids," demanded a fourth.

98

"You mean those two I had *experimented* with?" hissed a fifth. "Barely survived a few seconds before they gave in to the symptoms."

Lily gasped, Colton looked at her, her whole body quivering, scars slowly flaring up and cracking more. Her fists were balled so tight they turned sickly pale as they trembled.

He slowly backed away from her.

What the nosk is— uh oh.

Lily stalked forward, grabbing the attention of the guardians. All of them froze in shock, table still lifted between them. Colton stilled his breath, crouching more into the shadows.

"Prisoner out of their cell!" exclaimed the first guardian, grabbing a helmet and slamming it onto his head before reaching for a baton at his hip.

"Surrender yourself now or—" the guardian began.

Lily held out her palm, whipping before clenching into a fist. The helmet tore itself off the guardian's head, crushing like a can before smacking the guardian unconscious.

The second guardian held a rifle, which cracked and shattered into a thousand pieces with a wave, it formed a blade and skewered the guardian. The third hurled a chair at Lily, which only stopped and tore itself to dust. She whipped her hand and the table flew across the room slamming the guardian into the wall with a heavy *crunch*, falling limp.

Colton stared from the shadows, Lily's scars worsening, starting to bleed as she kept her eyes locked on the last two guardians.

Her eyes burned like blue flame as the fourth guardian rushed. A flick sent all of the playing cards flying around and slicing through the armor. The guardian cried out, swatting at the cards only for them to pile up into a dense small ball and smash the guardian to the ground.

The fifth guardian turned and sprinted down the hall, and Lily chopped downward, causing the ceiling to cave-in on the guardian, earning a scream cut short.

Once the rubble had settled, Lily stumbled sideways, shoulders shaking and head bowed, prompting Liam and Colton to rush forward, but she brushed them off.

"What was that all about?" Colton asked.

"To do such a horrid—to be so abominably—to treat such young and innocent as test subjects—" Lily struggled out, before giving a distressed shout, throwing her hands down to her sides, shredding the table into pieces, causing her scars to bleed a little more.

Colton and Liam started, flinching terribly before giving each other wide-eye looks. Colton's hair stood on end, and he made sure to keep his distance from her.

Lily shook her head, wiping the blood from her face on the sleeves of her cloak before giving the stain an annoyed look. She pushed off the wall and stumbled to the end of the room, tipping sideways a few times before regaining her balance with outstretched hands. She took a deep breath and continued to a flight of stairs, tipping slightly.

That's what Calibers can do? Scary. Colton thought, before following.

The steps were cracked and covered in damage, with plenty of crude drawings etched into the concrete walls. Light shone through a small dirty window in the only steel door at the top, with a noisy but muffled ambiance emitting from behind it.

There's people shouting. It sounds like something's going on upstairs.

Before they could climb the steps, an alarm blared, echoing in the halls in a shrill note, making them all clamp their hands to their ears. The door shook as locks were undone, and Lily shoved Colton and Liam away from the stairwell toward the hexagonal room.

"You nosking gjinxes!" shouted a raspy voice.

Colton ducked as gunshots rang out. They all sprinted for a hallway. The guardian, pinned against the wall with the table, a pistol in hand, fired shots that ricocheted off the walls, a bullet grazing Colton's ear.

Lily flicked her hand, and one end of the table lazily leaped upward, freeing the guardian, dropping him to the ground. She tilted sideways, crashing into the wall, almost fainting. Liam rushed to her side, while Colton rushed further into the hall, looking for a hideout as the sounds of marching footsteps echoed from the stairs.

He nosking set off the alarm!

Colton threw open a utility closet door, holding it open as Liam and Lily followed a second later. Shouts echoed as Colton slammed the door, locking it, and retreating in the dark as far back as he could go.

Outside were pounding footsteps, dozens of distorted radio-like shouts, and the clatter of armor and weapons. Colton watched Lily sidle up to the door, pressing her ear to the wood, listening carefully. She looked exhausted, her scars slowly fading again, but her eyes slightly sunken.

"Are they gonna find us?" Liam asked.

Lily held up a finger. "Quiet!"

They waited, the sounds of the guardians growing loud, their helmets twisting the shape of their voices to that unsettling digital tone.

Looking at his surroundings, Colton saw many tools, brooms, pipes and metal boxes on the walls. The room smelled unpleasant, especially strong where some pipes and wires connected, and others ran out of the room. Continuing his search, Colton pulled open the front of a metal box, revealing a myriad of switches, buttons, levers, and dials. Most were labeled with indecipherable letters and numbers, with some assigned to vaguely named places. A specific one was labeled 'Power.'

What are these things?

Colton cast another glance at Lily and Liam hyper-focused on the door.

Maybe she could tear everyone up again?

He frowned, his gut churning at the thought.

Dunno, she looks ready to pass out. And I don't want her to kill me like that. Or anyone else either.

He looked at the box again, his heart constricting as he considered the switch. Steeling himself, he flipped the switch, the control box beeping a little. Nothing happened and he frowned, hefting his baton and smashed it on the control box, causing a series of sparks.

Ow! What the—guess that didn't work.

A moment later, the booming sound of metal grinding against metal deafened their ears. Hinges creaked and an alarm blared before fading to silence.

The grinding continued, dragging on.

Time ticked by, and it dragged on.

The trio stood silently in the darkness, as the cacophony continued relentlessly, ending with a boom.

Did I just kill everyone?

It was so quiet, Colton could hear his heart pounding in his chest.

"What happened?" Liam asked, face hardly visible.

"I have no idea," Colton replied with a grimace.

Lily spun, grabbing Colton by the collar of his shirt and shoving him against the wall. Her gaze shifted momentarily to the open box, before hardening as it returned to him.

"For the love of the seven, if you have done exactly what I think you have done—" Lily hissed.

Colton held up his hands defensively. "I was just trying to help!"

You have released every prisoner confined in this dungeon, Lily conversed with him mentally.

So, we can get out, right?

Very angry, and mentally broken prisoners, hungry for retribution.

We'll be fine. I think.

Chapter 13
Out of the Frying Pan

A scream rang out, triumphantly cutting the silence before a cacophony of chaos broke out.

Shouts and screams, gunfire, banging, wails, the sound of ricocheting bullets. Footsteps pounded past. Something smashed and cracked. Chaotic yells of triumph, rapid metal banging.

Something crashed against the door. Colton snapped his gaze toward the noise, causing Lily to release him and he huddled deeper in the utility closet. Minutes passed. The ruckus from outside worsened. A baton smashed through the door, nearly hitting Liam in the head. Shouts and grunts before someone else slammed against the door.

Please don't let them in.

Lily reached forward to grab it, only for the baton to be yanked out by an unseen hand. A voice outside muttered angrily, seeming to grow distant.

"We should be—" Lily began to whisper.

The door creaked as someone rammed themselves against the door, a dilated eye peered through the hole, wild and insane. Colton froze, breath non-existent as the stranger's eye twitched, examining what little could be seen through the hole.

It vanished, leaving as suddenly as it had appeared. The owner's voice trailed from down the hall in a slithering sing-song tone, "Where's dat li'le boy, gone run away? I wish ter eat his flesh. Ter chomp an' chew while he n' screams. Where're them guardians sweet? I want ter cut them at ter seams."

That accent. Is that—?

Suddenly the singing cut off, followed by an eldritch scream. Colton huddled in the corner, trying to tune out the blood-curdling shriek as moist thumping could be heard. Cracking and crunching, followed by something skittering down the hallway by the door.

I never wanna hear a scream like that again, Colton thought, his gut twist and his throat knotting up.

Troubled relief came with a deafening silence, occasionally broke up by sounds of conflict. The time ticked by. Colton's discomfort grew with each beat of his heart, waiting for the next crazed individual to peer through the door again.

I didn't help at all.

Colton sat down in the darkness, straining his ears to hear something for what seemed like hours. He only got the buzzing of silence as nothing else seemed to move.

Please say they're all gone. Please say they're all gone.

At long last, Lily shuffled forward, cracked open the door, and poked her head out.

She muttered something about 'a barbaric prison' and vanished into the hall. Colton and Liam carefully followed, the hallway a new sight to them.

Lights were smashed, smattered debris, plenty of rubble on the floor, and an occasional corpse slumped in the shadows. Scribbles littered the walls, and an occasional broken weapon here and there.

"Perhaps it's best to vacate this dungeon," Lily stated, nudging a smashed helmet that had stains of red inside, a trail leading from it past the closet door.

"Again, what happened?" Liam demanded.

"I opened the doors," Colton hurriedly said.

Liam gave him a 'what-were-you-thinking' look, folding his arms, looking at Lily. She frowned, tilting her head slightly.

"In a way, it did work," she conceded, heading towards the stairs.

At the top of the steps, the scenery continued, with couches and rugs burned by logs taken from a nearby fireplace. A crystal chandelier laid in the center of the room, and a few office chairs sat outside on the sidewalk amidst shattered glass. A front mahogany desk was smashed in two, with a dozen fallen guardians littering the floor behind it. Outside, came an ambiance that droned on constantly. The distant sounds of life that dulled the unnerving edge of the room.

"What did we just do?" Liam muttered, eyes wide, voice pitching.

104

"Well, we've caused quite the mess, haven't we?" Lily huffed, casting Colton a dirty look.

Why's she so calm about it?

He returned the look as she kicked aside bits of glass, forming a path and strode to the door. Liam followed dutifully, while Colton surveyed the victims, weaponless and some parts of armor stolen.

Someone has a stealing problem, Colton thought with a wince. He frowned. *Or…no. There's no way—they're crazy if they think they can riot against the whole city.*

He frowned, heading outside, careful to avoid impaling his bare feet with glass. He wrinkled his nose against the smell of burnt oil and cleaning chemicals. He joined Lily and Liam in surveying the dusk-lit street, vacant with little sign of any damage or jailbreak. Citizens walked by at either end of the street, too focused on themselves to notice much else.

What's up with them? Are they blind? Mindless?

Turning his attention to the scenery, Colton craned his neck to see the tops of the buildings. Impossibly high, the structures held reflective windows set in shiny steel that gave the city a surreal look, with the buildings ranging widely in height, width, color, and shape.

It's… big. It's really really big.

"Quite the view, yet nothing compared to Novum," Lily said.

Colton looked to Lily, who answered his unspoken question with a gentle smile.

"It's yet another city, with technology beyond anything normal humans can create. However, for now, let us get somewhere not so exposed due to—"

She paused, frowningly slightly.

"—*some* people having careless natures."

"Where did they even go?" Colton asked.

Lily pointed to a grate in the middle of the road that had been lifted up out of a large hole, a bad stench coming from it.

Sewers? Right, no Richmen would follow them.

Lily turned on her heel before limping across the street. Liam looked at Colton, who returned with a sullen look.

Maybe I should just stop trying to help.

Lily led them past the street to a narrow alleyway filled with heaps of trash and a rusted motorbike missing its wheels. A series of metal balconies rose up the side of the building, connected by metal ladders that extended down to about six feet above the ground.

Lily touched the bottom of a ladder, looking upwards at something unseen hidden in the shadow. A few seconds passed of silence, before something clanged and a person emerged.

The person stepped off the ledge, expertly leaping from balcony to balcony, dropping from the last railing and landing with a heavy *thud*. Colton stepped back, fists raised, intimidated by the brawny, tan-skinned man dressed in camo-colored military gear, with a rifle in his arms.

I saw him earlier! He's definitely not a guardian.

"This is Ivan Pavlenko, originally from Popenko, far north near a place called Forzendum," Lily stated, gesturing to the man who saluted.

"I pleasured to meet you," his voice was deep, and his Plain-Speak was poor, with an accent clouding his words. "Why all people in prison run free?"

"An unfortunate occurrence to be dealt with later," she said.

The man held out a hand, which Liam shook, and Colton regarded coldly.

He got freaky powers too or something?

Lily cleared her throat and pursed her lips, raising her brows. Colton looked at her somewhat annoyed, keeping his hands to his sides.

"He's the expert when it comes to field operations," Lily said. She dropped her voice while looking sullenly at Colton. "And I'd suggest highly to not draw his ire. Of which he has plenty."

Colton folded his arms, raising a brow. *This is starting to feel more like I'm being kidnapped, rather than joining them.*

"We replace old clothes," Ivan said, "yours not fit with Auratus."

He reached into his combat-vest and pulled out two outfits before chucking them at the two boys.

106

They were vastly different from what Colton had ever worn and looked much nicer than what he currently wore. Primarily due to the lack of holes where holes didn't belong.

"Well, that's lucky you had to have these," Colton muttered.

Ivan shrugged. "We plan ahead. Know boys are poor."

Colton frowned, looking down at his own clothes, suddenly feeling inadequately dressed. Ivan gave a toothy grin.

"Change clothes. We get you safe. New home."

Liam looked at Colton, who returned with a bewildered expression.

"Who *is* this dude?" Liam asked Colton, gesturing to the military-man.

Colton winced. "I was put on death-row, met them, and they said they'd help us break out. But we'd have to follow them for a while."

"So, you joined a—a—"

"The Celestial Lumanine," Lily frowned. "Did he not—?"

Colton winced. "I forgot that part."

"This is why you don't attack the guardians when you have a bounty on your head," Liam said, rubbing his temples.

"I wasn't just *attacking* them."

"What were you doing? If you actually stopped being a criminal, we wouldn't be here."

"I was trying to—" Colton began.

"Liam, Colton," Lily said, "now is not the time. Resolve it later. For now, we must get under cover. We cannot be exposed."

"Exposed to what?" Both boys asked at the same time.

"Hell itself may soon break loose. If not, it's certainly on its way," Lily said.

Colton threw his hands in the air. "It always is! I might as well be a part of it, with my luck."

"That's not—" Lily said, giving him a dark look. "Don't be so harsh to yourself."

Colton frowned, but Lily once again turned and walked away briskly.

She knows something I don't. Why doesn't she tell me?
What does she know about me?

Chapter 14

Rain on my Parade

I dunno if I hate or love this.

He picked at the bandages around his right hand, itching horribly as his skin started sweating. However, he appreciated how the black shirt, pants, and boots gave a sense of 'stylishly cool.'

This feels—less—vulnerable. Only a little.

Colton glanced at his friend, seeing Liam was just as happy with his gray-sweatshirt and trousers, going well with the red shoes that looked way more expensive than his previous pair.

Lily ushered them out of the alleyway despite the boys being overly fascinated with their new apparel. Colton pushed back against her, staying in the shadow of the alleyway.

"Nobody will recognize you here," Lily said, causing Colton to relent.

Out onto concrete streets they walked, with crowds pressing in one direction or another. Everyone so often, a motorbike would zip by, humming loudly as the driver navigated the crowds.

"Why don't we use one of those?" Colton asked.

"They're reserved for deliveries," Lily said. "No other vehicles reside in the city. Only the guardians have anything larger."

"Uh-huh," Colton said, his shoulders itching.

He reached up, grabbing for a hood, his heart stopping when his hands grabbed air. He frowned, glancing behind himself constantly, considering the people.

Sleek, gray clothes with odd designs and shapes, some white or black mixed in. Hardly any color to be seen, with holes and blemishes non-existent.

Everything's perfect. Too perfect.

Tall buildings rose into the sky, full of sun-reflecting windows, and thin antennas poking out on top. The sickly green of a park could be seen here and there between the overly smooth buildings, bloated flowers standing stiffly.

Colton slowly shuffled through the city as Lily started giving a rambling tour. He opted to crane his neck upwards, walking blindly until he stood before the tallest of skyscrapers within the Auratus District, so far up its top was wrapped in clouds. It was nearly twice the height of the nearest competitor.

Framed against the gargantuan Montiwell mountains, which rose utterly out of sight, the towers were dwarfed in comparison, adding an impressive image of insignificance as both steel and rock were lit an orangish-purple by sunset.

How did they build things this tall?

"—Wallich tower is also well known for being named after the two founders of the city."

Lily was continuing her ramble of trivia about the skyscraper, all of which was tuned out by everyone, including Liam, to Colton's surprise.

At least we agree on something about her.

"And you guys are staying at the top of it?" Liam asked.

Colton threw his friend a look.

Or not, you backstabbing gjinx.

"We have secure base at top. Secure base nice," Ivan answered.

"Shall we?" Lily added with a suave gesture, walking toward the door.

Inside, the building's foyer was furnished to the teeth. Plush couches, expensive wood tables, crystal and gold chandeliers, stiff fur rugs and a thick lavender scent hung around like smoke. People dotted the area, milling about on the furniture, by crackling fireplaces, or walking in and out of tiny rooms sealed off by three-inch thick metal doors.

Everyone seemed too focused on their feet as they walked or sat with blank faces. Hardly any words being said as they entertained themselves with various electronic devices that played sounds or gorged themselves on glossy chemical-smelling foods.

Creepy. They're supposed to be eating healthy, but it's like they're kinda dead still.

Lily headed right for the tiny rooms, Colton hung back, especially as the doors opened and closed without a single person touching them.

Sure, get in a claustrophobic magic box with a bunch of strangers. Definitely no problem with that at all.

Colton only followed when he looked at Ivan, rifle in hand, and biceps flexing to the size of melons.

Once Colton was inside, Lily entered a series of numbers on a keypad. The thick doors closed, followed by the room shaking gently for a moment or two, and the sound of motors whirring in a muffled tone. A sign in the upper corner of the room displayed a slowly ascending number that beeped every time it changed.

That's gonna be annoying real fast.

Once the sign had illuminated the number eighty-six, the beeping and the shaking stopped.

The doors opened, revealing new scenery.

Did we just teleport? Or fly? Colton thought, *clutching the back wall. Or—what just happened?*

Colton admired a short hallway made of marble and curved windows. The floor was covered in carpet, and the walls lined with the occasional light fixture glowing softly.

Lily led the way down the hall, with Ivan staying guard at the door. Though Liam was eager to follow the girl, Colton hung back, narrowing his eyes at the room.

How much does living up here cost?

Ivan looked at Colton, gesturing toward the hall, a smile that made Colton swear he saw sparks in Ivan's teeth. He spoke in a gravelly language and Colton stood blinking at Ivan, not understanding a single word. Ivan nudged Colton down the hall and he complied, hurrying forward.

A set of double doors stood at the other end, made of pearly white wood ornamented with shiny gold-colored accents. Lily waited till Colton and Ivan stood beside Liam before gently knocking with her knuckles.

Colton raised his brows at the doors, finding the top at almost double his height.

Who in the world is tall enough to need doors this big?

Nothing happened for a few moments until a click came from within. The doors opened, revealing a man barely taller than Colton.

He was almost as tan as Ivan, brown hair nearly as dark as Colton's, eyes hidden behind a pair of aviator sunglasses, and a cocky grin.

Lily gestured to the man. "This is Admiral Tom Stockdale; He's the Airforce Grand Admiral in the Celestial Lumanine. He and Ivan work together often."

Tom adjusted his leather jacket before extending his hand, which Liam shook and Colton considered before averting his gaze, rolling his shoulder.

"He'll be leading out our small group for the next little while," Lily said, raising a brow at Colton.

Tom stepped back, giving access to the penthouse room. "Which leads you to your new home."

The penthouse was the most extravagant room Colton had ever seen, with a conjoined living room, kitchen, dining room, and wraparound balcony, all filled with the most elegant and comfy furniture. Windows gave views to impressive sights, making the entire city look like a sea of stars amidst the dim glow of twilight. A succulent meaty aroma wafted over them, making Colton's mouth water. A welcoming fire blazed in its hearth in the living room, inviting them into comfort.

What would I give to live like this for the rest of my life?

"You guys're rich!" Colton exclaimed.

Tom shook his head. "Couldn't be further from the truth. The Auratus District has been in heavy decline for the past year. This penthouse costs us very little."

"This is one of our command posts. It comes with an abundance of security measures that make it difficult to besiege," Lily announced. She cast Colton a glance. "Should one need to hide during a chaotic riot."

Tom laughed, clapping Colton on the back, earning a glare, before striding into the kitchen. "I bet these boys are pretty hungry, huh?"

"No, we don't eat food," Colton said sarcastically.

Liam nudged him in the side. "Just be grateful."

Colton repeated Liam's words mockingly but earned a glare from him, and he rolled his eyes, muttering a quick apology, making Tom laugh.

Lily led them into the kitchen, where two main dishes had been cooked. Colton's mouth began stinging, over-salivating from the irresistible entrées he could see, unfamiliar and exciting.

"What's this?" Colton asked, sidling up to a juicy meat dish covered in golden crumbs.

"Specialty from Khalas," Tom answered, "They prepare a type of fried bird. Apparently, they were owned by a white-dressed colonel in an eastern state, before surviving the First Great Calamity."

"Sandy or something similar was his name," Lily added.

Tom grabbed a set of towels before propping open an iron oven. Heat seared forth, tiny flames erupting from pipes beneath a series of iron racks. Tom deftly reached in with the towels and pulled out a steaming pan of some type of bread. He quickly set it down on the counter, wincing as he shook his hand rapidly.

"And this is what is called a cake," Tom announced proudly.

"Yeah, we have them in the Scintilla Initium District," Colton said.

Tom nodded. "Oh, right."

Liam resisted a grin, while Lily let out a slight laugh. Colton shrugged and reached for a bowl full of strange dark objects. Grabbing one, it partially melted in his grasp, looking like mud. Lily gestured for him to eat, and he popped it into his mouth, finding it sweet, but gritty.

"It's a type of chocolate," Lily said.

"Man, I feel like a king," Colton bragged.

Liam grimaced. "He means thank you."

"Yes, well, we've cooked something for a special occasion tonight."

Colton and Liam shared a glance before looking at Lily with expectant looks. Her smile fell, and Colton raised a brow.

Are we celebrating that I got arrested?

"Don't you know what today is?" she asked, hands limp at her side.

Both boys shook their heads, Colton ate more of the dark objects, and Lily appeared bewildered.

Some holiday the kretches in Auratus celebrate, Colton thought, reaching for more sweets. Lily slapped his hand away, making Colton throw a glare.

"How do they not teach you such things in Studia-Generalia?" Lily fumed.

"They teach us about the acunar money stuff, and some random bits of history," Liam replied. "And how Kekamotos and us have lived as the only two sentients."

"And I don't go to Studia-Generalia," Colton added. "Partly because Bristol ruins it with her theories about other races."

"Bristol actually believed me?" Lily asked.

"She's always been—wait you've been the one telling her that crap?"

Lily held her head in her hands, shaking it. Colton cast a glance at Liam, who warned him not to try for the sweets again by shaking his head.

"Firstly," Lily began, "Humans and Kekamotos are not the only sentients upon this earth, as Kekamotos are one of many creatures that came from the First Great Calamity," Lily explained. "Secondly, today is Trial Day. The day we celebrate when the Desolation Trials ended, when the Twilit Gate was sealed. No knowledge of it?"

Colton shook his head, looking at Liam who shrugged.

Yup, definitely sounds like Bristol. Or Nessa's folklore.

Tom chuckled. "They really aren't teaching you boys anything useful?"

"Whatever they know," Liam answered. "Which I guess is not much."

"It's quite convenient today happened to be the day of your liberation," Lily said.

Tom put out ceramic plates and metal forks before he served up portions of food, which the two boys took with wide eyes and drooling mouths.

"Ignoring poverty, the severe oppression on the Scintillia Initium would *also* cause quite the lack of education, I suppose," she admitted. "But not to that level."

Colton speared a piece of the bird-meat with his fork, wincing before switching to his left hand, and stuffing the food in his mouth. Flavor flooded his tongue from the taste of various spices on tender, white meat, making him mumble in satisfaction.

So, this is rich people's food!

"The Richmen treat us like dogs," Colton said while chewing.

"Are you guys' rebels against the guardians?" Liam asked, mouth half-full of cake.

"Nah, we're more of—" Tom paused, "heroes, to fight off what's known as the Heralds of the Damned. A real nasty group."

"Though, they have quite the influence over many of the city-states in Central Mesica," Lily added. "Especially over the guardians, as Malelentos as a city-state is failing."

Tom placed a folder on the counter, opening it to reveal various symbols, blueprints, and the like.

"And with that, we're sent here to extract you two outta here before the city blows itself apart or you two are killed. We're lucky we have no Heralds here. A demon is not easily fought."

"Demons? Those are real?" Liam asked.

Lily nodded. "Though they do exist. Fortune be ours that genuine demons are all behind the Twilit Gate, called Anti-Demons. But at times we encounter their imitations, called Proxy-Demons. The latter are experiments done long ago to create super soldiers, which have failed miserably."

"So, what does that have to do with us?" Colton asked.

Tom shrugged, taking off his glasses to reveal dark green eyes that hinted at his weary age.

Gotta be what? Thirty? Maybe forty? Colton thought.

"They sent an assassin after you two," Lily said. "Specifically, you, Colton."

"So, it's for the bounty?" Liam clarified, hesitantly scooping out a portion of a third dish, a type of macaroni salad.

"We don't believe so," Lily said. "The most professional murderers you can hire cost much more than your petty bounty."

"Mr. Daas wouldn't call it petty," Colton said.

Liam slapped his friend on the shoulder. "That's because you two don't get along. I hope he's okay."

Colton stared at Liam, earning an uncomfortable look from his friend, before turning to Lily.

"He doesn't know, does he?" Colton asked.

Lily shifted uncomfortably, and Liam looked between the two with confusion.

"What do you mean?" Liam asked.

"Liam, the thing is—" Lily began.

"It's nothing," Colton interjected, throwing the girl a glare, "just that Jace was imprisoned, too."

"Yeah, I saw him," Liam said.

"Well—" Lily began.

"Oh, forgot about that," Colton said, lightly kicking Lily in the shins, earning a glare.

He returned the glare, and her scars flared up slightly, turning from their pale to a light crimson.

"Lily," Tom began, "Maybe we should tell them about the Auratus experiments that—?"

"It's quite late," Lily stated with a forced smile.

Liam frowned. "What's going on?"

Colton looked between her and Tom, noticing Lily clutched her hands in fists. She gestured to an off-shooting hallway across the room from a flight of stairs. "Ivan?"

The soldier strode into the room, earning a wary glance from Colton.

So, he's the mutt of the group.

"Would you show them to their quarters? Lily asked.

Ivan nodded. "Follow. I show you sleep place."

He gestured for the two boys to fall in line, which they readily did. Colton looked over his shoulder at Lily, clutching the counter as Tom whispered something to Lily with a concerned look.

Liam looked at Colton with a question look, who only shrugged.

Down the hall, past a couple other doors, some partially ajar and showing bathrooms, a room with piles of clothes and large metal boxes, another with weights and machines, and a third holding arrays of metal cubes inlaid with glowing wide lights on a single desk, people busily mashing away on boards of buttons. Other doors were closed to any access or view. They stopped at the door at the very end, right next to a large window that allowed Colton to peer down at the city below.

Inside the room were two beds, each with a desk built into the end and padded chairs sitting adjacent. A large fan hung in the center, lazily spinning; yellowish light shone from a bulb in its middle. Between the two beds was another window, the outside fading twilight framed perfectly in its view.

"This room, your room. Pick bed, don't matter," Ivan declared, before leaving.

Colton entered after Liam, closing the door behind, and hurriedly taking the bed on the right, throwing himself onto the mattress. He laid his head into it, enjoying the soft feel, and light fragrance it had.

"Too slow," Colton teased.

Liam shrugged, taking the bed on the left. "Been a long time since I laid in a bed like this. Doesn't matter to me."

"When was the last time?" Colton asked.

"When I lived with my parents," Liam said, absentmindedly reaching for a rusty key that hung around his neck.

Why does he hang onto that? His family doesn't own the house anymore.

Colton frowned as Liam settled down, curling on the bed. A droning sound started on the ceiling above them as rain began to fall outside. Rumbling came from distant lighting and the gentle sounds of wind sung against the window.

I wonder how long this vacation'll last?

Colton resisted, but his eyelids proved too heavy a weight, and he felt himself slip into slumber. Just as he was enjoying it, along came the uncomfortable sensation of falling. Colton jerked heavily, snapping into a sitting position. He held up his hands, before frowning at seeing the lack of metal bars right above his head. He bit his tongue and rubbed his eyes, glancing around the room to find Liam missing again and the door ajar.

I couldn't have fallen asleep for that long, right?

Swinging his legs over the edge of the bed, Colton walked outside the bedroom, lingering as he looked at the black rain falling in the afternoon light.

116

Weird rain...How long did I sleep for?

Glimpsing down the hall, Colton saw it extended much longer than he remembered. He glanced at the window at the end of the hall, finding it gone, replaced by the endless hallway.

This is probably one of those tiny rooms that teleported us. Some kind of tech-magic.

Anxious, Colton jogged to the right, passing dozens of identical doors, then hundreds, prompting him to break into a sprint as the doors kept coming. He ran for as long as he could hold, racing until his body started groaning with a stitch in his side. He slowed to a stop, doubled over with hands on knees as he took greedy gulps of air.

Agitated, he peered as far down as he could for the end, which remained out of sight. Looking back, he saw the window only a couple feet behind him again, and the door he came out of was not much further. An eerie purple glow came from it, like a throbbing infected heart.

How? I just ran like a mile away from—this can't be a dream. I feel too awake. Did they spike my food with something? Did I hit my head too hard?

Colton glanced down the hallway again, and a sensation of vertigo overwhelmed him as the hall twisted like a ribbon. He crumpled to the ground, body as heavy as if all blood had been drained through his feet.

Pain blossomed on his neck and he clutched it, his hands going cold in a wet liquid. Pulling away, he gasped at the crimson staining his fingers. His head swam and his body felt disconnected.

Help me! I think I'm going to—

His mouth didn't move; the words stuck in his mind.

Somebody—

Silence.

Any—body—

Colton tried to crawl forward, trembling with each inch he took, fissures spreading from where his hands touched, extending forward down the hall. He paused, gasping for air, his entire body exhausted.

117

Caleb DM Smith

A shadowy substance slowly began emerging from the edge of the fissures, cracking the wood floors and crunching the marble walls as it boiled, becoming a tidal wave of venal darkness. It continued relentlessly toward Colton, only seeming to be slowed by the blazing light beaming through the window behind him in radiant shafts.

Colton dragged himself backward, using agonized hands and knees to prevent the shadowy substance from devouring him until he had pressed his back up against the windowed wall.

It felt like wires and metal were clawing at his limbs and throat as the shadow reached for him. His veins burned hot with adrenaline, and a harrowing writhing sensation bubbled beneath the surface, like a meal severely disagreed with him to the point he felt the urge to vomit. A triplet of intolerable twisted faces lurked in the shadow, leering at Colton with horns and scales but still humanoid before they morphed like liquid to charred buildings with shuffling corpses, slowly melting to dark spots in his vision. He blinked, rubbing his eyes as his vision warped in an array of dark colors and shadows.

He closed his eyes, taking a deep breath that froze in his lungs as the shadows warped, something appearing in the darkness *beneath his eyelids*.

He watched, terror seizing him, screaming as a spider-like monster lunged at him with an anger-filled hiss. Teeth clamped around his shoulder, *human teeth* that seemed to connect directly to his instincts, and he let out a scream, thrashing and kicking, waves of rage drowning him.

Colton felt a hefty slap on his cheek, knocking his head onto the soft bed. Blinking rapidly, he looked up at Lily towering over him, expression wide-eyed. Liam sat on his bed, an expression like he'd witnessed a murder. Ivan stood guard by the door, scowling at Colton.

"What in the love of the seven is it with you?" Lily asked indignantly.

Colton sat up, detached of feeling, the bed creaking underneath him. His veins still felt hot and his legs buzzed from numbness. He grabbed at his neck, and shoulder, relief flooding him when he couldn't find a bite.

Morning sunlight seeped directly through the window, illuminating the room, making Colton squint slightly.

Okay, that was all just a dream, right?

Colton swung his legs off the side of the bed and stood up before crashing back down. Lily tried to catch him, failing and uselessly clutching his right wrist as he fell to the bed and smashed his head against the wall. He winced and cradled his skull, jaw clenching in pain.

She froze for a few moments, her eyelids fluttering as she stared at Colton, her grip slowly tightening, buzzing in his head. The injury became aggravated, blossoming in pain, and Colton cried out, trying to pry her hands away from crushing his bones further.

Hey! Let go you—

Lily gasped, releasing and backing away from Colton, her expression jarred and the color drained from her complexion.

"What *are* you?" Lily mumbled.

Ivan stepped forward, throwing an accusing look at Colton, rifle at the ready, causing Colton to hunker down on his bed.

"Lily, what problem?" Ivan asked.

The girl looked between Colton and Ivan, swallowing hard and clutching at her chest. She took a few shuddering breaths before closing her eyes for a few moments.

"Go, arrange an appointment. *He* will surely wish to hear of this."

Ivan marched out of the room and Colton looked between the door and Lily as he slowly sat up.

"What appointment? Who's 'he'?" Colton asked.

Lily pressed her lips together, dismay evident in her harrowed voice.

"The leader of the Celestial Lumanine."

Chapter 15
Genesis Start

Protesting was his first thought, but with the dream festering in his brain, Colton sunk into brooding. His head throbbed slightly, and he felt very much awake. But his mind itched with small doubts.

He stood at the bottom of a flight of stairs next to the hallway leading to the bedroom. Just across the living room from him, in the kitchen still dirty from dinner, Lily and Ivan brooded by the counter.

Why're they doing this over a dream?

Colton was beginning to think his own restlessness would kill him before any mystery assassins could. The only indication of time passing was the rain outside, gently pattering against the windows.

Colton grew agitated, the blood pooling in his legs and causing them to grow numb. He impatiently rubbed his heel on the floor, his eyes willing the door at the top of the stairs to open.

Why is this taking so long? Come on!

Colton took a step forward, placing his foot on the bottom step, but earned a scolding throat-clearing from Ivan.

"Wait, he summon you."

Colton rolled his eyes, shifting back and folding his arms, biting his tongue as his sanity slowly decreased.

Is this guy asleep or something?

He threw a glance at the soldier, watching him focus on adjusting something on his rifle, with Lily watching Colton, picking at a loose thread. Yet her eyes were glazed over, causing her to *look* at Colton, but not *see* him. He waited, and her eyes continued to uselessly stare.

Let's just get this over with!

Colton rushed up the stairs, feet pounding on each step, causing Lily to call after him a second later. He reached the door and crashed into it, wriggling the knob and finding it locked, the door unyielding.

Lily and Ivan were at the bottom of the steps, rushing up to him. Colton jerked on the doorknob, twisting it with frustration until there was a click, swinging the door open and sending him crashing forward into the ground. He resisted the urge to cry out, his wrist wrapped in agony, and the instinct to clutch it only worsened the pain.

A strong smell of dust and a slight fragrance of something sweet hidden under the years suffocated him. He clambered to his feet, rushing into the new room and gave Ivan a glare before his eyes shifted to the other man holding open the door.

Woah, he looks a few hundred years old.

The old-man had long silver hair that entwined into his long matching beard, a proper pair for his pale and wrinkled skin. A set of opaque, quartz-like eyes gazed tiredly behind a pair of spectacles. His hands were laced behind his back, and he wore a navy blue robe around his hunched body. Down at the old man's feet, Colton glanced a pair of—

Bunny slippers? Really?

Clean and fluffy, donning button eyes that glimmered with polish, and a button-nose that featured tiny whiskers and a simple smile.

Colton looked up at the old man, who extended his aged left hand, looking more fragile than glass.

"Ah, thou art he whose name is called Colton Diaíresi Toa. Blessed be this hour, to behold thy countenance, and greeteth thy soul."

The old man's voice was kind and knowing, yet tired. It almost carried the same years worn into the wrinkles of the shrewd smile.

Colton glowered at the hand but wilted under the patriarch's warm gaze. Not frightening, but oddly commanding respect.

Colton reluctantly reciprocated the gesture with his good hand. The skin was like paper, and the wrinkles like creases, with it all feeling like an ancient document forgotten under a shelf. Colton found the old man's grip surprisingly solid, much stronger than his own.

"Why do you talk like that?" Colton asked.

The old man shrugged. "Worry not on the form of my words. Old age and outer beings bring a change."

"So, you're—"

121

Caleb DM Smith

The old man nodded, lacing his hands behind his back again, striding into the room as the door closed of its own accord, slamming shut on Ivan.

Did Lily do that? Or—

Looking around the room, Colton found it was akin to an undersized library, with bookshelves lining every wall, and a table in the center. Set between two bookshelves was a bed, with curtains wrapping around the edge, hanging from a raised frame.

"I am Oraculi Conditor, leader of the Celestial Lumanine."

A slight bow, a warm smile, and a twinkling in the ancient eyes, with the bunny slippers letting out a small squeak. Colton watched the man warily, who turned to browse a bookshelf, hands like spiders jumping between covers.

Seems like the classic cult-leader type.

"Tell me, what hast thou dreamed?" Oraculi asked.

Colton stared, reeling slightly, only for the man to give him an inviting smile.

"I barely know you," Colton said.

He groaned and rubbed the side of his head, headache pounding in his skull, causing Oraculi frowned and stepped forward.

"Lift up thy head," Oraculi said, stepping forward.

He reached a hand out to Colton, who stepped back. Oraculi froze for a moment, then turned his flat palm upwards, a gentle golden glow emitting from his palm. Colton considered the hand, weighing the risks in his mind.

At long last, he let out a sigh, relaxing his shoulders. Oraculi reached forward and gently pressed a couple fingers against Colton's forehead. Warmth spread over where Oraculi touched, the headache slowly ebbing away, and Colton felt his brain slowly ease up on its vertigo.

"Wow, that helps a lot!" Colton said

Oraculi smiled. "Take care from this time hence, and be wary, for I canst always heal thy wounds."

"Can you heal my wrist?"

"At this time, it should not be."

Colton frowned. "How'd you do that?"

122

"A gift given to me by a friend, one who's name is called Hazel. As such, I gave unto thee a portion of the gift."

"I don't understand what that means."

"In due time. Again, I ask thee, what dream hast thou dreamed?"

"Well, this last one, I woke up, the rain was black, and the hallway went on forever. I tried to walk down it, but whenever I looked back, I basically hadn't moved. Then this weird shadow with three faces attacked me. Afterward I saw weird dead things *moving,* and a massive half-spider-half-human creature come at me and bite me."

Oraculi frowned deeply. "And of thy other dreams which thou hast dreamt. What of they?"

Colton shifted, rubbing his right shoulder. "I had one about a random guy crawling away from a fire. He had some weird eye-like thing, and a stranger with a massive hammer got mad at him. The other one was when I had to leave my home because—"

Colton's throat tightened, shaking his head to clear the burning images of fire, his right shoulder stinging.

"This dream wast when thy friend perished, thy friend, Kai Winder. Burned to the flame, which hath swallowed up thy first home, Aquila Mons?"

"Yeah. That. Wait, how did—?"

"Out of the multitude of twenty-thousand, wast fifty counted to live." Oraculi said, turning to the books once again.

"Yeah, most still died of third degree burns though," Colton said. "Guess I was lucky."

"The flesh is weak of humanity. But thou hath not luck, but some *other* gift."

"Like what?"

"Many are called, but few are chosen."

"So, I'm a chosen one?"

"Nay for thou shalt die, but thou art blessed, and cursed."

Colton shifted, frowning and picking at the scabs on his hands. "They're just dreams, right?"

Pulling a book out of nowhere, Oraculi ambled towards Colton and set the heavy book on a table, making Colton cough from a plume of dust. A chair flew out and buckled his knees into a sitting position.

Caleb DM Smith

Did that just pop into existence?

While Colton questioned his sanity, Oraculi flipped through the book, displaying various creatures. A humanoid with odd colors and fragile wings on their back, large lizards with wings and breathing all kinds of elements, brutish humanoids with massive underbites and fangs, or horrid corpses with white eyes and purplish-black rotting skin.

"What's that?" Colton asked, just before Oraculi turned the next page.

"The Scourger, an abomination created by one having fallen to temptations of a wasted life."

Colton shivered at the shadow corpse, "Okay, never mind, keep going."

Oraculi nodded, continuing to flip through the pages, displaying more creatures of metal, magic, and the like, until he thumbed to a page with a humanoid lizard.

"Hast thou beheld such a creature?" he asked.

Colton shook his head as he examined the creature more.

Is that a Kekamoto? Or—a demon? Nessa always described them as more like spirits. What're these things?

Curling horns emitted from the creature's skull, like a ram, with bright orange scales covering its humanoid body and serpentine eyes peering out from a crocodilian head. The label above read: 'Homo-Saurus. The Proxy-Demon.'

Proxy-Demon? Like Lily was telling us about?

"That looks kinda like what I saw in the three faces," Colton amended. "They look like Kekamotos. Are they related?"

Oraculi shook his head, rubbing his chin in deep thought.

"These creatures are of utter darkness and wickedness, born in iniquity. The latter thou speakest of is born of waste and destruction of the First Great Calamity. Wherewith this creature, their very blood corrupts, and those of their race seek nothing but the vilest things."

"And what's that got to do with me?"

"Thou hast dreamed a dream, a calling to harken and take watch, for thy path may be treacherous. Doth thou knoweth what this meaneth?"

124

Colton looked briefly down at the demon and then at the old man.

"So, you think I'm *actually* going to turn into a—that?" Colton shivered, cold fear trickling down his spine.

"Thou wilst not become one such as this in the flesh, according to our knowledge. But like unto them in nature, for thou hast given into thy temptations."

So that's what this is all about?

Oraculi closed the book, rubbing the binding ponderously, the title of the book visible. *The Mystical, The Magical, and The Deadly by Fran Hewitt.*

"Hast thou witnessed thy right hand to disobey thy left? To act how it shouldst not?"

Colton stared. "What?"

Oraculi smiled. "Anything strange you've noticed about yourself?"

Colton rolled his shoulders, giving a long considering look at Oraculi before relenting to the old man's inviting smile.

"A lot, yeah. But I've got worse things to worry about."

"Expound."

"Getting me and Liam out of this stupid city, not dying to the guardians…"

The old man gestured inquisitively to Colton's bandaged hand. "May I?"

"Sure, I guess."

Colton held his hand out, and Oraculi reached forward and pinched Colton's wrist with his thumb and pointer finger. Colton yelped as pain washed over his muscles, not very intense, but permeating. The purple crystal residue emerged once again across his hand through the wrapped bandage.

What? How's he activating it?

Oraculi let it spread further, reaching past Colton's lower arm before the old man released him, stopping the growth and the pain.

"Thou hath a Caliber in awakening. Not yet ready to wield at battle, nor asleep to be surely safe."

"I don't have a Caliber. It's a disease.

125

Caleb DM Smith

"Yea, you were born with thy condition. A disease it may be, but a Caliber it remains."

Colton examined the strange residue, eyes transfixed on his arm as it tingled from the material. It was adaptable to the point he thought it had replaced his skin. Even when he twisted his hand to its limits, he felt no pain from injuries or the slightest hint of anything broken.

"What *is* this stuff?" Colton asked.

Oraculi motioned to the book again with an expression of grimness. "Demothest. The stones most precious of the earth, corrupted by Dark-Energy. The nature thereof the two is unsure."

"Demo—like the demons?"

"What believest thou hast?"

"I was always told I had some weird disease. Similar to epidermodysplasia, or something."

"Thy condition hath mystery. Yea, it is not a human condition. Not even among those who hold Calibers."

Colton couldn't help but be transfixed by the strangeness, twisting it back and forth as he marveled at it.

"Did it fix my hand?" He asked.

"Thy injury remains. Let it be and it shall heal in short time," Oraculi said, taking Colton's hand and retracting the crystal.

"How do I know this is real?"

Oraculi smiled, leaning close and holding out his hand, a few droplets of water emerging from the palm.

"Ask, and ye shall receive. Knock, and it shall be opened unto you."

The water slowly increased until it threatened to drip from the old man's palm.

"Verily verily, thou hath a Caliber, and thou shalt care for and grow it, awaken it by practice. Then thou shalt be free from the guardians through tribulation of moving darkness. From thence, thou needest discover *what* thou art, and overcome thy natural self."

Colton stared at the water as it slowly increased until it overflowed, flooding the ground in a dark pool. His reflection was clear, though not entirely recognizable, like someone darker had stolen his identity.

126

Colton frowned, his gut bubbling as the old man closed his hand, the pool vanishing as if being rewound through time, soaked up by the antique palm.

"What do you mean? What am I?" Colton asked.

Oraculi reached out and quickly grabbed Colton's wrist, this time being the left. The Demothest on his right pulsed like a heartbeat, throbbing darkly, while the veins on his left stood out in golden hue.

Woah, what's happening to me?

"Colton Diaíresi Toa. Harken, and watch therefore, for thou art strong. Thou art dangerous. Thou art an important child, who in no form, is ordinarily dull, nay not an unknown person."

Chapter 16
Respite Out of Spite

Boom!

Colton stared out the window, chin resting on his palm as the walls shook slightly from the rumbling thunder. The rain poured endlessly outside, abating any activity from people down in the streets below.

What would I look like as a demon?

Lightning flashed across the noon sky, snapping back and forth across the clouds before vanishing. The deafening boom came a few seconds later.

What Caliber am I supposed to have?

He sighed and slightly banged his head against the wall. He climbed off the padded bench and walked through the living room, walking past Liam sitting on a couch, book in hand. Ivan stood guard by the door that led out to the entrance hall, and Lily sat with Tom in the kitchen talking.

Colton threw himself on the couch next to Liam, sinking into the cushions and proceeded to stare at the crackling fire that burned in a hearth in front of him.

Liam looked up from his book, raising a brow at Colton. "Are you going to tell me what happened? Or make me guess?"

"I don't want to talk about it right now," Colton said.

"It'll help."

"It's fine."

"Not if it's bothering you this much," Liam said.

Colton stared at the fire, watching it pop before speaking. "He said I was gonna turn into a demon."

"Oh."

Liam winced, putting down the book, staring at the cover. Colton looked away from the fire.

"Whatcha reading?" he asked.

128

"It's something Lily gave me. It's a history book."

"About what?"

"Just the First Great Calamity," Liam replied.

"Sounds interesting."

"Speaking of interesting. . ."

Liam climbed to his feet, setting the book on the couch and taking off to the hallway. Colton followed him, passing by the staircase. Liam stopped at a door, throwing it open.

Colton stared at the orderly, minimalist room, with a couple shelves of wooden weapons against each marble wall, a wooden-board floor that shined with polish, and a soft glow emanating from lights that hung from a brass ceiling.

"What is this?" Colton asked.

"I think it's some place similar to what the guardians would probably use. Like where they get all their weapons."

Colton wandered over to one wall, examining the shelf that held an array of wooden swords, each varying in style, shape, and size.

He grabbed one, finding it lightweight, slim and elegant, like a thin rapier. He swung it, admiring the hiss sound it made. He swapped it for another, finding it heavier, bulky, and with a rougher grain, like a broadsword. Swinging it gave more of a whoosh as it hurled through the air.

"Wanna duel?" Colton asked, giving Liam a mischievous look.

Liam raised a brow before grabbing a large wooden greatsword, nearly dropping it to the ground before hefting it with two hands.

"I don't know," Liam teased, "I don't think we should use these without permission."

"Come on, what's the worst that can happen?"

"Someone gets hurt or something gets broken."

"Well yeah, but we'll be careful."

Colton swung the swords wildly, striking poses every so often as he imagined himself being a master weapon artist. He launched into a brazen combo with the two swords, swinging off balance only for the swords to clash into each other. The swords flew from his hands, vibrating somewhat and leaving his hands stinging. He winced, stepping back as the swords clattered to the ground, Liam shaking his head.

"What'd I say?" he asked.

"I—yeah," Colton said, grabbing the swords and putting them away.

He heard someone loudly clear their throat behind him, and he groaned internally.

Uh oh.

He turned around slowly, adopting a half-smiling-half-grimacing expression. Lily stood at the doorway, a curious look on her face as she held her hands laced behind her back.

"Well? Are you going to duel?" Lily asked. "There's no harm in practicing."

"I don't really know how to," Colton admitted.

"I do," Liam piped up, "but not well."

"What? Bristol taught you?"

"No, before—I got kicked out of Auratus," Liam said, hand straying to the key around his neck.

Lily frowned. "We might as well start. Surely Oraculi mentioned such in your meeting?"

"He didn't really tell me much," Colton said.

"Not a word about it?"

"Said I'd turn into a demon by nature."

"Already there," Liam remarked.

"Shut up, Liam."

Lily rolled her eyes. "Did he foretell you of anything else?"

"I mean, he said that whatever's wrong with me is strange even for you guys used to this stuff," Colton said.

"Really?"

"Yeah? No idea what it is still."

I don't know if I want to know.

Lily pounded a fist into her palm, smiling. "We must make haste in training to discover more of your situation."

"Can't we just ask the old man?"

"Old man not reveal secrets," Ivan said, stepping into the room. "He is mysterious, but smart man."

"As such, the best method to learn is through practice," Lily said.

Colton held up his right hand. "Remember this? When I punched a dude and broke my hand?"

"We would wait, but such is impossible when hunted by an assassin."

"Assassin? What assassin?"

"Remember that horrid figure in the fires of the Central Market?"

"Yeah, but that's just a guardian, right?" Colton asked. "Electric voice and all that?"

"Did you forget about Red Dusk?"

"But why'd they wanna send an assassin after me? All I've been told is that I'm weird."

Lily smirked, her eyes gaining a mischievous glimmer like shining spring pools. "That is what we wish to know."

Chapter 17

Inkling of Power

Crack!

Colton grunted, his arms smarting, his right hand in a supporting brace. He swung, his wooden staff whooshing through the air. He ducked, sliding across the gritty pavement, footsteps echoing loudly in the courtyard. He leaped, clearing a rusty barrel, landing and spinning, attacking with his wooden quarterstaff.

Crack!

"Don't swing so wildly!" Lily commanded from the sidelines. "Form a tactic and employ it. Control!"

Colton gritted his teeth, swinging again with more force, only to splinter his and Ivan's weapons. Ivan pushed back and swung downward, which Colton sidestepped and stabbed, landing a blow in Ivan's stomach against the padded vest, earning a grunt.

"Hah!" Colton exclaimed, "I actually—"

Ivan swung, cutting him off. The wind quickly left Colton's lungs, pain exploding in his gut as he fell down into a wooden barricade, toppling it to the weed-ridden pavement.

He curled up, nausea permeating him, threatening to make him vomit. He took a few shaky breaths, the scent of fresh rain serving a respite from the stench of the nearby dumpster.

"Not good enough," Lily muttered, turning to Liam. "Your turn."

Colton groaned, uncurling slightly as he watched Liam leap off the rusty barrel he had been using as a seat. He began sparring with Ivan, being light on his feet, and defensively blocking before quickly striking. He gained the upper hand and whacked Ivan on the side of the head, sending him staggering sideways.

"Good, Liam," Lily said, right before Ivan deftly knocked Liam's feet from underneath him.

Liam slammed into the ground, let out a grunt, tensing up before taking deep, greedy breaths, letting himself go limp on the pavement. Ivan rubbed the side of his head, a bruise matching the one Lily had earned from the guardian in the Auratus prison.

"We have a basis of your fighting capability," Lily looked at Colton, "or lack thereof."

"I have a hurt wrist," Colton protested.

"We came here to train you in a realistic dangerous scenario with obstacles. Your brace helps mitigate damage, but you need to learn to still be capable and fit despite injuries."

Colton gestured to the blue crystalline bow, and blue quiver wrapped around her waist. "Easy for you to say when you have that and haven't worked your butt off the past three hours."

He kicked a rock at her, which she stopped with her white combat boots, kicking it to the wall of the small, high-rise hidden junkyard and landing it in a rusty barrel.

"You're hardly worked up," Lily said. "You remember the promise I made you in the prison?"

"Yeah?"

"You want to make sure Liam's safe, then you need to be capable of it too. Use whatever righteous means necessary if you have to. Ivan?"

Ivan grunted, before turning to Colton and chucking his staff at the boy. Colton ducked, deflecting, his staff cracking more. Ivan ripped Colton's staff away and attacked with it, causing Colton to fall back, arms raised.

"Fight," Ivan commanded, "or I break bones."

"How the nosk is this supposed to help?" Colton exclaimed, scampering back.

"As it stands," Lily stated, "you need to be taught how to survive against someone trying to kill you. You've been told you have an interesting condition. Use it."

Colton threw her a dirty look, earning a heavy blow from the staff slamming into his jaw. His head snapped back and he cried out, losing footing and falling to the ground. Ivan placed a heavy boot on Colton and held the staff behind himself, winding up his muscles.

"Wait!" Liam cried, rushing forward, placing himself between the two, "don't you think this is a little far?"

Ivan swung with all his strength, the staff hissing through the air till it collided with Liam's hands. He grunted, keeping his footing as he withstood the blow, body shaking as he pushed against Ivan pressing down on him.

Colton held his jaw, watching through partly blurred vision, head swimming. Colton shook his head, his gut beginning to bubble again.

"Enemy no have mercy," Ivan said, shoving Liam aside, bringing the staff back.

"I don't know how to even fight or activate my disease," Colton protested.

Ivan grabbed him by the collar and hoisted him up until his feet dangled just above the ground. Ivan brought the staff back again, scowling.

"Do you submit?" Lily called. "Or do you let your darkness overtake you?"

Colton squeezed his eyes shut, the bubbling fire shot through his veins, gut churning.

Bury it! bury it! Bury—

His eyes were open, and he could see, but his brain couldn't register anything. The thrashing erupted, Colton tried to push it down, until he felt his consciousness nearly slip away, *something else* taking control. He felt his own veins tug inside his flesh, as if they had a will of their own.

Colton Toa, let him taste our hunger!

The staff came hurtling toward him and he shot out his hand, Demothest covering his skin in an instant. The staff cracked into his palm, splintering. He clenched it into a fist, twisting his wrist, turning the staff to shreds with ease.

"Enough!" Colton's voice roared, the words forcing themselves out of his throat like stomach acid.

Ivan grinned before dropping Colton and punching him in the stomach. The boy flew into Liam, crashing onto the ground on top of each other. Colton groaned, his head dizzy, the adrenaline pumping out of his veins, leaving him shaky and weak.

No! We were close. So close to satisfying our hunger!

Colton shook his head, gasping for air as he rolled to hands and knees, the dark, foreign thoughts echoing for a few moments before they left. The thrashing sensation simmered down to a calm beneath the surface. His eyes slowly regained their vision, and his body felt less on fire.

"That was much better," Lily said.

Colton blinked rapidly, looking between her, Ivan, and himself.

"Did I just—?" he muttered.

Colton groaned, climbing off Liam, his eyes settling on his Demothest covered hands, the crystal pulsing like a heart, glowing veins extending through it. The brace was torn, some trapped in the crystal with shreds on the ground. His gaze settled on the remains of Ivan's staff, half the size, with the remaining parts barely held together at the massive cracks.

Holy woah. Did I do that?

"Bad skill, good power," Ivan said.

"Yes, it does seem quite promising," Lily muttered.

"How long have you been able to do that?" Liam asked.

"Do what?" Colton replied.

"All that?"

"I dunno. Ivan was grabbing me and then—I like—blanked for a couple seconds."

Lily moved forward, grabbing Colton's wrist. He tried to jerk away, yet Lily held on tight.

What are you doing—? Colton thought.

Lily glared at him, *Remain still, you idiot!*

Let go of me! What's wrong with—

Lily smacked Colton on the shoulder, stinging the bullet scar. She met Colton's eyes and her gaze softened slightly.

I apologize we're so rigid with you. But you must understand that the gravity of our situation, especially yours, provides no leniency.

Yet you called me an idiot.

I—sorry. That was a mistake. I merely do not wish for anyone to come to more harm.

135

Caleb DM Smith

Yeah just—whatever. It's fine. Get it over with.

Lily frowned, sympathy bubbling in her irises, but she shook her head. She examined Colton's hand, twisting and turning his wrist, flexing the skin-like crystal.

"Oraculi discussed with you about Demothest, correct?" Lily questioned.

Colton nodded, finding his fingers a little more stiff than usual.

Did I break my wrist more?

"Then are you aware it's the crystal of the demons?" Lily checked. "And the mere fact you can produce it—well, only demons can do that!"

"But Oraculi said I wouldn't turn into an *actual* demon," Colton protested. "Claimed I might become *like* one. Whatever that means."

Lily shook her head and held up Colton's hand for display.

"Explain this."

"I can't! It just happens whenever I get a stomachache or I'm really emotional."

What are you? Lily narrowed *her eyes.*

Colton frowned. *What do you mean?*

You're very odd. You don't seem—

Colton pulled his grip from the girl's, trying to burn her with his glare.

"Stay out of my head!" Colton rubbed his wrist, hoping the crystal would vanish to no avail.

"An ability as unique as that—" Lily said.

"Thanks, I'mma demon," Colton retorted. "I get it! Look, I never stole 'cuz I wanted to hurt anyone. I never caused damage just to cause damage. But it clearly doesn't matter if I was just trying to survive one more day."

"That's not what—" Lily frowned, lowering her eyes. "You're not the only one who feels terrible toward yourself in that unnatural way at times."

Lily used a hand to fix her hair, subtly tracing the scars across her face, giving Colton a bittersweet-smile, her eyes like icy-pools that were very slow to melt.

136

Huh. I wonder how she really got her scars?

Colton opened his mouth to speak, but froze when a metal *clang* rang out, drawing everyone's attention upwards. His shoulders started itching, and the shadows cast on deeper shadows from empty balconies played tricks on his eyes, making him flinch every time he thought he saw a slight heat shimmer like mirrors moving amongst the empty steel barrels.

They waited, moments of silence ringing in their ears. Colton glanced all around, twitching at the smallest disturbance of the quiet.

"Who did you say sent the assassin?" Colton asked, "some news people or something?"

"Heralds of the Damned," Lily corrected. "The harbingers of chaos and Hell itself, arising from the First Great Calamity. They hired an assassin from a separate group, the Red Dusk."

"That's when the earth started, right?" Liam asked.

"*Restarted*," Lily said. "To put it simply, a world war that destroyed the earth, causing its current, almost magical state, fueled by inhumane experimentation of Calibers. How exactly it was all performed precisely is unknown. Yet all we know are that victims had Calibers horrendously, endlessly given to them, which was the spark to greater destruction."

She stopped, glancing at the balconies with a sullen gaze, grip tightening on her bow. "Imagine if eyes were added to your back, arms to your teeth, or tongues to your hair. Such is the birth of Proxy-Demons."

Colton shuddered, his skin crawling at the image. He imagined someone strapped down, machines jabbing into them, cutting and sewing body parts as they writhed. Helplessly becoming living weapons.

I hope I never experience that or meet anyone like that.

He scratched at his itching shoulders, the same sensation coming over him he had at Angel's Landing. Scouring the nearby balconies, or any of the heaps of trash for something off or ominous.

Looks like we're alone.

Yet his heart felt squeezed, as if wires were slowly wrapping around him and crushing his bones.

Caleb DM Smith

"History aside, we ought to return home," Lily pointed out, equipping her bow and an arrow with its tip covered by a red, bulbous end. "I'd rather not wait until a hostile reveals itself."

Colton pointed to the arrow. "What's that for? More torture?"

"Not at all! Rather, the Flare-Arrows, or flarrows are for—"

Her words were cut short as a horrendous high screech tore through the air. Colton cried out, hands clamping to his ears as his brain felt like it was tearing itself apart. His muscles went weak, dropping him to the ground with numbed senses.

The harder he pressed, the less effective his hands were.

A hand grabbed his wrist. *Stop it!*

It's not me!

"It's not me!" Colton shouted, his voice never leaving his throat.

The grip tightened, and the shriek redoubled. Something fell next to him, sending vibrations through the ground. A glance, and it was Liam, convulsing and eyes rolling into the back of his head.

He looked like he was dying.

Chapter 18
Blitzkrieg

No! Stop! Colton thought.

He started crawling toward his friend, and the shrieking stopped, being replaced by an alarm blaring in the distance, soon joined by another, then another, until the whole air was reverberating with wailing sirens.

Colton grabbed Liam's arm, and Liam slowly stopped convulsing, his breaths coming labored and eyes slightly red. He groaned and shifted, laying his woozy gaze on Colton.

"W-what did you do?" Liam asked.

Colton shook his head. "I didn't do anything!"

"Then who did that?"

The two of them looked to Ivan and Lily, the girl almost unaffected, and the soldier barely able to stand. Lily clutched a hand to the side of her head, groaning as she swayed slightly. Colton unsteadily rose to his feet, a migraine pounding the inside of his skull.

Shouts erupted behind them just as three brazen men dressed in rags, dirt, and burn marks rushed into the courtyard, brandishing pickaxes and sledgehammers.

Colton immediately moved to guard Liam, Ivan rushed by, half-staff gripped in hand. The first man raised a pickaxe, which Ivan sidestepped, knocking the man out with a slam of his staff. Ivan spun dodging a swing of a sledgehammer, dropping the second man to the ground, then striking the third with a punch to the throat. He finished them off with a solid whack to the head.

"How did they get up here from the Scintillia Initium District?" Colton asked, noting their tools.

"Not all poor people are from there. Some are servants bought from the prison," Lily replied.

She crouched next to the three men, picking up the wrist of one and examining it, pulling the sleeve back.

"No Ruling-Hand tattoo," she said. "They're indeed from the Scintillia Initium District."

"What are they doing up here?" Liam asked.

"It's unclear, but I possess a theory," Lily muttered.

She rose and strode toward the courtyard exit, the others following. The further they progressed down the narrow alleyway, the higher the temperature rose. The scent of burnt rubber wafted to them, along with dim, dancing orange lights on the walls.

The guardians're still looking for me?

With Lily in front, she emerged from the alleyway first, immediately freezing on the street. Colton hung back as Ivan pressed forward, grumbling. All Colton could see was the building across the street, an inconspicuous little store, windows smashed.

Lily ducked, and a large chunk of flaming debris flew over her head. The ground shook as the air reverberated from an explosion. Ivan charged forward, Liam following. Colton hung back, but curiosity won and he hurried forward.

Out on the street, carnage raged. Hundreds of rioters from the Scintillia Initium District and prisoners surged forward, trampling citizens of the Auratus District beneath their feet. Fires hissed, explosions roared, gunshots filled the air, and screams tore through it all.

"You've got to be—" Colton swore.

Guardians fled away, a large horde of rioters pursuing them, brandishing more crude weapons.

"What just happened?" Colton yelled.

"A riot—err no, an urban war They've already coordinated an attack," Lily shouted.

"Urban what?"

"Like a civil war."

"That fast?" Colton asked.

"A suppressed angry people are capable of much," Lily said, ducking as gunshots rang out. "We must return to Wallich Tower."

"No," Ivan said, "Too dangerous for us all to go. Take Colton, warn Tom. I take Liam to evacuate place, Angel's Landing."

Lily wrung her hands, frowning. "But we're stronger if we—"

"No! Better this way," Ivan said. "Our goal to escape Malelentos."

140

"I'm not capable of such—"

"You be fine. Go, now!"

Ivan didn't wait for Lily to respond before taking off running down the street. Liam followed for a few steps, slowed, stopped, and turned, giving Colton a look.

"I'm not the one who's always running," Liam said, "so don't do anything dumb."

Colton nodded, forcing a smile. "Who said I'll be walking?"

Liam chuckled, shaking his head as he turned and followed Ivan. Colton felt his heart sink, the fear spreading through his body as the chaos raged around them.

he looked at Lily, her eyes like shimmering pools as she helplessly wrung her hands, face melting into a pouting frown, staring after Ivan.

Is she going to cry? Colton thought.

"Hey, I think we should leave," he suggested.

Lily looked at him, before nodding, sniffing as she wiped her nose on her sleeve, drying her eyes and pulling her bow off her torso. She cast looks at the chaos around her, shivering.

"Yes, err, we ought to," she agreed, voice shaky.

She pulled an arrow from the quiver and nocked it to the bow, nudging Colton down the street as she took off running. Some people giving chase, only to swerve toward a closer target.

"Why're we going back to the tower?" Colton asked.

"Tom and Oraculi are still there," Lily shouted.

A massive explosion rang out in the building above them, and the two of them dropped to the ground, crouching behind a series of large bushes. More shouts, rioters storming past, gunfire. A platoon of helmetless guardians ran out onto the road, unleashing volleys of bullets on the rioters.

Colton watched, orange lights flickering in his eyes as the guardians were ran down, sloppily handling their weapons, or wearing terrified expressions.

The guardians aren't sloppy. Why're—wait, those're normal people! What happened to—?

Lily suddenly turned to him, bow pulled tight, arrow pointing right at his chest, a hard expression dominating her face.

Caleb DM Smith

"Hey, wait!" Colton cried.

He ducked a second before the string *twanged* and the arrow skimmed past his head. A heavy *thunk,* followed by a Kekamoto collapsing next to him, an arrow embedded deep in the chest. The body twitched slightly as the eyes rolled into the back of the head.

"Come on!" Lily shouted, grabbing Colton's wrist and leaping to her feet, dashing away as a trio of rioters rushed their way.

You almost shot me!

Lily's grip tightened momentarily. *I waited till you thought to crouch down.*

But how did you do that? You weren't touching me.

"I'm not sure. Perhaps something to do with—

Nosk!

Colton pulled against her grip, slowing her just in time as a large table plummeted into the ground, shattering into large chunks, accompanied by a rain of glass.

Nice job paying attention! Colton thought.

Sorry!

Lily tugged him forward till he ran beside her as they rounded a corner. They dashed down the street only to be met with a wall of citizens and rioters fighting. Colton threw himself back around the corner as projectiles flew their way. Rioters ran past missing the two of them.

Okay, so this is all happening because I freed everyone from the prison?

Yes and no. Remember in the prison I stated Malelentos failing as a city state? Everyone was biding their time until the right time. Your blowing up of the gallows and Central Market was a signal to others to start rioting.

So, this is my fault?

It's more complicated than that.

I freed the prisoners.

You aided, yes. But I wouldn't say you caused it.

Colton groaned and dashed forward, tugging Lily as he shoved a rioter out of the way, only for the rioter to grab his wrist and yank him back, pulling him to the ground. Colton rolled, wrenching himself

142

away just as the rioter swung. He ducked, meeting the eyes of his attacker.

It's Jace!

"Come back here," bellowed Jace, smacking Colton in the stomach.

Colton doubled-over, and Jace shoved him up against a wall. Lily leaped forward, smacking her bow uselessly against Jace's thick arm.

Jace sneered at her and knocked her to the ground. Colton thrashed, Jace hit him in the stomach again.

"Where Fisk at?" Jace shouted.

"Why would I tell you?"

"I'mma tear yo limbs off!"

Colton kicked Jace in the knee. Jace cried out, dropping Colton, clutching the new bruise. Colton smacked him in the head.

"Come on, Lily, get up!" Colton called.

Lily slowly climbed to her feet, reaching for her bow. Jace bellowed and charged Colton, throwing a wide punch. Colton ducked and countered, the two swinging at each other until Colton's legs were knocked out from under him.

"You're dead!" Jace screamed, eyes wild.

He pulled Colton closer, scraping his back on the concrete, cutting him on a piece of wreckage pipe. Colton grunted and kicked again, uselessly smacking Jace's flabby body. The boy's veins bulged, full of a dark liquid. Lily leaped forward, slamming her bow into Jace's head. He grunted, throwing Colton aside before turning to Lily.

Jace snarled, black bile spewing from his lips as he swung. Lily body-slammed him, and he didn't move an inch. She took a step back, scowled, and slammed again. He chuckled, grabbed her by the hair, and yanked her away. She cried out, grasped at his meaty hands, and he began shaking her, laughing with throaty sounds.

Colton coughed, stumbling to his feet unsteadily. He watched Jace a moment, his stomach curdling as Lily was jerked around like a doll.

Leave her alone, you kretch.

Caleb DM Smith

Colton grabbed the pipe, the rust biting into his skin. He rushed forward, hefting the pipe and swinging. Jace grabbed the pipe, countering and ramming Colton to his back.

"You weak," Jace said, "tell me where Fisk at, or I break your face."

"He's somewhere else," Lily said, eyes tearing up and scars turning red.

Jace yanked at her hair and she wailed, blood oozing from her head. Colton stared eyes wide, Jace sneered, pointing a fat finger at Colton, who began backing up.

"I'mma rip her hair out 'cuz of you," Jace said, advancing toward Colton.

Lily's crying. What can I do?

Colton scooted back, crossing most of the street. A few motorcycles rushed his way, and Colton curled up. They raced past, engines roaring and missing Colton. A truck manned by guardians raced their way from way down the road.

"Tell me now!" Jace said.

I can't—it's Jace. What am I supposed to do?

His muscles refused to work and heart raced.

"I count to three," Jace bellowed.

Colton looked between the bully and Lily, her expression wild and scared. Jace yanked on her hair again, and she began sobbing.

"One," Jace said.

"Colton, please help," Lily said, earning a yank, making her scream. "Please! Get him off! Use your—"

Jace smacked her again, and Colton flinched, climbed to his feet, causing Jace to threaten another strike.

How am I supposed to help? He's bigger, stronger, and indestructible. He's only more stupid and not fast. I could run away, leave her.

"Two," Jace said.

His feet felt glued to the ground, and any course of action seemed impossible.

I can't beat him. I can't run away. There's nothing I can do.

144

Gunfire rang out from the truck manned by guardians. Bullets whizzed past, a couple scratching Colton and plenty erupting in the ground.

They missed me—I can pretend I got hit.

Colton jerked, making his body go limp to the ground. The guardians cheered, the vehicle slowing down to take on other riots, and more gunfire rang out. Jace released Lily and charged away, hands covering his head as he beelined for cover.

Colton reached out, grabbing Jace's ankle and pulled, doing little but getting kicked in the head. He scrambled to his feet, and Jace towered over him.

No way he got taller!

Jace bellowed, grabbing at his own clothes and ripping his shirt off, causing a dozen rods of rebar to shoot out like tendrils, erratic and crooked, hissing in irregular directions from his body.

Colton curled up, the metal missing him as it struck randomly, cracking the ground or piercing nearby guardians. Jace roared again, and the rebar retracted back into his body, leaving small wounds that oozed darkened blood. His eyes were more sunken, his veins stood out, ready to burst.

"What did they do to you?" Colton asked, voice shaky and quiet.

Jace took a step forward, groaning as a guardian rushed his way, and Jace swung at him. The guardian dodged, striking Jace in the back. He groaned and curled up, before stretching himself wide. Rebar exploded in a lethal array.

This time it travelled much further, grazing Colton, shattering the windows of a building, raking the ground, and skewering the guardian. Concrete lifted up from the rebar, stray bullets ricocheting off the metal.

A cry of pain, and the metal retracted, wounds worse than ever as the heavy boy collapsed to the ground, barely conscious. Colton inched forward, and Jace's gaze snapped on him, burning with blood-shot eyes.

Jace stumbled to his feet, hunched over, sweat covering his skin. Colton backed away, another vehicle approaching them. He held his hands out.

Jace started curling up. "I've had it wit' you!"

Colton tripped over a pile of debris, falling and bruising, watching Jace start shaking, eyes bulging from his skull as something bubbled under his skin.

"I'm gonna skewer you! After what you did to Fisk and me," Jace screamed, "I'm gonna make sure you—"

The truck of guardians slammed into Jace. A sickening *crunch* and the screech of metal from its bumper. It roared past Colton, missing him by inches. The vehicle sped onward, barely slowed as shouts of shock and jeering erupted from the guardians. Metal bars erupted from the front of the truck in a massive storm, destroying everything nearby. They stopped, gunfire rang out, and the bars twitched, only to retract, causing the vehicle to burst aflame.

Oh nosk! Jace's—

Colton squeezed his eyes shut, keeping down the bile that crept up his throat. He shook his head, taking a deep breath that only worsened the tight pain in his chest. He tried again, and again, slowly calming down his breath.

Shaking his head and climbing shakily to his feet, he stumbled across the street, coming to stop by Lily, who was gingerly touching her crimson stained hairline.

"Are you okay?" Colton asked.

Lily nodded. "Oh yes, only minor damage was dealt. It'll heal quite quickly."

Colton held out a hand and Lily took it, climbing to her feet. She looked at him, her eyes widening.

"Colton, he's—" she began.

He shook his head. "Don't. I don't wanna think about it."

Lily nodded and they took off down the street, avoiding more rioters and guardians. They rounded a corner and came into view of Wallich Tower. They rushed toward the doors, broken and shattered. Glass crunched beneath their feet and debris fell from the ceiling. People screamed and leaped toward them. Colton landed a solid punch on a rioter's face, and Lily dropped another rioter with a blunt-strike from her bow.

They dashed to the closed tiny rooms, and Colton punched his fist into the buttons, smashing the tiny light in the process.

"Maybe we should've gone with Ivan," Colton said.

Lily grimaced. "We can't leave them behind."

Colton scowled, rapidly pressing the broken button again as the muted sounds of chaos raged in waves outside the building. He stepped back, looking for danger.

Come on! Why does this magic room take so long to work?

It's an elevator, Lily replied mentally. *The metal boxes work via—*

Not right now.

Colton moved to press the button again, just as the doors slowly opened, creaking and screeching their thick metal.

Colton rushed in, and Lily hesitated.

"I don't believe it's fully—" she began.

"Come on!" Colton said, yanking her in.

She hurriedly tapped in the numbers on the keypad, which only produced a long beep. She typed it again for another long beep. She pressed it a third time and it gave no answer.

A group of rioters rushed into the lobby, led by a large Kekamoto, brandishing sharp claws.

"Get those nosking Richmen!" the Kekamoto screamed.

Lily pressed the buttons again, only getting a fourth beep, and with the sign in the corner of the room displaying 'error.' The elevator shook and the lights flickered.

"It's not functioning!" Lily cried.

"They're almost here!" Colton shouted.

Lily stepped into view of the rioters, held out her hands, and slammed them together. Debris flew together, slamming into the rioters and crushing them. Lily teetered against the wall, looking utterly drained.

"Filthy rats!" screamed the Kekamoto, slashing away the debris and leaping forward.

Colton backed up to the wall of the tiny room, his heart racing faster as the rioter's outstretched hand reached for his throat. Lily shouted and smacked it away with her bow, the doors slowly closing on the lizard-humanoid. Metal squeaked and bones creaked as the Kekamoto thrashed despite the crushing force.

Caleb DM Smith

"Gotcha!" the Kekamoto screamed, grabbing at Lily, catching hold of her bow, nearly tearing it from her hands.

"Let go of it," Lily screamed, pushing against the rioter to no avail.

The Kekamoto slowly forced open the door, and surviving rioters behind pried for entry. Colton stared, body frozen solid as he helplessly watched.

"Help!" Lily cried.

Her scars flared up, expression wild and terrified as the elevator began groaning and shaking.

Colton gasped, blinking rapidly, his body starting up. Pushing down the fear, he threw himself forward, driving his leg into the Kekamoto. He let out a shout, the Kekamoto snarled. It released Lily, wriggling out of the doors.

Lily held her hands out as if grabbing two objects before forcing them together. Subsequently, the doors screeched shut as if grabbed by a giant, warping and breaking in the process. The tiny room lurched upward, jerkily moving slower than before. The sounds of chaos gradually faded away, giving way to quiet that drowned out all other sounds except for the faint scraping of metal against metal.

Colton fell back against the wall, his mind working once again. His body felt ready to break, legs aching. His limbs felt jittery and he slid to the ground as he took quick, shaky breaths.

"Thank you," Lily said, collapsing beside him.

Her eyes were shimmery, and her appearance was messy and blood-stained.

Colton nodded, the silence eerie to him. Every so often the room would lightly shake from a dull boom.

"What just happened?" Colton asked, his eyes trained on the damaged door.

Lily hugged her knees to her chest. "Kekamotos are violent creatures, especially here. The revolution is a great opportunity to gratify their murderous desires against those who oppress them."

"I meant with the gjinxes and the guardians and everything."

"A civil war. Smoldering hatred turned into a flame."

"There's not any Kekamotos in the Auratus District, are there?"

148

"No. They're even more hated here. They'd be killed on sight."

"Where did they come from?"

"With the rest of the rioters."

They sat in the silence for a while, Colton's heart pounding as he stared up at the ceiling.

How'd it end up like this? Rioters everywhere and with those crazed lizards killing everyone. Holy kretch, I hate Kekamotos. Why does something like that exist?

"They're one of the many creatures that have been living on earth ever since the First Great Calamity," Lily said, her head resting against the metal wall. "Perhaps once human, but changed from the disastrous events, surplus of energies and radiation from who knows what. At least we suppose."

"So, where'd we come from then?"

"All humans originate from bloodlines coming from shelters buried deep in the earth. And each was based on nationality to protect their languages and way of life. Thus, diversified towns and cities were created."

"So, did the—"

Colton never finished his question. A boom exploded in their ears, causing the elevator to shake horribly, leading to the lights flickering, and the tiny room slowly coming to a stop.

Silence.

It's gonna keep going up, right?

The lights flickered again, then died.

Darkness.

We're still alive. For now.

They sat there in the darkness. Colton began to berate himself for not counting the seconds as he soon forgot whether the darkness lasted for a few minutes, or hours. His adrenaline became replaced with restlessness, and he laid his head against the wall.

The room shook heavily, causing Lily to whimper and curling up and hug her legs. A single emergency light flickered to life in ominous red glows, humming slightly.

"How's that supposed to help?" Colton protested.

"Would you rather sit in the dark?" Lily asked, voice wavering.

"It's very helpful," Colton amended.

Caleb DM Smith

He sat patiently, tapping his knee as he strained his ears to hear any sign of the chaos or a rescue. Small sounds here and there, barely audible. The red light never dimmed, barely illuminating the room. Lily sat next to him, quiet as she shook slightly hugging her knees.

"I wanted to ask about this Caliber magic—" Colton began.

Lily held up a hand, taking a deep shuddering breath, slowly letting it out, then another. She took another, repeatedly taking purposeful breaths, her shakiness slowing. She sniffed and stopped hugging her knees.

"Not magic," she said at long last, "magic is simply an occurrence without a scientific understanding. Calibers are scientific developments with sentient beings and their biology. Everything unordinary you see is a product of unseen science applied in some way. Whether It's Calibers, demons, Kekamotos, or anything else."

"Scientific basis, yeah? What's that mean?"

"Think of how you feel tired when in a bad mood or full of energy when excited. All based on the Bio-Energy I mentioned a bit ago. Think of when you've been sitting for too long, too much energy. You burn it off by getting hyper, restless, and so on. As humans lived longer due to increased health, medicine, and surgeries, they gained more energy than they knew what to do with, and Calibers formed as a result to burn off the energy. Of course, if you lose it all, you die."

"Like you mean when you were using your Caliber in the prison, and you tore those guardians to shreds? That can kill you?"

"Depending on your Caliber, one usage may be lethal. Other times, it's quite impossible, even if you tried to end your life via Caliber use. But, yes, theoretically."

"Why use Calibers? Safer not to, right?" Colton asked.

"Not everyone has a Caliber as simple as that," Lily answered. "And in some cases, if an individual is distressed to a sufficient extent, their Caliber could activate on its own. Such as—" she paused, "with me in the Auratus prison. Or perhaps with you and your condition?"

The elevator room shook, rumbling slightly as it jerked slightly downward. Lily grasped at the string of her bow, starting to twang it rapidly. Colton felt his hairs stand on end for a few moments, waiting for everything to start falling apart.

150

The moment never came, and he found himself settling into boredom again. Lily stopped twanging her bow, making the quietness grow louder. His mind started going stir crazy, and he rested his head against the metal wall.

He cast a sideways glance to Lily, who sat with eyes scrunched shut, hands in her lap, and controlling her breathing. Her scars were slowly pulsating as if they were cords holding something captive that was trying to break free.

I wonder where she got them, Colton thought.

Lily sniffe*d. A childhood lesson.*

How did you—?

The metal floor and wall.

Oh, right. Your telepathy.

You must have a lot on your mind to forget that, Lily teased.

Gimme a break, I knew about it for one day. And I— Colton began.

Lily smiled, shaking her head. *Don't fret about it. It's an easy remembrance for me due to living with it most of my life and being harmed consistently by it.*

Colton frowned. *Did using your Caliber make your scars?*

Lily reached up a hand and gently touched the raised bumps, her eyes opening, dull gray puddles.

Yes, as much as my scars have caused my Calibers. The two are inextricably linked. A painful loop. As would be with anyone else who was given a Caliber through unnatural means.

You got a Caliber artificially? Like those Proxy-Demons?

Lily nodded. *Yes, my father, in his obsession to perfect humanity. Too prideful to see his erroneous ways, until they consumed all that he was, in every aspect of the meaning. Unlike Proxy-Demons, I've retained my humanity.*

Colton thought back to the images he had seen in the prison, of the machines and the scientist. He shuddered, his insides crawling at the possibilities.

Yes, not very pleasant, Lily conceded.

You said your Caliber had mind manipulation?

151

Caleb DM Smith

Yes, if I overpower your will, or you submit, your brain becomes malleable like clay. Memories, thoughts, ideas, identity. All of it eager to be changed.

Colton shook his head. *No thanks. I don't want to be someone's puppet.*

There exist other ways to manipulate someone besides simple telepathy, you know, Lily replied. *Best to be careful.*

Lily returned to her breathing exercises, closing her eyes. Colton frowned and began hugging his knees, resting his chin on them.

Man, I wish this—

The elevator jerked, the light flickering.

Oh no! They both thought.

A dull boom sounded out, trembling the tiny room. Metal screeching, followed by debris pattering against the elevator top.

I think we're fine. Colton thought.

The room shook again, a long metal groaning like the building was collapsing, causing the light to flicker and die.

Darkness surrounded them, trapping them in the tiny room, an untold height above the ground.

Please tell me we're gonna be fine.

Chapter 19

Elevator to Hell

"Let's try it one more time," Lily said, stepping onto Colton's hands.

He hoisted her up, grunting as his arms complained under the weight. He clenched his jaw, forcing himself to endure the strain as she balanced on one foot, her other foot against the wall, and glowing flarrow hovering beside her.

So heavy! Colton thought.

Lily knocked Colton in the shoulder with her heel. *I am not at all so cumbersome.*

Yeah? Doesn't feel like it.

I'm precisely—uhm, lightweight.

Lily shook her head, staring at the open panel, fingers dexterously working at the wires in the ceiling. Electricity suddenly arced between two wires, the white lights of the elevator flickered, only for one to burst, showering Colton with glass.

"Try *not* to kill me!" Colton called.

"My deepest apologies," Lily muttered, flarrow bouncing dangerously.

She let out a yelp as the wires zapped her, dropping the flarrow, and it flickered from the impact against the floor. She fiddled around a bit more before there was a *zap,* followed by the broken lights sparking heavily, filling the room with acrid vapors.

"Oh, goodness, no!" Lily exclaimed, breaking the circuit, leading to ending the salvo of tiny embers.

Colton nearly buckled as Lily leaped down from his hands, landing gracefully on the floor, giving her grime-covered hands a disgusted look.

"It's quite pointless," she said.

"What caused—" Colton paused, unsure of the wording to use as he grimaced, "what just happened?"

Caleb DM Smith

The wires began sparking again, and Lily flicked a hand, sending the ceiling pane up to the ceiling with a *click*. The sparks could still be heard skittering over the metal, a dim orange glow growing in the center.

"Perhaps a surplus of electricity?" Lily groused. "Or merely as simple as damage to the infrastructure. Regardless, what we need—"

The panel popped off, the metal molding to a lump upon crashing to the floor. Sparks showered down on the pair, forcing them to cover their heads.

"Oh, for the sake of the Higher Ones!" Lily exclaimed.

She clenched her hand into a fist and twisted, causing the wires to flatten themselves into the steel ceiling, whirlpooling with a horrendous screech of metal.

It was ill-lit and quiet, and Lily sighed, turning to Colton and opening her mouth to speak, only for a massive metal snap to echo around them, as if occurring underwater.

"What was—?" Colton began.

Another snap, and another and another. Colton felt himself get lighter, his gut rising into his throat as the tiny room rattled.

"Oh, dear, we're falling!" Lily blanched.

"We're *falling*?" Colton asked. "Isn't that a big problem?"

Lily squeezed her eyes shut, muttering something to herself. She held out her arms to either side and closed her hands as if gripping ropes before pulling them close to her body.

Immediately, Colton felt himself pressed into the floor, his guts falling to his feet. An ear-shattering noise of something tearing bits off the elevator came from outside.

Are we slowing down?

Colton watched as Lily groaned, beads of sweat building on her brow, expression contorting, and the elevator rattled heavily. The ceiling completely tore off, revealing a series of thick steel cables grasping at the elevator like tentacles. One grabbed hold of the elevator-room's wall and the metal stretched, on the verge of tearing the whole box in two. The cable reached its limit, the fibers snapping taut before bursting, sending sparks and metal wires bouncing.

"It's not working!" Colton cried, an intense whirring audible as the elevator plummeted faster and faster.

154

Lily tightened her grip and the remaining cables squealed against the friction. Another snapped, and she tumbled to the ground. Colton felt the wind whip at the edges of the platform as his ears were deafened by the high-whine of wheels reaching their speed limit. He noticed Lily climb to her feet, reaching her hands out again before he was thrown to the floor by an impact, his body momentarily being crushed beneath itself from the abrupt deceleration.

The elevator significantly dropped speed and began slowing down, and Lily cried out in pain as the elevator still raced too fast. Colton could barely see her in the darkness, the array of sparks and screeching metal above them as the wires gripped at and slowed the elevator greatly.

A second impact hit, much harder than the first. All movement stopped as the floor slammed into him, cutting his vision black.

Chapter 20
Somewhere Deep

Consciousness returned in waves, and Colton laid still for a good while, not daring to move for fear of his whole body falling apart. Sporadically, dust and small debris would clatter onto the floor beside him from higher up, making him cough on the dust clouds.

He slowly rose to his feet, wiping his eyes and groaning, feeling the dozen new bruises across his whole body and a gritty taste of dirt in his mouth. The elevator had been completely shredded with only the floor and first few inches of the wall remaining. Wires and debris piled around them, nearly burying them.

"Am I dead? Please tell me I'm not dead," Colton began, wheezing out the dust. "Lily, you okay?"

No reply.

Uh oh. No no no.

Colton stumbled over, blindly searching in the dimming light of a few fires, hands grasping past sharp rubble and steaming metal. His hand closed around a warm wrist, and he felt a jolt of relief. He paused, listening to her, slow breathing, weak, but existent.

Okay, she's alive. Come on, wake up!

Lily groaned, stirring, but not much. The buzzing began in Colton's ears, and her muddled thoughts floated subconsciously into his head. He couldn't pick out any words or images clearly. Just something stirring beneath the murky surface.

He sighed, falling back as he bowed his head on his knees.

Some situation we're in. She better have a hidden ability to fly.

Lily gave a hollow laugh, and Colton jolted so hard his leg muscles groaned. He heard Lily stirring, rising to her feet, followed by a *thud* as she collapsed to the ground. Colton moved toward her, only to retract when she retched, followed by the splash of chunk-filled liquid.

"You okay?" Colton asked.

156

Lily took a few deep breaths. "I-I should be fine. I just over-worked—"

Colton averted his attention as she retched again, making his own insides crawl. He only just managed to keep the bile from rising up in his own throat.

Once Lily had overcome her nausea, she rose unsteadily to her feet, stumbling a little, kicking metal debris.

"Sorry. I don't normally overdo it," Lily mumbled.

"So that's what you were doing. With your Calibers," Colton said, standing up.

"Yes, I slowed us down enough to survive. Seems my body could only handle—" Lily paused, and Colton worried she'd retch all over him.

He felt a hand on his shoulder as Lily steadied herself, breathing shallow.

"I defentalee overd'det," she said weakly, her words slurred slightly as she swayed, face tinged green.

You think? Colton thought.

Lily began rummaging for something in the debris. A loud *scratch*, and a flame flared to light, lit atop an arrow with a bulbous red sack tied to the tip, casting a diminutive light on the two of them.

Lily looked worse than ever. Her hair was a frizzled mess, face a tinge of green, and covered head-to-toe in soot and scrapes. Her eyes were dull gray puddles, and she had blood leaking from a couple of her scars.

Colton felt like he might not be looking much better.

Lily grabbed the flarrow and waved it around, casting dancing shadows on the walls as something glinted amongst the rubble. Lunging at it, Lily pulled out her crystalline bow, dusting it off. She wrapped it around her torso before retrieving the quiver punctured through with a metal shard.

"Could have been worse," she said, pulling out the shrapnel and donning the quiver.

"So how do we get outta here?" Colton asked.

Lily stumbled over to a portion of the shaft wall, partially hidden by the wreckage. She waved the flarrow, casting the light to reveal a doorway, barely visible beneath the rubble.

"Hold this," Lily said, holding out the flarrow.

Colton gingerly took it. "Uhm, sure."

Lily held her hands out and pantomimed ripping something open. The metal complied, the wreckage screeching to the sides, before the door itself crunched open just enough.

She collapsed to the ground, face slick with sweat, scars standing out starkly, and expression ghostly pale. Colton rushed to crouch beside her, shaking her gently. Her chest rose and fell rapidly, hyperventilation, and Colton let out a sigh.

"She's gonna kill herself at this rate."

Colton stayed crouched by her until her breathing had calmed down. He stood, kicking a piece of debris through the doorway, followed by a bubbling hiss from the darkness beyond the doors.

Where did that go? It didn't hit any metal or concrete.

Colton navigated from the wreckage to the door, squeezing through the small opening, and his feet splashed into murky water. He nearly got knocked sideways by the stench, gagging at the fleshy, brown objects floating in the water, illuminated by a single buzzing light above the shaft door.

From what little luminance shone forth, he could see the circular tunnel extended into darkness, water trailing in from several rusty pipes, mixing in with the sounds of something moving ahead him.

"What is that?" Colton muttered.

He flung the flarrow into the tunnel, the red glow harsh against the concrete, lighting up the inhabitant of the sewers before being extinguished. A harsh hiss, the creature racing toward him, grisly teeth and matted fur. Its claws clicked against the cement as its beady eyes stared furiously. It leaped, tail thrashing horridly as it flew forward.

Colton grumbled, sidestepping the small rat before kicking it away into the sewage. It squeaked, baring its teeth at him. He sloshed forward, chasing it off as it squealed in indignation, squeezing itself into a pipe.

"First the otters, now the rats," he said. "Animals just love me, don't they?"

He picked up the flarrow again, separating it from brown chunks floating amidst soaked trash in the greasy soup. He gave the doused, soaked tip a deep frown, tempted to retch and vomit.

"This is just disgusting. I thought I'd be sleeping in soft beds and eating good food," Colton grumbled, "not exploring sewers."

He chucked the flarrow down the tunnel, the bulbous cloth end falling apart and the metal arrow clattering along the cement and into the water.

Sounding like something was sloshing toward him.

Colton peered into the darkness, the noise growing louder, echoing with unclear direction the closer *it* came.

It's just another rat, right?

Step…by…step.

No, that sounds much bigger.

Closer…and…closer.

That's not a—!

Something cold grabbed his shoulder from behind, accompanied by heavy breathing. He spun, fists ready to punch, only for a hand to shoot out and land a blow on his cheek.

Chapter 21
Shadows on Shadows

"Cease your panic!" someone demanded. "You are not in danger."

It took Colton a few moments to realize it was Lily who had grabbed his shoulder and slapped him. Though she was awake, her eyes were sunken and she looked ready to pass out again.

"You look less dead," Colton said.

Lily huffed, clearing her hair from her face, adjusting the bow in hand. "Fortunately, Caliber exhaustion is less likely to be lethal if one is healthy and well-rested."

"You still look 'bout ready to die."

"Exhaustion isn't what'll kill us down here."

"You mean the sewage?"

"Let's just say it's best to keep quiet."

Lily hefted her bow as she crept down the hallway. Colton glared at her back but still felt his shoulder itch. He glanced back to the destroyed elevator, the light puny against the darkness. He shook his head, steeling himself as he followed her, leaving behind the comfort of light.

"Do you know where we're going?" Colton asked as they reached an intersection off shooting in four different directions.

"I have failed to explore the sewers in my time in Malelentos," Lily expressed, gagging, "for *very clear* reasons."

"So how do we get out?"

"We shall explore until we are free."

Colton peered down one route, eyes narrowed against the darkness. A chittering sound wafted to him, faint but clear.

"Plenty of happy rats," Colton said.

"Those are not rats," she replied softly with a grimace.

"Mice?"

"Incorrect. Far worse than any rat or rodent."

"More rioters from the Scintillia Initium?"

"Not quite."

"What are they *exactly*?"

Lily nocked a flarrow to her bow, the string creaking as it was pulled back, then twanging as she released it. Colton could hear the flarrow whistle softly down the tunnel before it lit up with light a good ways away, a red glare casting harsh shadows.

"Scourgers," Lily answered.

"Like, those rotting purplish black skin, white eyes, and dead-looking things?"

"Precisely. Though, they're not dead."

"What are they again?"

"Individuals who've perished in an intense and synthetic urge-seeking state. Think of how one can become severely addicted to substances or content. But as their urges were artificially amplified, upon death, they kept such desires."

"Can they feel anything? Since they're—dead?"

"They're not wholly dead. It's an odd state. But yes, they do not appear to feel much. Rather they seek for pleasure in the consumption of living hearts."

Colton shivered. "How'd they end up here?"

"The Auratus District is a stiff, stagnant place. Anything below perfection is discarded, and with how selfish and senseless they are, it would not be uncommon to see them perform the same with their own. Not to mention, the gallows were not just designed to kill those that bothered them. They needed servants who were more—mindless, obedient, loyal. But their attempts never worked, and so they ended up here."

She shot a flarrow down each pathway, examining it before moving to the next one. Colton watched, his unease growing as the chittering noise grew to be quite noisy, though the source was nowhere near in sight.

"I believe this one's the safest," Lily gestured to one tunnel.

At least it's opposite of that weird noise.

The girl marched down the tunnel, Colton in tow. At length, they reached the flarrow, and Lily bent to pick it up. She paused, shaking her head as she leaned against the wall for support. Colton walked

161

Caleb DM Smith

over and picked it up from the sewage. Lily waved her hand, drying out the flarrow, and it sizzled to full strength again. Another wave and it was cleaned of sewage before they marched down the tunnel.

A cold draft blew through the tunnels, making Colton hug himself for warmth. His feet grew freezing as the temperature of the greasy-soup-sewage plummeted.

The chittering grew louder, as if excited and howling. Lily tilted her head, listening to the ruckus. A clacking started up like an unnatural chomping of teeth. Colton froze, peering ahead at the darkness. The shadows moved, slowly shuffling to one side of the tunnel. The shadows threw its head around, a grotesque creaking like old joints followed.

Colton stepped forward. "What is—"

"Quiet!" Lily whispered, barely audible over the chittering.

Something groaned, the noise raspy and dry. The clacking sounded again, followed by the shadows wading toward them, carrying a heavy stench that nearly knocked Colton sideways.

They can't see you. Lily had grabbed his wrist. *But they can hear you.*

So, what should I do?

Don't breathe.

Colton nodded slowly, glancing at Lily out of the corner of his eye, following her lead to remain completely still. The flarrow extinguished, plunging them into pure darkness while rocketing Colton's panic through the roof, making holding his breath difficult.

He could hear slow, shuffling steps, sloshing noisily. He could smell a stench so vile it made his lungs shrink. The shadows groaned right next to him, nearly making him flinch, rotten breath on his cheek. He held still, the clacking unnerving as the shadows twisted and shook.

What kinda monster is this? Colton thought.

More groans, and light swishing of the water. The teeth clomped again, and Colton's throat began to itch. He squeezed his eyes shut, the urge to cough rising up.

Please don't, please don't.

162

He waited moments of eternity; his brain screamed at him to breathe as his chest burned. He let out a muffled huff, his insides twisting, his lungs vying for air.

The shadows shuffled forward, and the stench intensified, the chittering louder than ever, as the shadows clicked right in front of him.

No more than half a foot from him.

"Where are yooooooo?" the Scourger rasped.

Colton flinched, his skin tingling as he lightly brushed against the edge of rotting cloth. The shadows began cackling, devolving into violent hacking, ending in chittering.

No! Don't cough.

Colton, ease your fear. It'll help.

Clomping and rasping from the Scourger. Colton could feel the breath on his face. Alive and strong, but empty.

I can't—it's gonna—

At long last, the sloshing of the shadows shuffled away, slowly fading out till it gave way to silence. Lily took a deep, slow breath, cautiously moving forward. Colton followed suit, gasping quietly for air as he walked onto the curve of the cylinder, holding the wall for balance, lightheaded.

"What the nosk was that?" Colton asked between breaths, his chest physically hurting from his heart hammering.

Lily ignited another flarrow, wincing at the loud hiss and sizzle it made.

"*That* was a Scourger," she whispered. "You were lucky it hadn't bumped into you. It would've found you."

"I thought it would be like, a dead corpse thing. Not a talking person!"

"He was only partially one."

"But don't you have to die to become one?"

"Yes. But the body remains animated due to its intense hunger and drive of its urges, almost like an odd addiction. The person's body is still imprinted so as to cause some mimicking of the person when they were alive. But they retain some cognitive function if they die slowly until they've fully perished."

"They're not that strong, right?"

Caleb DM Smith

"Not entirely. If any part of a Scourger mixes with your body, it will infect you to increase your carnality and vileness. But you won't become one of those until you perish."

"So, a disease huh?"

"I believe through Dark-Energy, which is Bio-Energy corrupted with vileness and hatred. As such, it corrupts others with the selfsame attributes."

"Then why not just kill it first?"

"Should one Scourger directly affect or be affected by you, the rest will know via hive-mind. And if the rest know where you are—"

A Scourger clacked their teeth off in the dark, and Lily sniffled, eyes wide and shiny in the dim red light, glancing behind herself quickly.

She really hasn't been in danger before.

Lily held the flarrow in hand aloft to provide light and continued through the tunnels. The temperature dropped cold enough Colton's fingers had become numb and stiff.

They reached the end of the tunnel, finding it open into a rectangular drainage-type chamber that extended left and right into more darkness. To the left, the concrete walls became more cave-like and rough. To the right, black moss and plants grew between puddles and mini waterfalls of the disgusting mixture.

The chittering had risen to a cacophony, seeming to come from every direction as Colton felt the air reverberate with it, forcing his heartbeat to match pace with the fast rhythmic noise.

Did we loop around? There's no way we could've.

"Let's go this way," Lily muttered, jerking her head to the left. "I'd prefer to avoid moist areas when dealing with Scourgers, as it makes them hold a lethal advantage on many fronts."

Lily stopped at the edge of the circular tunnel, and Colton hopped down to the rectangular one, falling a good four feet or so. He landed in a crouch, feet giving dull thumps as if muted underwater.

The chittering stopped.

The cold burned away.

Why did—? Oh no. Oh kretching nosk.

"What did we step into?" Colton hissed.

164

There was warmth. A sickly warmth, like being pressed up against a fresh carcass. Though dead, the heart of the corpse was still beating, loud and filling the tunnel with thumping. Then dozens, growing to hundreds, like one amassed creature rasping amongst the vines to the right.

"Colton?" Lily asked breathily.

Colton peered into the darkness toward the vegetative tunnel, only to see the shadows twisting and deforming, filling the entire tunnel. Hundreds of white dots emerged, groaning and teeth-clacking.

"Colton?" Lily asked again, voice shrill.

He continued to stare, mesmerized by the corrupted starry sky appearing before him, each blinking like a set of eyes as it slowly advanced. The sound of shuffling clothes, scraping skin, and tearing vines filled his ears.

He watched the very shadows coming alive in the red light. Hundreds of bodies, hundreds of living corpses, that surged forward, covered in invading vegetation that visibly ate away at their bodies, leaving gaping holes.

"COLTON, RUN!" Lily screamed, grabbing at his shirt.

Torn from his trance, he turned and ran, Lily beside him, a collective shriek erupting behind him, and the warmth increased to a disgusting scorch. He raced down the cave-like tunnel, heedless of the splashing bile at his feet.

Lily turned at an intersection, sprinting down a tunnel, Colton followed, slipping. She stopped and Colton ran into her. A second horde of shadows blocked their way. Lily screamed, and the duo dashed to the intersection, raced the other way. The two hordes collided and surged after them.

Colton's lungs burnt. Groans filled his ears. They turned another corner, feet sloshing. they turned again, then a third time, racing the length of the tunnel.

They hesitated at a three-way intersection, then dashed right. They sprinted more corners, more wrong turns, long tunnels, avoiding Scourgers. Hands grasped at them, rotten fingernails scratching at their clothes, and decayed teeth nearly chomping on their hair.

The cave-like tunnels vanished, giving way to metal piping flooded with bile. Colton felt light-headed but kept up his pace, body sore.

They passed a set of black vines and a Scourger leaped out, grabbing Colton's ankle. He tripped and slammed to the ground. The Scourger moaned and crawled forward. Colton kicked at it as the horde tumbled over his way, a hand grabbing at his shirt. He leaped to his feet and sprinted off, tearing apart a rotten hand.

More water from the pipes slowed them down, the Scourgers were unaffected. Lily ran on the side of the pipe, nearly slipping. Colton followed, rusty metal scraping at his shoes and hands as he balanced on the side. They traversed the pipe till it became a dry, upward slope, a dim light slowly growing.

They turned another corner, and daylight flooded them, the pipe ended up ahead, a grate hiding the view. Colton raced forward, slipping on wet shoes, nearly sliding back into the Scourgers behind. He pushed forward, crashing into the grate, and pulled on it.

"Take this," Lily commanded, handing Colton her bow and arrows. "Fend them off!"

Colton examined the items before slinging the quiver over his shoulder and nocking an arrow to the bow. He struggled to pull the string back at first, the draw-weight too heavy. He strained, groaning as his back arched, creaking the string and letting fly a flarrow without aim. It flew, thudded into the convulsing shadows, and flared up, fully revealing the humanoid appearance of the Scourgers.

"Those aren't human at all!" Colton screeched.

Lily twisted and pulled her fingers like handling a metal bolt. "Obviously! They're Scourgers."

Colton shot another arrow, hitting pure, milky white eyes. Another arrow impaled purplish-black skin clawed or bitten away in spots, the impact splintering yellowed bone. Colton sent a flarrow flying, and it landed in a forehead, flaring up in red light, and setting fire to the clumped and sludgy hair.

"They're not slowing down!" Colton called.

166

He smacked away a Scourger with a *crunch*. Another leaped forward, bile-filled mouth wailing. Colton blocked with the bow, landing a kick on the Scourger's torso, the tight skin ripping against the ribcage.

Another crawled toward him on its stomach, fingers ruined, and legs only bones. Colton stared, frozen as he watched the wretched creature draw closer. Lily snatched the bow out of Colton's hands and dealt a powerful blow to the head of the Scourger, then kicked a second away, before nocking an arrow and shooting a third.

"The grate's loose. Kick it off!" Lily shouted.

Colton rushed to the edge of the pipe, sending himself crashing into the metal mesh. The grate felt like a wall, but popped off, stopping Colton's momentum enough to prevent him from falling hundreds of feet down to the ground.

"I said kick, not tackle!" Lily admonished.

She ran up the side of the pipe before leaping and grabbing the top, hoisting herself up. Colton stood awe-struck for a few moments before a Scourger snapped him back to reality with a wail. He dodged to the side, and the Scourger missed its leap, falling off the edge. More rushed him. Colton ran forward, ascending the pipe wall before leaping and missing the top of the pipe. Colton's gut rose to his throat and Scourgers surged under him. Lily grabbed his hand, slowly lifting him up until he could grab the pipe edge.

He pulled himself up and scrambled across the top to the cliff face, heart pounding and lungs wheezing as he stared forward blankly. The groans and bemoaning echoed up to him.

"Ah, holy—" Colton began, stopping for lack of breath.

"First time running for your life?" Lily asked.

"I've run plenty," Colton replied, "but not from things supposed to be dead in dark places."

Lily grimaced before nocking another arrow to her bow. "Best to grow accustomed to it. It's one thing I've heard happens on field missions."

"Wait, you saying this is your first time being out?"

"My expertise was used in arranging missions, reconnaissance, and research. Intel and such. Not nitty-gritty combat."

I knew it! Know-it-all-girl hasn't even done this before!

Caleb DM Smith

Be quiet! Lily's voice snapped mentally.

"Tell me how we're not dead," Colton muttered.

"A severe amount of training leading up to this. And you don't seem to be lacking survival wits."

Colton took a shuddering breath and rose to his feet, making sure he was a good distance from either side of the pipe before moving to stand with Lily.

"Then we should be able to get off Vagabond's Venture, right?" Colton asked.

From his position, he could see most of the Scintilla Initium District, and only the tops of the tallest buildings of the Auratus District, the latter which was covered in smoke and fire.

"Best for us to descend, rather than to climb," Lily commented, noting the many ledges that wound down the cliff face to the ground, serving as a makeshift staircase.

Colton watched her stride to the edge of the pipe, crouching down. A black hand grabbed her ankle, she cried out, kicking at it as a Scourger grabbed the pipe edge, hauling itself over the edge.

Lily screamed, kicking the Scourger off, only for another to reach for her. More came, like a black sludge of corpses that seeped over the edge toward Colton and Lily.

"How're they doing that?" Colton shouted, shoving a Scourger that leaped at him.

"They work like ants!" Lily replied, smacking her bow against a Scourger, knocking it to the ground. "They're half hive-minded!"

She kicked two more away, opening up a gap between their numbers. Colton took the opportunity, dashing through to the rounded edge of the pipe. He skidded to a stop, Lily sailed past him, landing on a stone outcropping a few feet out.

"Oh, nosk!" Colton swore, his feet nearly slipping off.

"Just do it!" Lily shouted.

Colton glanced back, Scourgers leaping at him. He sucked in his breath, vaulting as he swung his arms. Scourgers screamed in his ears as he fell through the air, falling short of the ledge, and feet plummeting past the outcropping. He grabbed the edge, hands slapping on smooth stone, slipping over the dirt.

"Grab me!" Colton shouted, frantically grasping at what little leverage was there.

Lily grabbed his hands, stopping his momentum. He felt something dig into his ankle, immediately pulling him down, jerking Lily to the edge of the outcropping.

Colton cried out, the Scourger painfully gripping his ankle, flailing and snarling. Its rotten mouth gaped open to bite him, a swath of rot burning Colton's nostrils, his eyes starting to moisten.

Colton kicked it in the face, but it dug deeper, nearly breaking the skin. He gritted his teeth against the pain, kicking again. His pants ripped, the Scourger clawing at the shred of fabric before it plummeted.

Quickly, Colton scrambled up with the aid of Lily. More Scourgers leaped their way, all missing and falling with screeches, with most staying on the large pipe and staring at them.

"I thought you said they couldn't see," Colton said.

Lily nodded as some of the Scourgers began crouching, teeth clomping as their heads twisted and twitched.

"They can't. Half hive-minded, remember?" Lily whispered. "They rely on dispensable numbers to test what they hear. The deaths and injuries are felt by all, making known the obstacles, which are solved by a leader."

Colton watched the Scourgers as they chittered at the edge, feeling forward with their feet.

"Then let's get outta here before their boss arrives," Colton muttered.

"I concur."

Colton turned and stepped to the opposite edge, leaping to the next stone outcropping. Lily followed, and Colton leaped to the next, landing less solidly and nearly slipping.

Outcropping after outcropping.

Leap after leap.

Slowly.

Sluggishly they made their way down, winding around the cliff until they reached a switchback. The next ledge was twice the distance, spanning ten feet of air.

Colton took more of a running start before leaping the extra distance, barely clearing the edge and slipping slightly on the sandy surface. His gut twisted, panic rising as his momentum forced him to the edge. He cursed and hopped down to the next outcropping, halfway back to the previous ledge, Lily flying overhead.

Colton paused, hands on his knees as he doubled over, legs ready to break. Lily landed beside him a few moments later, not looking much better.

A glance down showed they were still high in altitude. Looking up, they could see the Scourgers shuffling around like demented penguins huddling together.

One stood away from the rest, testing the edge. It let out a groan, before swinging its arms wildly and leaping.

It's not gonna—

Colton froze as the Scourger tumbled on top of the stone outcropping, chittering its teeth. All the others had stilled and looked toward where the first now rested.

"Lily we gotta go," Colton began.

The rest of the Scourgers surged forward, throwing themselves wildly, most making it onto the outcropping. The first began running and leaping, clearing each jump in half the time Colton and Lily had taken.

"Lily, Run!" Colton cried, running and leaping to the next outcropping.

Lily looked at him with raised brows as he took off. He didn't stop as he heard her exclamation of surprise, followed by her landing next to him.

They quickly descended, the Scourgers gaining as most made it to subsequent ledges. The rest fell and rag dolled, hitting other outcroppings as they became deadly projectiles.

Colton leaped to an outcropping, pressing himself to the cliff as a Scourger smashed into the stone next to him. Black sludgy remains splattered all over.

At least it's dead. Its head is nearly gone. It's—

Colton bent on heads and knees, stomach twisting as he felt his throat burn, keeping down the acid. He closed his eyes, fighting the nausea until the Scourger let out a gurgle, slowly stirring, pushing itself to hands and knees.

"OH, COME ON!" Colton staggered forward, slamming his foot into the Scourger. It rolled off the edge, flailing again as it plummeted.

More Scourgers fell down, only a couple managing to stay on the outcropping, most slamming and spinning as they fell. Colton forced his eyes shut, breathing more controllably until he turned toward the next outcropping.

He leaped away, continuing his descent, Lily close behind. He leaped again and again, pushing himself at a brutal pace. The ground drew closer and closer. The further he went, the less Scourgers lived.

Colton leaped more, at long last clearing the last eight feet to the ground, landing in a crouch. All around him, the corpses of Scourgers laid still, most crumpled to heaps. Only one or two stirred slowly, now severely crippled.

Lily dropped beside him, not pausing as she clutched his shirt and tugged him forward. They took off running, and Colton stumbled, his legs shaky and weak. He coughed and picked himself up, dashing away from the groaning horde.

I just need to find Liam.

The buildings slowly turned grayer, with the dirt becoming more afflicted with silver dust. The chaos of the riot in the Auratus District echoed down to them, gunfire, screams, and sirens echoing in the otherwise silent Scintillia Initium District.

They rounded a corner, jogging down a street devoid of life. The quiet hum of nothing filled their ears, and Colton's heart constricted.

What the kretch? There should be people. He swallowed hard, throat twisting as flashbacks to Aquila Mons played in his head.

He looked in the windows as they passed by, not seeing anything stir. Doors stood open as if waiting, and personal items lay strewn across every open surface. He stopped at an intersection, breathless as he turned around in circles, peering down every which way. Lily stopped beside him, face twisted with a frown, and Colton shook his head.

"Where *is* everyone?"

Chapter 22
Absolute Fallout

"No no, they must be in the Auratus," Lily gasped between breaths as they ran. "Otherwise, where would the corpses be?"

"But they had to have started rioting down here before they got up there," Colton countered.

He glanced up toward the richer district, flames billowing from buildings, smoke wrapping around towers, and chaos erupting from every visible point.

Are they really fighting a civil war up there?

They turned onto another street, a large area visible ahead of them. Lily had fallen behind considerably, looking ready to pass out. Colton's body was starting to mimic Lily's exhaustion as the ground became mucked and gray.

They burst from the road, entering a flat wasteland of black soot and glowing embers. Dozens of buildings were now heaps of rubble, with odd, charred pieces sticking up sporadically. Blackened hands petrified in place, as if begging for help. The place looked empty, but Colton felt claustrophobic. The echoes of once loud, shuffling crowds whispered in his ears, each wisp of smoke almost making a sad face before it was snuffed out.

"Did the fire do this?" Colton asked, his voice feeling amplified as they wandered.

Lily frowned. "I don't believe so. Fire doesn't destroy stone buildings into utter ash and rubble of this degree."

They reached what used to be the Central Market, now a flat field of ash. A few smoking piles of wood and stone here and there, scorched and drowning from a large puddle in the center.

Hundreds of blistered bodies littered the area. Many were trapped beneath rubble, a mixed scent of charred wood, burnt plastic, and overcooked meat. Others were piled on top of each other as if they were merged, blackened arms vying for escape.

Everything was dead.

Nothing moved.

It's all gone.

"Colton," Lily said, gently tugging on his sleeve.

He looked over at where she was pointing at someone peeking out with wide eyes and a rat-looking face. The girl looked their way and gave a yelp, vanishing from sight.

"Wait, Bristol!" Colton called, running after her.

He dashed into the alleyway, slipping on the dirt. Bristol was running away toward the exit, kicking up ash. Colton stumbled to his feet, racing after her.

"Woah, hold on," Colton called, throat burning.

Bristol slowed, glancing back. Her eyes widened as she came to a stop. "Colton! Did—you go crazy to?"

"What? No! Why would I have—?"

"The others did."

Colton tilted his head. "What's that mean?"

"Bristol!" Lily called, coming around behind Colton.

The younger girl's eyes widened and she dashed to Lily, catching her in a hug. Colton stared for a moment, his torso aching.

"Wait, you two know each other?" Colton asked. "I thought Bristol was just nerd."

Bristol nodded, pulling away. "Yeah, Lily's been teaching me a lot about what's really out in the world."

"Explains all her crazy theories."

"Hey!" both girls protested in unison.

"What happened down here, Bristol?"

Bristol shuddered, eyes darkening. Colton frowned, shifting his gaze from her to the landscape. He looked up, squinting against the snow that fell, warm and gritty.

That's a lot of ash.

Silence reigned, the Auratus District smoldered with fires, and not a sound came from it except for the occasional distant wail. Colton glanced at Lily, and her face paled. Bristol shook her head and hugged Lily tighter.

"It would seem those from the Scintillia Initium were intent on not merely rioting," Lily said, eyes closing for a second.

Colton tensed up. "If I was in their spot—"

"You'd be capable of such utter bloodlust?"

"No one liked the guardians. I don't know if I'd go that far though."

"Because you care for other things," Lily said. "So long as they kill the focus of hatred, that is all that matters to them."

Colton looked up at the Auratus, shivering at the thought. He rubbed his shoulder, the skin rough from burn scars as it tingled with phantom heat.

"We should go," Colton said.

Bristol pulled away from Lily. "Wait, what about Liam?"

"He's gonna meet us somewhere."

"So, he didn't come down with you?"

Colton shook his head. "No. We got separated during the riot."

"We need to go back for him."

"On the contrary," Lily said, "we must wait for him at the rendezvous."

"He's not gonna be there," Bristol said, frowning.

"How would you know?" Colton asked.

"Because I know you."

"I didn't abandon him!" Colton said, heat rising into his face.

Bristol folded her arms. "Like you've never done that before."

"You're really obsessed with him, aren't you?"

Bristol's face turned red and she stomped forward, throwing a punch, hitting Colton with a loud *smack!* He cried out and stumbled back, the side of his head smarting.

"You kretch!" Colton shouted, his voice ringing out uncomfortably loud.

"Colton did not abandon Liam," Lily said.

Bristol threw her a glare. "He's still back there, isn't he? We have to go back for him."

"We cannot."

"*No,* we have to go *back* for him. I'm *not* leaving him"

"Why is it so pertinent?"

Bristol scowled, but a glint of fear flashed across her eyes. "Because if we don't—anyone who didn't go to the Auratus is dead or—

or—" Bristol shook her head. Someone thumped somewhat nearby, and her head snapped in the direction. "They're not *normal* anymore."

Colton exhaled sharply. "Look, Bristol. Let's just get to Angel's Landing. Liam *will* be there. He's with one of Lily's friends. They'll be fine."

"One very capable in military terms," Lily added.

Bristol pursed her lips, wrinkling her nose as she looked at Colton for a long silent moment. She sighed and nodded, opening her mouth to speak. "Alright, but he'd better be—"

The sound of her voice cut out, and Colton felt something smash into him. He blacked out for a moment, before snapping back to consciousness on the ground. The echoes of a boom reverberated off the nearby buildings, but there wasn't any fire or smoke.

What just happened? What kind of explosion doesn't use fire?

His body hurt, bruises and cuts stung all over his body, and his ears rang. The ground shook with small aftershocks, twinging his injuries.

That wasn't the Scourgers—was it?

"Colton, come on, get up," Lily said, grabbing his shoulders, bruised and scraped.

He stumbled to his feet, slipping on the rubble that littered the alleyway. One building was destroyed, only a single wall still standing, with a large chunk taken out of the other. Rubble covered the road, and everything besides the buildings had been blown over.

"What—why'd the building explode?" Colton asked.

Lily coughed and started helping Bristol out from the rubble. "Someone fired at us with something. I couldn't tell who or by what method."

"It's gotta be one of the crazies," Bristol said, spitting up blood, lips bleeding profusely. "They've all got freaky powers."

Colton shivered. *Like Jace?*

Lily started jogging toward the outskirts of the Scintillia Initium District, leaving the others behind her, weaving and winding between roads and alleyways. Ash stuck to their clothes and shoes as they ran. Pungent smells burned their lungs, making things worse.

This is almost like Hell.

Someone wailed in the distance, their tone wild and gleeful. Bristol paled, eyes wide as she shook her head, picking up her pace. Colton followed suit, glancing behind repeatedly as he rolled his shoulders. They wound past shacks and decrepit houses, the fields on the outskirts coming into view.

"We'll take the forest path to Angel's Landing," Lily called.

Colton winced. *Not so loud!*

Something crashed into Lily, sending her tumbling into the ground, followed by wailing elation. Colton slowed to a stop as Lily rose shakily to her feet, bow in hand. Someone beside her stood up, dressed in rags, hair stained a crimson dripping red, and deep gouges in the ashen skin.

"Liam?" Bristol asked, taking a step forward.

The boy whipped around, smacking her and sending her to the ground, before turning to Colton with wide crazy eyes, bloodshot and twitchy. Broken teeth and a crooked smile that trembled.

That's not Liam.

"Well, looky who decided ter to show up?" Fisk asked, licking blood off his lips and flexing bony hands, the nails yellowed and long.

"How'd you get down from the Auratus?" Colton asked.

Fisk sneered. "At no thanks ter you."

"I'm sorry about—"

Fisk lunged and Colton dodged out of the way. The deranged boy began snarling as he stood up, scratching at his own skill until he started bleeding.

"Shut up! Shut it, shut it, shut it!" Fisk hissed. He grabbed at a spot on his torso, a dark ooze drenching his clothes. "I'm tired o' hearing yer stupid voice. I'm tired o' hearing any o' y'all."

Lily inched closer to Colton and grabbed his shoulder, making him flinch. *Careful, his torso…*

What about it? Colton thought.

"Well, looky looky," Fisk said, "someone's got a li'le girlie."

It's the origin point of his dark veins. He's been infected. Lily thought.

So. he got bit?

No, tested on.

176

"I was talking ter yoo!" Fisk screamed, making Colton's blood curdle.

"Look, Fisk," Colton began, "just let us go. We're not tryin'g to cause you trouble."

"That's where yer wrong, boy. Yoo caused me enough o' trouble. And now? I want you *dead*."

"But what would—"

"*DEAD DEAD DEAD!*" Fisk screamed, stomping with each word. He grabbed handfuls of his hair and tore it out. "I wanted my money. I wanted you ter worship me. And now yer problem in my side. I'm going ter slit yer throat."

Lily readied her bow, nocking an arrow and aiming right at Fisk. "Not while we're here."

Bristol began creeping toward an alleyway, and Fisk laughed, massaging his jaw, popping coming from his joints, streaks of red permeating his eyes.

"This ain't no place for a li'le thing like you," Fisk said. "I'll have *fun* with you once I'm done. An' Bristol too. Yer both will be beggin' fer me to treat yah kindly."

Colton and Lily shared a glance before Fisk inhaled sharply, lungs visible standing out against his chest. Colton's gut thrashed and he tackled Lily to the ground, right as Fisk made a coughing motion and something almost invisible shot out from the crazed boy's mouth.

Fisk staggered back. A small shockwave slammed Colton's back. A nearby house exploded without fire or smoke, looking as if the house tore itself to shreds. Dust and debris flew everywhere, pelting Colton as his ears rang.

Did he just do that—with his voice?

Lily rose to her feet. "You—they injected you, didn't they?"

"How'd you know, li'le girlie?" Fisk spat, sporting new bruises on his jaw, puffed slightly from internal bleeding.

"You didn't have a Caliber before."

Fisk laughed. "Yoo darn right. And now it'll be all I need ter rule this nosking place. To *own you*. Just *die die die!*"

Fisk laughed and began inhaling. Lily nocked an arrow to her bow and let it fly, sinking the shaft deep into Fisk's chest. He stumbled back, grunting as unnaturally dark blood oozed out.

Did she just—?

Fisk laughed again, yanking the arrow out, shivering as his wound worsened. His body convulsed and his eyes twitched as his jaw came fully dislocated, hanging by the skin.

His laughs reached maniacal hysteria as he let out a roaring shriek. Colton clamped his hands to his ears, his muscles seizing up with pain. The ground vibrated beneath him, the dust forming patterns as he felt his brain rattle in his skull.

Fisk's shriek cut out, and he laughed, blood spilling from the sides of his mouth. He glared at them with a wild hunger that made Colton's senses go numb with cold.

"I've had it with yoo!" Fisk screamed, spit flying.

He inhaled again, and Lily shoved Colton out of the way just as Fisk fired another sound-bolt, stumbling back enough he nearly lost his balance. Colton felt the sound bolt shoot past him, slamming him with a residue shockwave before the bolt hit Wallich Tower in the Auratus, exploding without flame. The skyscraper creaked, shifting and tilting slightly, but staying up.

"Colton, run!" Bristol called as she grabbed a piece of rubble.

The bolt slammed into a far house, exploding it, a second shockwave making Bristol stumble. Fisk laughed and ran at Colton. Bristol tackled him, swinging her rubble piece. Fisk howled and struck her with his fists. Bristol fell. He kept attacking.

Her head smashed to the ground.

Colton paused, watching in horror. He glanced at the edge of the district, not more than a hundred yards. Fisk wailed and Colton flinched, watching Bristol vainly struggle.

I could run away, and I'd be safe. But maybe should I help? No, I can't do anything. I'm just a normal, nobody kid.

"Yoo see, yer only as good as *I allow* yoo ter be," Fisk wailed, slamming the girl by the shoulders. "But now that them rules are gone, it's 'bout time we civilized people *eat each other!*"

Fisk laughed, throwing his blood-stained head back, body convulsing and mouth drooling black ooze. He screamed and held high his fists, stained red. Bristol breathed weakly, hands twitching.

Lily shot an arrow, piercing Fisk through the shoulder. He laughed and struck again. Colton ran forward, throwing himself at

Fisk, who shot a sound bolt, forcing Colton to duck. Fisk laughed and grabbed Bristol by the hair, lifting her up and sneering at her.

"Colton, get out of here!" Bristol cried, batting at Fisk's hands.

Colton clambered to his feet, grabbing a piece of rubble and swinging. Fisk grunted, dropping Bristol before smacking Colton, sending him flying.

"Yoo are smart for a little girly," Fisk sneered, towering over Bristol. "If you beg an' say you're mine. Maybe I'd just let yoo live."

Bristol scoffed. "I'd never date a creep like you."

"That's a shame," Fisk said, grabbing a shattered wooden board. "Yoo were pretty."

"Bristol!" Colton called, standing as his face stung.

Fisk laughed and slammed the broken board, impaling Bristol. Colton moved forward and Lily grabbed him. Colton watched in horror as Bristol flinched, mouth agape as words failed to come out. She glared at Fisk as her body started to relax before he twisted the board, and she went limp.

"No. There's no way you just—" Colton muttered, trying to wrestle Lily off him.

Fisk twitched, head hanging back as he laughed at the sky. Lily let go and flung another arrow, piercing the boy in the leg. Fisk laughed and snapped his glare onto the two of them.

"Come on, we have to go," Lily said.

Colton gripped a slanted wall as his head swam. *Fisk just—Bristol can't be—*

She's already dead.

But Fisk—

He's been infected and then tested on. He's hardly human anymore. And once he dies, he'll be a Scourger. We must leave before we join Bristol's fate.

Colton nodded, letting Lily pull him away. They ran down the road, and Colton looked back repeatedly, Fisk still laughing at the falling ash, his wails carrying like a gunshot. Colton shook his head, Lily's voice echoing in his brain.

He's become a demon.

Chapter 23
Rotten Dead

The view from the mountain side was breathtaking, mostly due to the heavy ash that fell or the thick smoke that billowed from the ruins below.

The air was stifling, lacked any breeze, and Malelentos had become a dull grey. Silent, withering, and haunting. Like a dead spot on the world.

Colton slowed to a stop, lungs burning as he collapsed onto a large boulder, his head swimming. He clutched his temples with his hands, trying to squeeze out that headache.

"Are you alright?" Lily asked, stopping beside him.

Colton scowled. "Malelentos just got destroyed, I saw one of my friends die, and I got chased by things supposed to be dead. And I'm starting to hate breathing right now."

"Apologies. But such things are going to be commonplace in your life."

"Why's that?"

Lily sniffed. "Scourgers or crazed individuals are not the worst you could meet. Malelentos was very sheltered. Hidden behind walls, in a way."

Colton hung his head in his hands, groaning as he let out an exasperated sigh. He stood up and took a deep breath, the falling ash making him cough, burning his throat.

"We'd better keep moving," Lily said, adjusting the quiver on her back. "Fisk may very well be following us."

She turned and trudged up the slope, Colton following her. Winding along the familiar path almost hidden by the gray blanket until they reached the broken window of a skyscraper buried on its side into the mountain. Dirty and rust infected, now filthied with ash.

Colton grabbed a metal bar jutting from the concrete as he hauled himself through, glass crunching underfoot. Dim light fell into the main room, the rotting couch somewhat in the center, with the overturned fridges resting near the back wall. The distant roar of the waterfalls was still audible, and water dripped from the ceiling.

There's no waterfalls this far over Colton thought, looking up.

He winced as a raindrop nearly hit his eye, followed by another. Starting slow at first, then building to a gentle but constant rain as water spilled into the room, forming puddles.

"Glad you guys could make it," someone said.

Colton started, whirling at Liam emerging from their makeshift bedroom. The boy grinned, sporting new cuts and bruises, but otherwise unharmed. Colton ran to him and hugged him, making Liam grunt.

"Sorry," Colton said, pulling back.

Liam shrugged. "At least I still got arms to hug ya back."

"How'd you guys get out of Auratus?"

"Not easily. We hid out, went from place to place. Ivan took a couple bad hits, especially when he cleared out the road going down. He's got a way powerful Caliber."

"Really? What kind?" Colton asked.

Liam gave a sly smile. "You've gotta wait to see for yourself."

"So, he's not—dead, is he?" Lily asked tentatively.

"No, he's just resting," Liam said, jerking a thumb at the room behind him.

Inside, Ivan lay flat on an overturned cabinet, a thin scratchy blanket beneath him. His kevlar vest was dirtied, and a bandage was wrapped around his lower torso, a red stain dominating it. Another bandage was on his leg, with a couple of wounds on his head.

"Oh goodness, Ivan," Lily said, stepping to his side.

The soldier sat up. "Small wound, normal in war."

"We were watching the city from up here," Liam said. He folded his arms, giving Colton a raised brow. "It looked like something flooded out of Vagabond's Venture."

"Scourgers," Lily said with a dark look.

"What're those?"

Ivan rose to his feet. "I go keep watch, Lily explain creature."

Caleb DM Smith

He hefted his rifle and limped out of the room. Lily frowned, twanging her bow string. Colton watched her for a second, his gut twisting.

They seem close.

"Imagine a dead person chasing you," Colton answered, turning to Liam. "They can bite or scratch you. And if they infect you, you turn into one when you die. You get all mad and stuff, too, when you're infected."

Liam shivered. "No wonder Malelentos is kinda bad right now."

"It's not our biggest problem right now, though."

"What is?"

"Fisk," Colton said glumly.

"Shouldn't Ivan be able to deal with him?"

Lily shook her head. "Not with the current state of your friend."

"What happened to him?" Liam asked, looking back and forth between Lily and Colton.

"He uhhh—" Colton began, "he kinda went berserk."

"What did you do?"

"Colton is not as responsible for much of what has transpired," Lily said. "At least not knowingly in many matters. Fisk was a result of corrupt authorities."

"I'm not even sure what happened to him," Colton said, looking to Lily.

"As far as I can tell, he was involved in experiments performed by the Auratus in order to create more obedient servants," Lily said. "They attempted to remove the desires and wants of an individual but failed and thus created the perfect urge-driven specimens for Scourgers. We suspect the Herald's of the Damned may have sponsored their attempts."

"Whole lot of good it did them," Colton muttered.

"They may have known it'd fail."

"So, what's wrong with Fisk?" Liam asked.

"Well, he likes killing things, and he can blow things up with his voice," Colton replied.

"So, he has a Caliber now?"

182

Lily nodded. "And one that grows stronger with passage of time."

"That's bad."

"Quite so. But it may return fire on him if it overpowers his body."

"How would it do that?" Colton asked.

"You saw him flung back upon usage of his Caliber, correct?"

Colton nodded, and Lily gestured her head toward the entry to the ruins, pantomiming falling off the cliff before grimacing. Liam's eyes widened and Colton raised a brow.

"But that's so barbaric," Colton said, mimicking Lily's voice.

She threw him a glare, and he grinned back, resulting in her shaking her head as she resisted a smile. Liam looked between them, before elbowing Colton in the side.

"Ow!" he exclaimed.

Lily laughed softly. "Yes, it would be a bit barbaric. I prefer not defeating my opponents in brutal ways, if possible. A fall off a cliff is quite horrifying."

"Why's that matter?" Colton asked, rubbing his side.

"If you're willing to throw away your morals at a certain point, it makes you breakable. Thus, a weakness that can be exploited to corrupt you."

"But if it's life and death, it's fine, right?"

Lily frowned. "Well—we haven't much time. Let's focus on our current trials before speaking philosophy."

"We've still gotta deal with Fisk," Liam reminded everyone.

"Is there not a second way down?" Lily asked.

"There's a lot of ways down," Colton said. "But only one you can survive."

"Then we must deal with Fisk."

"Why do we have to deal with him at all?" Colton asked.

"I do not think your so called 'friend' would simply let you slip away."

"He doesn't know where I am."

Liam grimaced. "I think he knows about our hideout here."

"But not that *I am* here," Colton stressed.

"Where else would you hide in a destroyed Malelentos," Lily questioned.

Colton looked at her, gut twisting. He frowned and ran a hand through his hair as he leaned back against a metal pipe. "So how much time we got?"

"Not likely much. I believe it took…what…about a rough hour to hike?" Lily asked, grabbing the pipe. "I would think no more than half an hour?"

"Okay, look," Colton began, "he wants me, not any of you. So—"

"Not happening," Lily began.

"I didn't finish."

You didn't need to.

Colton scowled. *Stop reading my mind.*

Lily pulled away from the pipe. "You *cannot* serve as a diversion."

"Why not?" Colton asked. "He doesn't hate you, or Liam. He probably doesn't know Ivan exists. So, if I get him to come after me, you guys can get away."

"Because it's not like us to run away," Liam said, stepping forward. "You are."

"I've got a bounty on my head, and some guy I've never met hired to kill me. Plus, Fisk, and who knows who else."

Lily threw her hands in the air. "So, you wish to throw your life away?"

"What's it to you?"

"I—" Lily paused, face reddening slightly. "—have a mission to prevent you from capture, if not recruit you. If you remember. I cannot allow you to place yourself in such danger."

Colton dropped his gaze down to the floor. Shuffling over until he sat down on the overturned cabinet. He rested his hands on his neck as his mind raced, the itchy sackcloth beneath him.

How did this happen?

He took a deep breath, hiding his face in his hands.

First the guardians, then being imprisoned, Jace, the Scourgers, and now Fisk. When's this gonna end? It feels like it's gonna go on for years.

He dropped his hands, staring at a cracked spot on the concrete floor.

I can't beat him in a fight. He's physically stronger, and his Caliber could kill me in one shot. The only way I can think of is to get him off the cliff.

Colton growled, clenching his hands into fists.

Can I really do that? I can't—fight him directly. I didn't beat Jace head-on without help. Can I really beat Fisk? I'm gonna die, aren't I?

Colton shook his head. *No. I have to beat him. At least enough that he won't hurt others.*

He rose to his feet, his gut thrashing. He glanced at his wrists, the veins glowing a dark magenta, the Demothest replacing his skin pulsing like a heartbeat.

"When he gets here, we'll try and fight him together," Colton said, looking at the two others. "And if that doesn't work, I'll fight him on my own, deeper in Angel's Landing."

Lily stepped forward. "Did you not hear what—"

"I heard what you said. That's why me being solo is second."

"If he captures you, that could be very catastrophic."

"You heard Fisk chanting, right?"

Liam folded his arms. "'Don't do anything dumb,' remember that?"

"It's not stupid, it's the best option we have," Colton groaned.

"Why not just run from him?"

"By doing what, Liam? Leaping down a cliff?"

"We can find a way through Angel's Landing," the boy suggested.

"There *is* no other way," Colton said, punching a metal pipe, causing it to bend with a raucous creak and spewing water. "Fisk wants me. *I* have to fight him. If I don't, he'll keep coming, probably even after he's dead."

Gunshots rang outside, repeated and loud. Everyone froze, the gunfire going silent a few moments later. A loud boom shook the structure, glass shattering and rubble crumbling outside the room.

"Oh, goodness!" Lily blanched, rushing outside.

Caleb DM Smith

Liam followed her, with Colton hesitating. He took a deep breath, clenching and relaxing his hands before moving to the door and throwing it open.

Ivan flew toward Colton, who dodged out of the way as the soldier slammed into the back wall, slumping down with a grunt.

"Small boy strong," Ivan groaned.

Colton dashed to Ivan's side. "What happened?"

"I shot boy," Ivan said, taking a deep breath before coughing. "Boy dying slowly. Becoming Scourger. More dangerous."

"Wait, you *shot* him? Shouldn't he be dead?"

Someone screamed outside, and Ivan struggled to his feet. Colton beat him to the door, running out to the main room filled with dust.

Fisk stood by the entrance window, looking more wild than ever, and with a few bite marks visible across his body. Gunshot wounds bled profusely from his head and torso; the blood mixed with black ooze.

Lily lay on the ground, hands clamped to her bleeding ears, her bow beside her and string snapped. Liam was against a wall, unconscious and with more wounds than before.

"Yoo fool!" Fisk spat, whirling at Colton. "Yoo left me ter die to them shamn dead things."

Colton frowned. "That sucks. Maybe you'd like the Scourgers better than me."

"I'd like you better *dead*."

"What makes you think you'll be able to kill me?"

"I'm stronger, Colton," Fisk said. "I'm different now. I could be a god!"

Colton shrugged, and Fisk's face grew red, inhaling sharply. Colton threw himself behind the couch, hands on his head. The rusted fridges exploded, sending coins and shrapnel everywhere. The structure rumbled and dust filled the air.

"Fisk, we can—" Lily began.

Fisk screamed. "We ain't talking 'bout nothing!"

A quick inhale, followed by a sound bolt blasting apart a section of the wall, the bedroom metal door flying to the side. Fisk's body snapped back, sending him to the ground as the concrete cracked.

Colton climbed to his feet and grabbed a large chunk of concrete. Ivan rushed past him, leaping at the boy. Fisk caught the soldier and threw him to the ground. They wrestled for a moment, with Fisk pinning Ivan to the ground, inhaling rapidly.

"No!" Colton screamed, hucking the rubble.

Fisk grunted, head bleeding as he turned to Colton. His veins bulged full of black ooze and his eyes, almost milky white, threatened to pop out of his skull.

The image burned into Colton's brain.

Colton, duck!

He felt someone tug him to the side just before Fisk shot out another bolt. Colton crashed on top of Lily as more of the wall exploded, collapsing part of the ceiling. Rumbles echoed loudly, distant and near as it felt like the whole mountain was shifting.

He's gonna kill us, Lily thought inside Colton's mind.

He wants me, Colton winced, his side bruised. *You and the others need to get out of here.*

No. Our mission was to—

Yeah, and I never do what I'm supposed to.

Colton shot to his feet, Fisk immediately inhaled, and Colton dove for the entrance. He felt the residual shockwave slam into him, strong enough to lift him in the air. His gut rose into his chest as he slammed back to the ground, tumbling a little down the slope. The wall collapsed, burying the others inside as Fisk laughed, marching toward Colton.

"Yoo can't run from meh!" Fisk said, voice hoarse.

Colton struggled to his feet, muscles groaning as his bones felt ready to break. His gut thrashed worse than ever, and he felt dizzy. Fisk grabbed his hair and slammed him in the stomach, doubling him over. Colton coughed, followed by a punch, and another, before a third knocked him back to the ground.

"Weak!" Fisk said, spitting on Colton and kicking his side. "Yoo ain't deserve life *ever!* An' now, you ain't gonna deserve it when I'm ter one in charge here."

"Charge of what?" Colton asked, spitting up blood.

Caleb DM Smith

"Malelentos and the whole shamn world. They made me stronger than all y'all. And now, I'm takin' what's mine."

Fisk laughed before whirling and kicking again. He continued his laughter, maniacal and unhinged as he convulsed, stumbling off slightly. Colton groaned, silently climbing to his feet. He focused his gaze on Fisk, who's back was to him.

"Yoo really were a thorn in my side, boy," Fisk muttered, scratching at his skin, angry, red, and bleeding.

"Then I'll leave."

Colton took off running, his muscles immediately burning. He forced himself to continue as Fisk screamed behind him. The distant roar of waterfalls drawing closer as he came closer to the cliff face, the path becoming narrower. He wound around a corner, nearly slipping. Otters scattered before him, and Fisk came around the bend.

The crazed boy grinned, inhaling again. Colton ducked, slipping on the rock and smacking to the ground. The bolt flew overhead, slamming into the cliff face and tearing out a chunk, scattering it down to the forest below.

He slowed down, Colton thought as Fisk was sent back by his own bolt. *Maybe I can beat him.*

Colton dashed away, the waterfalls coming into view, and the rocks becoming more slick. He felt friction against his shoes lessen, and he instinctively slowed down. Another turn, and the broken railing stopped him from falling off the cliff.

He hid around the corner, testing the rock with his foot as Sudsrea Moss squelched underfoot. Fisk ran into view and Colton lunged, ramming him. The boy stumbled, slamming into the railing, the metal creaking as it collapsed under the strain. Both metal and Fisk vanished below line of sight, and Colton took off.

Fisk screamed and sent another bolt, blasting the ground close to Colton. The eruption sent him flying, sliding across the concrete of a partially buried structure. He stopped right at the edge, scrapes smarting across his body. He groaned as Fisk climbed back onto the path, hands digging gouges into the stone and disfiguring his fingers.

Colton leaped up and ran toward the next building, recklessly leaping through the window and landing on the catwalk. It shook beneath him, metal groaning as he felt his weight drop for a split-second.

He ran into the stairwell, ascending as fast as he could. He heard Fisk below him, crashing into the walls like a cannon shot.

Concrete exploded and the stairs jerked, dropping partially. Colton tripped, smashing his knee. Fisk caught up and lunged. Colton kicked, breaking a few teeth.

"Dead, dead, dead," the crazed boy chanted, spitting out blood.

Colton kicked free, scrambling the rest of the way and raced across the roof. Fisk came close behind, limbs flailing, closing the gap with insane speed. Colton reached the edge and leaped, Fisk smashing into him a second later in the air.

They spun midair, and Colton collided with a ladder, and they dropped, stopped by Colton hanging onto the last rung. A sharp pain blossomed in his ankle, and he cried out.

Where's that net?

"Yoo comin' with me," Fisk howled, nails digging into Colton's skin.

"Get off!" Colton snapped, kicking Fisk in the face.

The two boys struggled, with Fisk slowly climbing. The ladder creaked, dropping downward, jerking to a stop. Colton paled, hauling himself upward as Fisk snarled. The ladder dropped another foot, metal groaning as bolts began bursting.

"Fisk, you'll drop both of us!" Colton shouted.

Fisk grinned. "That'll be fine by mae! I want you *dead!*"

Colton kicked Fisk again, and the ladder creaked. Another kick, something groaning long and loud. A third kick followed by a loud pop. Colton's gut thrashed and the ladder dropped a yard. It caught and started leaning away from the wall.

"Oh no no no," Colton muttered as the ladder fell, scraping against the opposite wall, forming a bridge. He hung from two of the rungs, Fisk holding onto his legs. His ankle joints felt ready to pop.

"Drop us, boy!" Fisk spat, lifting himself up enough and baring his teeth.

Colton looked down, the cliff narrowing the further it went, a small dirty window visible near the bottom. He looked up at the metal rungs, creaking and groaning as the ladder slowly began sliding down.

"I've got to be out of my mind," Colton muttered.

Caleb DM Smith

He gripped tight with his Demothest hands, the metal squeaking before he let go. He plummeted, Fisk below him before they slammed into the sloped cliff. Rocks scraped them painfully, the bottom of the cliff quickly rushing up.

Colton gritted his teeth, righting himself just enough to push off, smashing through the window and slamming to the concrete ground. He felt his whole body creak from the impact as glass shattered around him. Fisk howled outside, and an explosion rang out.

Silence fell for a few moments, the dust settling as Colton lay still for a moment. A massive groan sounded out, followed by the floor tilting beneath Colton.

No way! Colton shot to his feet, wincing as the structure tilted more and more. *How powerful has Fisk gotten?*

Another explosion, and the structure shook, followed by cracks breaking their way through every visible surface. The windows shattered and Colton felt the floor begin to shift. Rubble caved in, and furniture began sliding to the lower wall.

Colton cursed and raced to the other side of the room, leaping through a large crevice in the wall into the next room. More furniture whipped by as the room behind caved in, collapsing into dust and tumbling down the cliff face.

Explosion after explosion rang out, shaking the ground and causing rockslides. Room after room Colton raced through. A chair swiped his legs, tripping him. He slid to the wall, cracks forming beneath him. A large desk slid his way. He rolled to the side, leaping up and catching a door frame as the wall collapsed. Everything plummeted into the open air, the forest yawning beneath him.

"Son of a—" Colton spat, hauling himself in the door.

He climbed through the next room, maneuvering around until he found the next doorway. He leaped through, entering a side-ways basement just as the building collapsed behind him. The door frame stood in place, an entryway to a bare cliff, ragged and torn with a crushed forest below it.

Less than a hundred feet away on the crumbled cliffside stood Fisk, crazed and angry eyed. He twitched and the air shimmered in front of him. Colton narrowed his eyes, before shouting and diving to the ground. The walls around him shattered, rocks pelting him as the rest of the building collapsed, leaving him on a concrete platform.

Am I dead? Colton thought, groaning as he climbed to hands and knees.

"You darn near killed me, Colton," Fisk called, appearing over the edge of the platform. "And yer harder ter kill. You learn that from runnin'?"

Colton coughed again, rising. "Why do you want to kill me so bad?"

"I don't need a shamn reason. Yer a waste of space. Waste of my time. Yer a *shamn weakling who's better off dead.*"

Colton balled his hands into fists, feeling adrenaline rush through his veins. *One shot from him and I'm dead. But I can't keep running. Not while others could get hurt.*

"No," Colton said.

Fisk tilted his head. "No?"

"I'm done running. And if I have to fight you, then…" he took a deep breath. "I'll make sure you don't hurt anyone else again!"

Fisk laughed, convulsing violently before snapping rigid, body completely still. "Yoo *think* yoo can kill me? Yoo of all people?" Fisk shook his head. "I am a *god.* I *can't* be killed, and whoever I want, *dies at my word.*"

"Then why'm I still alive?"

Fisk glared at him, face twisting so badly it looked ready to implode. Colton's body tensed up, adrenaline flooding his veins as Fisk boiled like a teapot, growing angrier and looking more lethal.

No going back.

Fisk inhaled sharply, and Colton felt his instincts go wild, gut thrashing. He ran forward, his veins glowing as he let out a battle cry. Fisk glared, eyes popping wild with maniacal hunger.

This time, I've got to win. One on one!

Fisk's jaw slammed shut and Colton ducked the bolt that blasted past him. Fisk went flying, almost to the edge as the bolt smashed the cliff face, collapsing large portions of rock down onto the platform. The floor shook beneath them, making Colton lose his footing. Fisk rose to his feet and charged, tackling Colton. They flew off the platform, tumbling down the steep slope into another building.

Colton slammed on top of a wooden desk while Fisk rolled across the moldy carpet. The boy leapt to his feet, inhaling quickly. Colton rolled off, dodging the bolt that collapsed part of the wall. He lunged forward and slammed Fisk with a fist. The boy cried out and inhaled, and Colton swung again.

Inhale, punch, inhale, punch, inhale. Colton swung again, and Fisk dodged, letting out a small burst. Colton raised his hands, the bolt hitting the crystal and he was sent sprawling.

"Give up while yoo can," Fisk said.

Colton grunted, standing. "I'll die either way."

"Then quit wasting my time!"

Colton ducked another bolt, the wall exploding. He rushed, grabbed a chair, and hucked it. Fisk ducked, got tackled, and the wall behind cracked. Colton rained blows.

A quick inhale, and Colton spun to the side, a shockwave hitting him, and another wall going missing. The ceiling crumbled, raining chunks of concrete on them. Fisk took a hit, while rubble glanced off Colton's arms.

"Just die!" Fisk screamed.

Colton grabbed a long metal object, smacking Fisk's head, making the boy howl. A metal staple stuck out from the object, and Colton struck again, marking the boy's head. Fisk landed a haymaker on Colton, and they wrestled.

"I'm not—gonna—lose to you," Colton grumbled. "Not while my friends are in danger!"

Fisk grinned and headbutted him, before unhinging his jaw. Colton lunged and swung, with Fisk side-stepping each swing, inhaling the whole while. Colton grabbed another chair and threw it. Fisk side-stepped to the last wall and shut his jaw, cheeks puffed.

I'm dead! I've gotta— wait. It always has two shockwaves. One passing by, and upon impact. Can I hit him with it?

"You think that'll kill me?" Colton spat. "That's weak. That much air wouldn't even hurt me."

Fisk's eyes flared and he took a deeper, longer inhale, his chest bulging as his head seemed ready to explode. Colton gritted his teeth, dropping his stance as he readied for the sound bolt to rip him to shreds.

One is gonna die, and I won't let it be me.

Fisk let the bolt fly, flying into the wall, and Colton lunged, bringing his arm back and swinging with everything he had. The bolt collided with his fist, sending tremors up his entire arm, but the crystal held, ripping apart the sound attack. He felt intense pressure on his hand as he swung through.

The bolt shot back, slamming into Fisk, tearing the wall apart, and shaking the whole cliffside. Rubble tumbled down as Fisk went flying, spinning spread-eagle through the air, well above the forest. The boy screamed, throwing one last hateful glare before he plummeted, vanishing beneath the tree line.

Colton groaned, collapsing to the ground as his whole arm hurt, bruise marks appearing all along it. Small rocks and rubble tumbled onto him, partially burying him but not crushing.

Am I dying? I don't think I'm dead.

He gritted his teeth and pushed himself to hands and knees, rocks falling off. He climbed to his feet, legs shaky as he grabbed a piece of rubble for stability. He surveyed the area, finding much of the forest below had been crushed by rubble, trees knocked over and riddled with concrete.

Colton stood still and listened, squinting into the evening light that blanketed the vista. The sound of the waterfalls roared in the distance, and some birds chirped in the forest below. He let out a sigh and sat down on a large boulder, shoulders slumping.

"I survived," Colton muttered. "I—" he shook his head.

He looked out at the view, Malelentos's edge visible around the mountain's corner, with the Endless Fields spreading out ahead of him. Off in the distance, a trio of collapsed buildings rested against each other in a triangle shape. Dozens of ruins rested much further out into the field, but none quite as big.

"Guess I gotta go there," Colton said, sighing as he looked back at Malelentos, "and say goodbye to that place."

He slowly rose to his feet, wincing at the pain. He looked around, before heading toward the safest looking parts of the cliff face to look for a way down. By the time he got down, the sun was nearly set, and he set off toward the trio-ruins. Wheat rustled as a breeze blew past, slowing him to a stop while he glanced back at Malelentos.

Now silent and a dark mark on the terrain, seeming much less imposing and suffocating as it had been. Wallich tower was leaning much worse than it had been, on the verge of collapse as it sloped at a forty-five-degree angle. Colton took a deep breath before turning back to the ruins and jogging again.

I'm finally leaving it. Once and for all.

Chapter 24

Only a Warmup

Colton reached the crumbling buildings miles away from Malelentos, and he collapsed next to a pile of concrete rubble. He scraped his knees as he felt his muscles groan. He gritted his teeth, bile rising in his throat.

My whole body feels like it's on fire.

He stayed there, squinting his eyes while his head swam. Slowly, the sensations ebbed away, bit by bit. He took deep breaths to stabilize himself, trying to stop his limbs from shaking.

I can't lay here, or else the Scourgers might find me. Where's Lily and Liam?

After a good while, he unsteadily climbed to his feet, swaying slightly as he looked up at the towering ruins. They looked like a yawning opening to a concrete jungle of debris and history.

These things are all over the mountains, but I never explored the ones out on the plains.

Colton crept forward, eyes roving for dangers, and flinching at the creaking and groaning as the buildings slowly shifted in their ancient graves. He followed a cracked concrete walkway, winding past ancient houses and offices. It looked like the Auratus District, if not forgotten, and hugged by vegetation.

As he ventured in, he looked at the buildings that had collapsed into one another, forming a massive, enclosed space, like a tent. The tops were cloaked in shadow, with the hundreds of spaces, entryways, and windows dark, showing strange objects he had never seen.

He came to a small park, mostly covered in rubble, with trees that grew resiliently, some from windows, others almost sideways from the piles of debris. Vines hung down like spiders, flowers blooming on the ends. Every now and then, a bird would tweet out of sight, or some small animal would scurry across in the tall grass.

Whatever ground was left was taken up by a machine, similar to the trucks the guardians had used, except larger, painted with splotches of tan hues. It had much bigger tires and a large rack on top, carrying a dozen red canisters with spouts.

Did they steal this—car? Or whatever you call this thingy, from the Auratus District? No. It's different. Must be one of their own.

Colton walked up to the machine, running a hand along the hood and feeling the cold metal on his palm. Tapping it slightly, it gave a dull thud. He kicked the tires, and his foot bounced off, proving how solid they were.

It looks like it could ram down any wall.

Colton meandered to the door, grabbing a handle and yanking at it. It was locked, and he backed away. He looked around the space, rolling his shoulders as they itched slightly.

All of them are back there, right? I think I'm alone. No assassins, Scourgers, or deranged bullies.

Colton shook his head, rubbing his temples, resisting the urge to doubt his sanity due to all he had seen. It still felt like a dream.

Meandering over to one of the buildings, Colton peered through the dirty window, seeing a minute dining room, the table still set. A nearby counter held shriveled remains of food, some in brightly colored bags.

Colton moved to the next window, peering in, finding it much darker. He narrowed his eyes, perceiving something moving inside. It slowly drew closer, beady eyes peering at him. It leaped out, and Colton fell back, landing on his hands and bruising his tailbone. Looking up, he spotted a bird, vainly ramming itself into the window, fluttering back and forth in its panic.

What's with animals trying to attack me? It's not like I ever did anything—oh. It's stuck.

Colton grumbled and climbed to his feet, watching the poor animal, with its green coat, wings near invisible from their speed, and long beak as it hovered by the window. Curious, he watched it for a bit longer, as it slowly realized it was trapped, stuck with the consequences of its actions.

It looked at him, eyes almost pleading with him, and he frowned.

I'll forgive you for scaring me.

Picking up a piece of rubble, Colton tried to shoo the bird away from the window, but when it refused, he aimed at the lower end. Throwing with all of his might, he sent the piece smashing through the glass, causing it all to shatter and fall to the ground with a crash.

Immediately, the bird flew out, a *buzz* as it flew right by Colton's ear, making him flinch.

"Perhaps try not to break anything else?" someone suggested.

Whirling around, Colton caught sight of Lily standing with hands on her hips, and somehow looking worse, now with black sludge all over her face, and her clothes in tatters.

Wiping the blood that oozed from a fresh cut on her cheek, she forced a smile that really looked more like a disgusted grimace.

"What happened? Like to the uhh—you?" Colton asked.

"Well, after you ran off, all the rest of us decided to retreat here," Lily answered darkly. "But the Scourgers made it a tad difficult."

Colton nodded. "Makes sense why I got here before you."

"Barely. We saw you running ahead of us. You look like you had quite the fight."

"I got rid of Fisk," Colton said with a shrug.

"How so?" Lily asked, eyes widening. "Is he—"

"His bolt always hit us with a shockwave before the actual attack, so I figured maybe I could send that shockwave back at him."

Lily tilted her head, reaching out her hand tentatively, as if she'd be electrocuted on contact. "May I?"

He nodded and held out his arm. She took it and her eyelids began fluttering. After a few moments she stepped back, eyes wide, face a little more pale.

"Risky," Lily said, "that could've torn you to shreds, had your Demothest arm absorbed all of the shock. Let alone, reflecting the strength of the sound enough to push Fisk that much. But…I suppose it suffices…"

"Yeah, well, he's not coming after us."

"Yet, I do not think Fisk was the only one after you. Best not to chance getting attacked while waiting here."

She strode to the truck and flicked her hand, opening the door. She placed her arrow and quiver inside, dusting off her hands, wiping some of the grime from herself, gagging as she shook her head.

Not used to dirt, huh? Colton thought. *And I'm the one who's supposed to be new to the real world.*

"Weird truck," Colton commented, rolling his shoulders.

Lily looked at him, her head tilted. She laughed, making Colton frown, folding his arms, only to wince as his right arm protested again.

She's making fun of me, isn't she?

"Oh yes, I suppose so," she replied. "This little thing is a Mine Resistant Ambush-Protected All Terrain Vehicle. Also known as a M-ATV. Often used for transportation through rugged terrain of military troops. Though they require quite the costly amount of gas."

"Gas? Is that some form of electricity?"

"Not at all," she said, smiling wryly, "but rather a liquid chemical makeup of Alkanes, Cycloalkanes, and aromatic hydrocarbons, called diesel."

Colton gingerly rubbed his arm, disliking the throbbing pain sensation. *Diesel? That sounds made up. How would a big machine like that run off a liquid?*

"By the process of science," Lily said.

Colton raised his brows. "I didn't say anything.".

"Didn't you just say—"

"I thought about it…"

"Ah…" Lily tilted her head, eyes closing partially.

Something crashed off toward the entrance, followed by a faint voice, and coughing. She gave Colton a stern look, holding a finger to her lips.

"Stay here, and stay low," Lily muttered, jogging away.

Colton watched her leave, his muscles tense. He looked around for any sign of danger, before his gaze strayed to the M-ATV, and he moved to peer inside.

Leather seats filled most of the space. At the front, was what looked like the driver's seat, where there was an odd circular wheel, and an array of buttons, switches, dials, and screens.

Climbing in, Colton sat in the driver seat, grabbing onto the strange wheel device. Beside him, a little stick stuck out, with numbers going up beside different slots. Looking over the buttons, most were labeled in ways he didn't understand, except for one with the word 'start.'

He reached for the button and pressed it, only for silence to echo back. He pressed it again, getting no response. He slammed it repeatedly before giving up.

"Don't break anything," someone admonished.

Colton jerked heavily again, looking back to see Liam leaning against the entrance to the M-ATV, looking almost as roughed up as Lily had.

What the—! Why do they keep doing that?

"I would've thought you beat me here," Colton said, breaking into a big grin.

Liam shrugged. "It took a while to get down from Angel's Landing."

"Did you fight Scourgers?"

"Yeah, they're scary. I recognized a few people."

"It gets real creepy fast," Colton said. "Nearly killed us in the sewers."

"You think the sewers were bad, try landing a jet full of those blasted Scourgers," Tom said, popping into view.

Colton's eyes widened. "How'd you get down from the tower? It got hit and kinda broke."

Tom grinned. "Oraculi is a living short-cut. He knows things ahead of time and has the abilities to keep us alive."

"So where is he now?"

Tom pulled out a little key and climbed into the vehicle. Colton moved to the passenger seat and Tom inserted the key into a little slit, turned it, pressed down on some pedals hidden near the floor, and thumbed the button. The engine roared to life, shaking the whole vehicle as an acrid stench wafted around them.

Caleb DM Smith

"Oraculi has—" Tom paused, "other things he needs to do. He kinda goes off on his own a lot. Doesn't tell me or others. Just pops in, gives you a little push in the right direction, and vanishes."

Wouldn't he die? He looks so old and weak, Colton thought. *Maybe he's avoiding all the danger.*

"So, where're we going?" he asked.

"We're headed somewhere safe," Tom answered.

"The penthouse didn't seem very safe."

"Not when a full civil war gets mixed with Scourgers, yeah. But this place is far from any potential enemies."

Colton sat watching Tom for a few moments, his gut twisting. He rose from his seat and popped out of the door. Liam gave him a questioning look, following him.

"Where're you going?" Liam asked.

Colton stopped. "Just—somewhere."

"And that is?"

"Why does it matter?"

"I don't think you being on your own is a good idea right now."

"I'm not a child."

"I don't mean because you'll do something. You have an assassin hunting you down, remember?"

Colton bit his tongue, giving Liam a long look, who splayed his hands.

"Look," Liam said, "if you want to tell me or not, it's your choice. But at least let me help in some way."

Silence, and Colton's gut twisted a little. Birds chirped off in the ruins.

Tell you what? Oh what, I have something simple, like tough homework? Right... easy... huh...

Colton looked at the ruins, taking a deep breath before letting his gaze fall to the ground. He shook his head and looked at Liam.

"How'm I supposed to react to me being told I'm weird, that I'm being hunted, and now my home city just got destroyed from living dead things and my bully who had screaming powers? And if I hang around you guys, you'll get hurt too. Look at Ivan, or even yourself."

"It's—a lot, I know," Liam said.

200

"This isn't the first time I've had my home destroyed, Liam."

"What happened the first time?" Lily asked, walking up.

"A big fire," Colton said, throwing his hands in the air. "Don't remember what caused it. Burnt the whole town down."

Lily frowned, folding her arms as she considered Colton. He sighed and shook his head. He ran a hand through his hair, grabbing a fistful.

"I still don't understand why there's an assassin after me," he said.

Lily tilted her head. "Because the Heralds of the Damned will stop at nothing to lay hands on you."

"Did I tick them off?"

"No, you are valuable. Our goal is to get you safe at Magna Arbor, and study you to know why."

"The krik is that supposed to mean? I'm not an animal."

Lily frowned. "Well, no. But to be honest, we don't know *what* you are. Only that you're partially non-human."

Colton stared, his gut boiling quickly. He felt his mouth go dry and his limbs numb. He remembered Lily saying something similar in the prison, only now felt less of a joke.

He looked down as his body tensed. "I'm just a normal, nobody kid."

That can't be right. No. There's no way—I—I'm normal. Unimportant.

"I used to think such things of myself," Lily commented. "I was naive to the world, until my father tried to *engineer* me into something. He had a goal and it drove him to madness. But you cannot ignore a disease that poses such danger to you. Especially when the Herald's hunt you for it."

"What do they even want with me?"

"We're not sure. But we do know they want to open something known as the Twilit Gate. In other words, the literal doors to Hell."

Colton scoffed, shaking his head. "Why's it so hard to live a normal life?"

"We have the life handed to us, whether it be normal, dangerous, dull, or unreal. All that we need to do to acknowledge it, dissect it, and then act on the plan we make to improve."

201

Caleb DM Smith

"You know how exhausting that is?"

Lily nodded. "I do. Which is why we'll take you to Magna Arbor. A place to escape to for a time, then to return to your own battlefield to fight your own demons."

Lily extended a hand, giving Colton a long look, irises a calm sea.

"The demons have taken much from you," she said. "And I ask you again, and this time without the pressures of prison. Do you wish to join us?"

Colton considered her hand, avoiding eye contact.

If there's more than Fisk after me, not much I could do. Is Fisk even that relatively strong? I've never met this assassin after me yet. Or maybe I have. I don't know. I can't fight back like this, I'm kinda a mess right now. Maybe things will change finally.

Colton looked up, meeting Lily's eyes, his gut twisting slightly. He stepped forward and shook her hand.

"I still don't fully trust you, but I'll fight with you."

Lily nodded. "Welcome to the Celestial Lumanine."

202

Epilogue

Most Scourgers lay slain, their heads wounded, hearts pierced, and corpses left in piles to rot. Others survived, meandering around listlessly.

A guardian shuffled along, helmet smashed and rotting mouth drooling a vile sludge. Bite marks covered any exposed skin, black veins infesting outward on the dark-purple skin.

A woman with a book in hand pressed her head on a wall, her glasses fell, dangling by beads hanging to her ears. Her mouth drooled black ooze as she groaned, teeth clacking.

Someone watched them from atop a crumbled building, eyes shifting with the sound of mechanical whirring. Fingers twitching as they extended into thin wires before retracting.

The assassin grunted, pain coming from every movement as his metal skin rippled.

"Destruction and death," the assassin said, "left by the Eclipse in every breath."

The assassin looked up to the Auratus District, the buildings blackened and smoldering, smoke wafting around them, and most skyscrapers missing their tops, with the highest tower leaning dangerously over the Scintillia Initium District.

"You've let the Eclipse escape," said someone behind, voice curt and cold.

The assassin turned, laying eyes on a woman standing below him on the ground, dressed in a black military uniform, back as straight as a board, and hair combed back severely, mildly resembling cornrows. Her eyes were a cold gray and face twisted into a permanent frown.

"The Eclipse is strong," the assassin said, "but he does not know his song."

"So, his Calibers are awakening?"

"A Caliber is their name, but a different condition is the game."

The officer shook her head, a Scourger approaching her before she dropped it with a pistol shot to the heart and head.

"Enough riddles," she said. "We've wasted enough time with—"

The assassin vanished for a mere second, appearing right in front of the officer as the small building collapsed from the force of leaping from the roof. The assassin let out a growl, muffled behind a black respirator that covered the lower half of the face. The irises, like yellow camera lenses, twitched, widening and shrinking.

"Idiot general! Naive woman! Gruntheart fool!" the assassin hissed. "The Eclipse is no child, but a tool. To kill again, he surely will."

"You have enough agility to destroy your surroundings with sheer force," General Gruntheart scoffed. "And you're an assassin of the Red Dusk, are you not?"

"No, no no no," the assassin hissed. "They forced me in there. I had no choice but to join the ranks and breathe the guild's air. The Herald's *made* me as I am."

"Made to capture a simple boy."

"No! No no no no. He's similar—no! He *is* me. He is yet to become me, as his Venal Darkness still thrashes and boils."

The assassin started laughing, and the general shook her head.

"You ought to be repaired," she said with disgust. "We must leave."

The assassin knelt on the ground, bowing his head of wires to the earth, grinding them into the dirt as he groaned and trembled. Scourgers started swarming their way, chittering and groaning as they moved with shuffled steps.

"I am *not* broken," the assassin wailed. "I am not some *mere* puppet token."

Gruntheart shifted, eyeing the Scourgers. "We must leave, *now*."

A Scourger came close to the assassin who snapped upright, left hand extending into wires before piercing the Scourger, lifting it up six feet above the ground. The assassin let out a growl before the wires retracted, dropping the Scourger to the ground, lifeless.

204

"No," the assassin said. "Yes, it would be so easy to tear him apart."

Gruntheart scoffed. "He's a child! How hard can it be to—"

The assassin whirled, his face inches from hers. "I must corrupt his heart. I've been hired to sway him. But turning a foe to a friend, that line is very thin."

"You're a mindless assassin. What do you know?"

"His heritage says it's so. I was made to kill but now must capture. It's not easy to do the latter with one so ill."

General Gruntheart paused. "His *true* parentage would indicate he's already corrupted. I will appeal to Ikumonos for more time."

The assassin laughed maniacally, grabbing at his hair of wires, and tore them out with a grunt.

"I will make Colton become me. I will make him become as I have. I will corrupt him into a *demon*."

Secrets are revealed in book #2:

Scourge of Dawn: Designed Heritage

Reading Guide

Pronunciation for odd & custom words/names.

(Colton) Diaíresi(διαίρεση) Toa - Dee-yeh-eh-reh-sea, Toh-u

(Mr.) Daas - Dah-s

(Fisk) Rels - Rell-ss

(Lily) Scientia Reine - S-eye-en-see-ah, R-ay-en

Oraculi Conditor - Oh-rak-oo-lee, con-dee-toh-oor

(Ivan) Pavlenko - Pah-vv-lee-en-koh

Kai Winder - Kah-eye, Win-dur

Dromus - Droh-muss

(Fran) Hewitt - Hue-witt

Nessa - Ness-suh

Theos Mortem - Tee-oh-s Moh-r-tem

Amicus (Desert) - Ah-mee-coo-s

Aquilla Mons - Ah-kwil-lah, Mah-nz

Ardens Terra - Ah-rr-den-ss Teh-ruh

Auratus (District) - Ow-wur-rat-toos

The Baranile - bah-rah-nee-leh

Centum Turris - Ken-tum Too-riss

Dunae Cranii - doo-nay crah-nee

Feram - fee-rum

Ferus (Frontier) - feh-roos

Fyamber - fee-am-bear

Forzendum - Foh-zen-doo-m

(Mt.) Hephaestus - Huh-fay-stuh-s

Kataramenos - kah-rah-tah-men-noh-s

Laborkinder (Woods) - Lay-boh-r keen-door

Magna Arbor - Mag-nuh-arr-boh-r

Malelentos - Mah-leh-lent-toe-ss

Malum - Mah-luh-m

The Mar Devorador - Mah-r Deh-vor-rah-door

Mershanti - Mur-shah-n-tee

Montium - Moh-n-tee-um

Montiwell (Mountains) - Mon-tee-well

New Lothdon - Lah-th-dun

Novum - Noh-vuh-m

Parvus Frater (Mountains) - Par-voo-s Frah-tur

Plummeth (of) Groff - Pluh-meth (of) Graw-f

Priroden (Wilds) - Pur-d-rear-roh-den

Reges Opidum - Reh-jes Ah-pih-dum

Salus - Sah-loo-s

Scintillia Intium (District) - Shin-teel-luh, In-nish-ee-uhm

Segregare - Seh-greh-gah-reh

Senile - Seh-nee-lay

stor gård - St-oor Goo-oord

Teafil (Mountains) - Tah-feel

Tenebris - Ten-neh-brih-s

Wangling - wah-ng-goh-lung (亡灵)

Demothest - Deem-mow-thest

Saelfite - Sah-el-f-eye-t

Homo-Saurus - Hoh-moh, Sah-russ

Kekamoto - Keck-uh-mow-tow

Scourger - Scur-jur

Celestial Lumanine - see-lest-shee-all, loo-mah–n-eye-n

Caliber - Cah-el-lee-bur

Gjinx - Jee-nks

Kretch - creh-etch

Nosk - naw-sk

Shamn - sha-ahm

Skiff - Sk-if

Calitch - cah-lich

Acknowledgements

There're so many people I'd love to acknowledge for ways they've helped this book come to fruition, whether directly or indirectly.

I'd like to thank the dozens of my friends that were willing to beta-read and give feedback on my book, as well as encouragement and critiques; to Connor Walker and Jeramie Juber for showing me what true friends are; to Amos Olsen for providing so much feedback and strategy for orchestrating this project; and a lot of thanks to Aimee H. and Meg Jensen for helping out in the early process.

Special thanks to my mother, Alison Smith, for applying the finishing touchups to make this book shine like it should; and to my father, Samuel Smith, who aided me so much in making the magic system actually work, and fit my vision; to my brother-in-law, Jared Jeffery, who shared his experiences he's had writing to help me get started; and to my sister, Monica Moore Smith, who gave me pointers on making my female characters realistic and relatable.

Of course, my appreciation goes to my two editors, Allister Thompson, and James Powell, who helped so much in making the story, characters, and world come to life in such an awesome way!

A huge thanks to Tathena Tubbs, who made the amazing artwork, and suffered through all of the little alterations I asked for. And to the many people who were willing to help do photoshoots of all the main characters to bring them to life: Boston Crier, Natallia Joy, Ian Hopkinson, and Lexington Holman.

As well as special thanks to those who I may not have gotten along with earlier in life, you taught me hard-learned lessons that ultimately aided me where I would have otherwise struggled more.

And of course, last but not least, a great thanks to you, dear reader, who decided to pick up, and buy my book, and also took the time to reach the acknowledgements. Keep reading on to the next book, and the next book, and the next!

About the Author

Caleb DM Smith is an author, filmmaker, and lifelong adventurer. *Scourge of Dawn: Ashen Genesis* marks the debut of his first book series.

While bringing his stories to life on the page, Caleb also stays busy behind the camera. He's worked in a wide range of roles on film sets—from writer, director, and DP, to editor, costumer, and prop master—collaborating on dozens of music videos and short films and learning from some of the industry's top talent.

Originally from Utah (with a couple of adventurous years in Texas), Caleb has a passion for travel and draws inspiration from the places he's explored and the people he's met along the way. He likes to put it simply: he either writes about adventures—or goes out and lives them.

www.ingramcontent.com/pod-product-compliance
Lightning Source LLC
Chambersburg PA
CBHW020411180626
46812CB00003B/920

*9 7 9 8 9 9 3 4 1 2 1 0 8 *